The Windermere Inheritance

Steffie Glen

AUTHOR'S NOTE

This novel's vocabulary reflects my mother tongue, UK English, to preserve its authentic British tone and atmosphere. I live and work in Florida, and my publisher is based in the USA. Therefore, in this edition, American spelling conventions are used for accessibility by US readers—for example, color instead of colour. On the other hand, the vocabulary is UK English, influenced by East London speech and early forms of what is now called Estuary English. For example, reckon instead of thought, mashed potato instead of mashed potatoes, got instead of gotten. This combination is deliberate to offer an authentic English voice while maintaining US spelling familiarity.

1 GASLIGHT SHADOWS

Rain turned London's pavements into mirrors, reflecting everything Eliza tried to hide: her worn, plain bonnet tied tightly under her chin, the patched sleeves on her cloak, her cheap shoes cobbled more than a dozen times. October's bite cut through her thin cloak, making her shiver as much from cold as from nerves.

She rested against the wrought-iron railings as darkness pooled at her feet. The Windermere mansion loomed ahead, its Georgian elegance softened by the London fog. Warm light spilled from tall windows.

The iron gate stood open, which was unusual for a house this grand. Invisible protection wards pushed back against her approach, shields against dark magic that felt like walking through cobwebs made of lightning. The layers of protection spoke of serious money and serious paranoia. Yet the gate remained open, the wards clearly designed to scan rather than repel—measuring whatever magical signature she carried before allowing passage.

They were expecting her, of course.

Her hand touched cold iron. She could turn around. Walk back to her cramped lodgings and abandon her fruitless search through servant networks and society gossip.

Yet something about this felt inevitable. Like turning twelve and starting work in the laundry. Or turning fourteen and being expected to find a husband before she turned into an old maid. But this wasn't a path of societal expectations; this was a path drawing her in with the promise of answers about her memory gaps, the nightmares that woke her screaming, the certainty that something vital had been stolen from her.

Whatever lay beyond this gate might hold the key to who she really was.

She pushed through the gate, raised the cast-iron door knocker, and rapped twice.

A well-groomed footman in a velvet livery coat answered before the echo of her knock faded. "Miss Clarke. Lady Windermere is waiting."

He led her through the front hall. The warmth inside was a blessed relief after the damp chill outside.

Marble floors bore intricate patterns that shifted in the gaslight. The chandelier's glow was met by unmoving faces in heavy gilt frames, each one fixed in the same strange half-turn toward her passage. In the morning room, carved wainscoting lined the walls, every panel inlaid with mother-of-pearl. The fireplace gleamed with polished marble veined in delicate lavender, unlit but immaculate. A silver-trimmed tea service rested on a lacquered table, radiating warmth.

Lady Windermere rose from a divan of pale blue silk taffeta, her movements fluid despite the tightness around her eyes. She was poised and luminous, her beauty preserved through wealth—and likely, magical anti-aging potions. She was perhaps the same age as Eliza's adoptive mother, but that's where the similarity ended. Lady Windermere bore no weary expression, no unbathed odor, no skin drawn tight from missed meals.

"Miss Clarke." Relief flooded her voice. "Please sit."

Eliza settled into the offered chair, her spine straight. "You mentioned urgency in the advert."

"Yes." Lady Windermere's fingers worried her lace trim. "Tea?"

"No, thank you, ma'am." While Eliza reckoned she probably could do with a cup after her long walk, she didn't fancy having a week's wages docked if she dropped the gaudy cup.

"You come highly recommended." Lady Windermere sipped her tea, little finger out. "Lady Ashworth spoke favorably of your time with her daughter."

Eliza nearly choked at the hypocrisy of the upper class. Lady Ashworth had dismissed her for refusing to beat a child, yet she was apparently willing to pass her on to another family. "Lady Ashworth was... kind with words, if not much else."

Lady Windermere raised an eyebrow. "She said you were stubborn and opinionated. She also mentioned that you spent your early years in India. It must have been difficult—such a savage place for a young girl."

Eliza's hands tightened into fists. "I don't remember much. I was just a little thing then."

The tea's steam curled upward, and it looked like smoke. The fragmented memories surfaced unbidden—fire consuming jasmine gardens, powerful arms raising her to safety, a voice whispering, "Run." Gone as quickly as they came, the memories left only the familiar ache of incompleteness.

"Of course not. Children are so resilient, aren't they? Able to forget such unpleasantness." Lady Windermere tapped the side of the cup with a fingernail. "Lady Ashworth also said her daughter learned more in six months with you than in two years with her previous governess. That you treated her like a person rather than a problem to be solved."

Heat spread through Eliza's chest. She'd grown used to being dismissed for her methods. "Treat a child fair, you'll get further than scaring 'em."

"Exactly." Lady Windermere's cup rattled on the saucer when she set it down. "That's what we need. Someone who sees children as people. Not weapons."

The word lingered in the air. Weapons. Eliza had heard the rumors, of course. But to hear it from a toff? She hadn't expected that. But it was not her place to ask questions. It was her place to seem agreeable and obedient.

"Tell me about Miss Madge, then." Eliza leaned forward. "No need to dance around things. I know when folk are holding something back." Damn. She'd opened her mouth again. She waited for the admonishment and dismissal—the *How dare you question my veracity*. But instead, Lady Windermere said,

"She's twelve. Exceptionally bright. Too bright for her own good." A pause. "She's different, Miss Clarke. Not in obvious ways, but different nonetheless. There are those who would see that difference as something to be managed. Controlled."

A shudder skittered down Eliza's spine. She recalled her own strange episodes, where her shadows refused to stay still. She had to be careful here. If the Windermeres even suspected that she had unregistered magic, she'd have more than a dismissal to worry about. "What sort of different?"

"The sort that attracts the wrong attention," Lady Windermere whispered. "What I'm about to tell you cannot leave this room. Do I have your word?"

Every rational thought screamed at her to decline. She had enough secrets of her own—she didn't need the burden of someone else's.

But she thought of the steady paycheck. She thought of the child—this Madge, different in dangerous ways. And she thought of the connections this position would give her.

"You've got my word, ma'am."

Lady Windermere closed her eyes as if to gather strength. "Madge has abilities. Magical abilities that are extremely rare. The sort that certain government institutions take a keen interest in."

The Imperial Magisterium. Unspoken but clearly heard.

"How rare?"

"The last documented case was over a century ago." Her hands twisted in the silk taffeta of her dress. "We've managed to keep it quiet, but she's growing stronger. More difficult to contain."

"You want me to teach her how to keep it bottled, is that it?"

"I want you to help her learn to hide." The words seemed to rush out. "I want you to teach her to be ordinary. To blend in. To be invisible."

"Forgive me, ma'am, but I'm not sure I'm qualified to—"

"Pish posh," Lady Windermere said, staring at Eliza's feet. "I saw the second you walked in that you are more than qualified to understand the dangers associated with unregistered magic."

Eliza swallowed hard. She looked at the floor—under the table, next to the sofa—anywhere but at her feet. Her shadows were playing games again. Games that were getting more obvious and harder to control with each passing day.

It was dangerous territory. The Empire's magical registration laws were strict and unforgiving. Every magical citizen was cataloged, monitored, and regulated. At least, those who could afford the two shillings registration fee. Those who couldn't pay risked forced conscription into the Royal Forces unless they stayed in the shadows—the irony of which was not lost on her. She *was* the shadows, and unless she could learn restraint, she would end up as cannon fodder in some foreign crusade.

"Let's talk compensation. How does room and board plus twenty shillings a week sound?" The sum widened Eliza's eyes. Twenty shillings was three times her last position—enough to secure her future. Surely she could show restraint for a few months—long enough to build some savings. It was an offer she couldn't refuse, even though a niggling feeling in her stomach told her that's exactly what she should be doing.

"And what exactly would you be needing from me?"

"Protecting a child who needs protection. I will be honest with you, Miss Clarke. The job will not be an easy one; hence the generous salary. Madge can be... difficult to control. The question is—are you brave enough to take the position?"

Eliza thought of her closet-sized room in the back of the King's Head Tavern, where she had to re-plug the holes in the skirting boards with rags to prevent the rats from getting back in at night. But more than that, she thought of the years of searching for answers and getting nowhere.

Most of all, she thought of finally having access to the sort of circles that might hold answers. "When d'you want me to start, then?"

Lady Windermere's smile transformed into something genuine. "Immediately. Madge has been quite eager to meet you."

Rapid footsteps echoed in the hallway, followed by a shrill voice that brooked no argument.

"Mama, you've been in there for ages, and I'm positively dying of curiosity. Is she here? Because if she is, I simply must—"

The door burst open. A girl who could only be Madge Windermere stood there—all dark brown curls and bright eyes. She skidded to a halt, expression shifting from eagerness to frank assessment.

"Oh." She tilted her head like Eliza was an interesting insect in a jar. "You're younger than I expected. And prettier. Most governesses look like they've been sucking on lemons."

"Madge!" Horror threaded Lady Windermere's voice. "Your manners!"

Eliza laughed. "It's alright. And you're spot on about the lemon-suckers, Miss Madge. I've met me share of 'em."

Madge's face lit with delight. "Excellent! I knew you'd be different the moment Mama started acting mysterious." She paused, head tilting further. "You have interesting shadows."

Eliza's pulse jumped. *Be still, shadows, be still.*

"Margaret Elizabeth Windermere," her mother snapped. "You will apologize this instant—"

"It's perfectly fine." Eliza rose from her chair and curtsied, stealing a glance at her feet to make sure her shadows were where they were supposed to be. They were. "Pleased to meet you, Miss Madge. Reckon we'll get on just fine."

2 THE WINDERMERE TOUR

Lady Windermere stood. "Madge, run along and get dressed for dinner while I show Miss Clarke the house."

Madge skipped away, and Eliza's tour commenced in the front hall. Power hummed through every surface like blood through veins. Ward stones masqueraded as decorative molding, their defensive energy vibrating in Eliza's bones. The marble floors displayed intricate patterns that weren't merely artistic—they were magical circuitry, designed to channel hostile spells away from the house's heart.

"You've got some proper safeguards," Eliza said.

"Essential ones. We've entertained unwanted visitors recently." Lady Windermere's tone could have frozen fire. "The Imperial Census Bureau has shown remarkable persistence in its neighborhood assessments. Last year, my neighbor Lord Aston was forced to pay a fine of ten shillings for not disclosing that his daughter knew how to spell."

Apparently, rich people in Mayfair got "assessed" for non-disclosure of magical powers, while East Enders got raided and sometimes truncheoned to death.

Lady Windermere must have seen the look on Eliza's face, because she said, "Oh, dear, I apologize for my insensitivity. I heard about the ongoing raids in the East End. I do hope it didn't affect your family."

"It didn't, ma'am." Her adoptive mother's only power was

wielding a switch with deadly accuracy, while her father's superpower was draining their coffers for Winslow's Soothing Syrup to "keep Eliza quiet."

As a child, she'd swallowed the bitter liquid, because that's what children do—take whatever their parents give them. Only years later did understanding dawn: her parents were suppressing her shadows with laudanum, because it cost a fraction of the exorbitant registration fees.

Weaning herself off the syrup after leaving home had been agony. Shaking hands, cold sweats, nights when her bones felt like they were dissolving. But during that time, when the opium devil called her name, she gritted her teeth and endured. She'd refused to become another East End addict drowning in what her kind called "The Real London Fog."

"Magical incidents," Lady Windermere said, pointing at scorch marks on the wallpaper as they progressed through the morning room.

The crystal chandelier bore signs of recent replacement—several chains gleamed newer than others, fittings mismatched like broken teeth.

"What sort of magical incidents?" Eliza asked.

"Madge's abilities have been... temperamental."

Eliza's stomach twisted at the vagueness of the statement. Was Lady Windermere too afraid of telling her exactly what had happened? Or was she blaming her daughter for her outbursts?

As she ascended the main staircase, Eliza's attention snagged on the gaps in the portrait arrangement. Empty spaces suggested missing frames, and the wallpaper showed faded rectangles where pictures had once hung.

Lady Windermere followed her gaze. "The frames were broken one night. Madge's power... well, you'll see for yourself, Miss Clarke."

A chill ran through Eliza's body. Magic strong enough to shake pictures from walls? What was she walking into? "What 'appened to the other governesses then?"

Eliza chastised herself for dropping the "h." As much as she tried to sound proper, polishing her dialect proved more challenging than working as a chimney sweep's assistant as a child.

"Nothing dramatic. They simply... departed. Usually, after witnessing the first manifestation." Bitterness laced her voice. "It's difficult to retain staff when fixtures explode regularly."

The upper corridor thrummed with a different energy that was heavier and more oppressive. Protection spells layered thick enough to suffocate, pressing against her consciousness like fog made of lead.

"The family quarters," Lady Windermere gestured vaguely. "Madge's room occupies the hall's end. The blue door."

Even from here, Eliza sensed power radiating from behind that barrier—wild, barely leashed, like lightning seeking earth.

"And the others?"

"My husband's study. My private retreat. Guest chambers that haven't welcomed visitors for a considerable time."

* * *

Dinner at the Windermere table unfolded like a chess match played with crystal and cutlery. Eliza had never eaten with her charge's family before—she usually dined with the servants. But now, staring at her plate of chicken, mashed potato, and a vegetable that looked like spindly green fingers, she had no idea where to start. In front of her were no fewer than six sets of knives and forks. She'd used one of the spoons to eat her soup, but there had only been two of those, and she knew enough not to use a teaspoon.

"The outer fork," Madge whispered. "And the second knife in from the right."

Eliza picked up her knife, sliced off a tip of green finger, and placed it in her mouth. She chewed it slowly and almost gagged at the grassy, bitter taste.

"How is the asparagus?" Lady Windermere asked.

Ispirigiss? What the devil was that? "Yes, ma'am. It's quite pleasant, thank you."

She would have swallowed it down with a glass of water—if she could sort out which of the five glasses to use.

Lord Windermere dissected his chicken leg like a surgeon amputating a gangrenous foot. "Miss Clarke," he said without lifting his attention from his plate. "My wife mentions you possess experience with... troubled children."

Lord Windermere twiddled the ends of his handlebar

mustache, seeming not to notice Madge's glare.

"I'd say they were remarkable rather than troubled, my lord," Eliza said.

"Remarkable?" He paused on the word, his gaze as cold as January drizzle. "Yes, Madge certainly qualifies. Tell me, what's your perspective on Imperial registration requirements?"

Her opinion was that the requirements had led to a generation of opium-addicted children—that was if their parents didn't toss them into the sewers as babies.

"I reckon," Eliza said, "that all children deserve protection no matter what gifts they got."

"Protection." Lord Windermere's laugh could have shattered crystal. "A lovely sentiment. But what occurs when protection conflicts with civic obligation?"

"Harold." Lady Windermere's voice carried a warning.

"No, Charlotte. Miss Clarke should comprehend what she's accepting." He leaned forward, voice dropping to a deadly whisper. "My daughter isn't merely 'remarkable.' She's dangerous. The sort of dangerous that makes Imperial agents lose sleep. The question becomes whether Miss Clarke prioritizes Madge's welfare above Imperial expectations."

The conversation stopped as if a guillotine blade had descended. Madge stared at her plate, her shoulders slumped with shame. Lady Windermere's hands trembled around her wineglass, so much so that the red liquid sloshed over the edge. A butler materialized from the edge of the room, wiped up the spill, and retreated.

Eliza chose her words carefully. "Children's welfare comes first with me. Imperial expectations can please themselves."

Something shifted in Lord Windermere's expression: approval, perhaps, or weary resignation.

"Then you understand why our last three governesses proved inadequate."

"They put their own safety before your daughter's needs."

"Self-preservation is a powerful motivation." His face didn't change as he looked at his daughter. "But it is usually not an honorable choice."

Eliza stilled. Lord Windermere's statement was loaded with

meaning, namely that he questioned her honor. Stay, and that was the "honorable choice." Leave, and she'd be admitting she was just another street rat who always chose self-preservation.

Madge looked up then, hope flickering in her brown eyes. "You won't abandon me when circumstances become difficult?"

The question held such raw vulnerability that a sharp ache flared in Eliza's chest. "I plan to stay for as long as I am needed, Miss Madge."

"Even if my abilities worsen? Even if government people arrive with questions?"

"Especially then, miss."

Relief flooded Madge's features. For the first time since Eliza's arrival, the girl resembled what she was—a twelve-year-old child desperate for someone to choose her over their own comfort.

"Well then," Lord Windermere raised his wineglass. "Welcome to the family rebellion, Miss Clarke. Try not to destroy us all."

* * *

The governess's quarters whispered stories to those who knew how to listen.

As Eliza unpacked her meager possessions, she cataloged the room's hidden chronicles. Scorch marks scarred the windowsill. Salt lines traced the doorframe, hastily scrubbed but still visible— protection spells against magical intrusion. A loose floorboard concealed a hiding place containing a half-burned letter in feminine script.

The child grows more perilous daily. I cannot in good conscience continue this arrangement. Find another sacrifice for your family's ambitions.

Eliza crumpled the letter, understanding flooding through her. The previous governesses hadn't simply departed—they'd fled, terrified by Madge's escalating power and the family's refusal to surrender her to Imperial control. But even with fifty-shilling rewards posted for reporting unregistered magic, no governess would risk her reputation. Word traveled fast in London's servant networks—betray one employer, never work for another.

After depositing the letter into the waste-paper basket, she arranged her clothes in the chest of drawers.

Footsteps whispered in the corridor outside. Light, careful steps that paused at her door. A soft knock.

"Miss Clarke? It's Madge."

Eliza opened the door to find the girl standing in the hallway wearing a nightdress and an expression of barely leashed terror. "What can I do for you, Miss Madge?"

"I can't sleep," Madge whispered. "When I close my eyes, I see things. Terrible things."

"What sort of things?"

"A man with silver threading his black hair, watching people die." Madge's voice came out hoarse. "And you're there. Sadder."

Eliza had experienced similar nightmares more times than she'd stood in a gruel line at the workhouse. Part of her wanted to shoo Madge back to bed so that she could unpack. Still, Madge was in distress and needed someone to listen to her.

Eliza drew the girl into her room, closing the door softly behind them. "These dreams—how long they been bothering you?"

"Since my twelfth birthday. They strengthen every night." Madge perched on the bed's edge, small hands clenched in her nightdress like claws. "Mother says they're ordinary nightmares. But they feel too real."

Eliza knelt before the girl, meeting those frightened eyes. "I don't reckon you're losing your mind. I reckon you're seeing maybe-futures."

"Maybe-futures?"

"The future's not carved in stone, Madge. What you see in dreams... that's what might 'appen if we make certain choices. But we can choose differently."

Hope flickered in her eyes like stars through storm clouds. "You truly believe so?"

"I know so." Eliza thought of the path chosen for her as a working-class girl. She'd dodged a certain path of servitude as a scullery maid or laundry worker by learning from books at the parish lending shelf.

She took Madge's hands in hers. Power trembled beneath the girl's skin like a coal furnace about to blow. "How about I read you one of me favorite stories?"

"You brought a book?" Madge asked.

"Nah, it's up 'ere," Eliza said, tapping her head.

She led Madge back to her room, settled her into bed, and

tucked the coverlet under her shoulders. Then, she began to recite the only story she knew by heart: *The Voyage of the Lightbinders.* The battered book had been her only possession when she had been dumped on Bow Church's doorstep all those years ago.

"You stay here," a deep voice had told her. "The doors will open soon. They'll find you a family to take care of you."

She'd read the book twice before the doors opened, thrice more before they introduced her to the Clarkes, and a hundred times after that. Mary Clarke burned the book a year later as kindling, but by then Eliza had memorized every word.

She began telling Madge the story. "Once upon a time, light and shadow swirled together on the great continents..."

When Madge finally succumbed to sleep, Eliza sat by the window watching London's lights glitter like scattered embers. Outside, Big Ben chimed midnight, and she felt a familiar warmth settle in, the one she got whenever she read the book. Someone special had given it to her, long ago.

If only she could remember who.

3 QUESTIONS AND ANSWERS

A knock on the door woke Eliza from her slumber.

"Beg pardon, miss, but it's morning."

For a moment, Eliza lay still, absorbing the luxury of clean sheets that smelled of lavender instead of soot, of a mattress that didn't sag toward the floor. Eliza's adoptive mother paid a knocker-upper threepence a week to shoot peas at the windows to wake the house at 5 a.m. Here, a servant gently rapped on the door like Eliza was the queen herself.

Moments later, she dressed in her nicest outfit—a brown cotton dress that hid the stains of daily life—and made her way downstairs. The morning room blazed with an unusual display of late autumn sunlight, and the sideboard groaned under silver chafing dishes that released tantalizing aromas.

"Good morning, Miss Clarke," Lady Windermere said. "Breakfast?"

Eliza was still full from the previous evening's meal. "No, thank you, ma'am. "I was 'hopin to get an early start on lessons if that's alright."

"Where is Miss Madge this morning, ma'am?"

"Still abed, I'm afraid. She had another of her episodes last night." Lady Windermere's voice tightened. "Half the street saw our windows glowing at three in the morning."

Eliza hadn't heard a thing. She'd slept like the dead, most likely because of her two-hour walk from the East End to Mayfair the previous day. And she wasn't sure if she should reveal last night's chat with Madge, so it was best to hold her tongue. "What sort of episode was it, ma'am?"

Lady Windermere cut her egg into tiny pieces with her knife and fork, but didn't eat anything. "She unleashed a fearful energy while describing a man with a silver streak in his hair who called at the house."

A chill spider-walked down Eliza's spine. She hadn't given Madge's mention of the man with the silver streak in his hair much thought, but now that she'd heard the description again, why did she feel that she knew someone with such a streak?

"Perhaps I should check on her, then?"

"Please do. She specifically asked for you to wake her after breakfast." She nodded. "You may be excused."

Eliza exited the morning room and climbed the stairs, noting the way shadows seemed deeper here, more responsive to her presence. Everything about this house felt alive with magic barely held in check.

At the end of the corridor, Eliza knocked softly on Madge's door.

"Do come in." Her voice was thick with sleep and fear.

Madge sat propped against lace pillows, her curls tangled around a face too pale for a child. Faint traces of light clung to her fingertips, guttering like dying candles.

"Rough night?" Eliza settled into the chair beside the bed.

"Strange night." Madge rubbed her eyes. "I keep seeing things. Faces I do not recognize. The man with the silver streak spoke of tournaments and service to the Crown."

Eliza's blood chilled. The Imperial Magisterium's recruitment methods were legendary. Perhaps that's where Eliza remembered the man with the silver hair streak—not from an encounter, but from East End gossip or perhaps a penny dreadful.

Madge's hands clenched the coverlet. "Do you think dreams can come true?"

"Some dreams are just dreams, right. Others are warnings. The important thing is you learn the difference."

"Mama thinks I'm losing my mind. Father pretends nothing unusual is happening at all," Madge said, the words barely a whisper. "Sometimes I wonder if it would be easier to pretend the power doesn't exist."

"Would it? Could you stop seeing light as something to shape, stop feeling 'ow it responds to your emotions?"

"No. It's like asking me to stop breathing." Madge held up her hand, watching golden threads weave between her fingers. "It's part of me. The most essential part."

"Then we'll work with it, won't we. Not against it."

She let out a tiny gasp. "Really? You won't try to make it go away?"

"I couldn't get rid of magic even if I wanted to. That's like trying to change the color of your eyes. But you can learn control. How to use your gifts safely."

"And you'll stay and teach me? Not go away like the other governesses?"

"I'll teach you everything I can. And I ain't going nowhere. Now, shall we start? What do you already know?"

Madge's face lit with a genuine smile. "I know quite a lot, actually. I've read everything there is about magical theory."

"Everything?"

"Well, everything I can access. Father's library has some interesting texts, though most of the good ones are locked away." Mischief sparkled in her eyes. "But locks are remarkably easy to manage when you can manipulate light to pick them."

Eliza laughed. "Clever girl. What have you learned, then?"

"That magical abilities usually follow bloodlines. That power manifests differently in different people, even within the same family. That the Empire has been documenting magical lineages for centuries." Madge paused. "Do you know where you got your power from?"

"Nah. Far as I know, no one in me family's got magical powers."

And that wasn't far from the truth—she didn't know anyone in her real family. She remembered a woman with hair the color of coal, a kind smile, and a blue circle on her forehead. But was that her mother? Perhaps. But she certainly didn't remember any magic.

"Mother says it's probably hereditary," Madge said. "She said there was a great-uncle with strong light powers. His name was...

hmmm... Uncle Leonard, I think? He left for foreign lands when he was quite young. Magic skips generations in our family, she thinks."

The name sounded familiar—had she known someone called Leonard? A friend of the Clarkes', perhaps, or one of her old teachers in India. It was a common enough name, though, so she dismissed the thought as a coincidence. "Sometimes it does," Eliza said. "I 'ad a charge once who got his grandfather's ward-power. He used to spin a ward when it was time for sums. I couldn't even get through the schoolroom door."

Madge chuckled. "Don't you have any family stories? Tales about ancestors who were different?"

"The Clarkes were simple folk. Me adoptive dad collected scrap metal and rags. Me mum washed clothes for toffs." The words felt hollow, like she was reciting someone else's story. "Nothing magical about either of them."

"Adoptive?" Madge seized on the word immediately. "So you don't know your birth family?"

A prickling tension crawled over Eliza's skin. She'd let the girl's easy manner trick her into honesty. She had asked the same question about her heritage twice, albeit in different tones, like she knew Eliza was hiding something. It wasn't like Eliza was being dishonest, but how could she explain to a privileged young girl that something traumatic had happened to Eliza in India? That she barely remembered her parents at all? "I was a little girl when they took me in. There ain't much to know."

"That explains why Mama was so interested in hiring you. She spent a whole day researching your background, making inquiries through channels I'm not supposed to know about."

"What sort of channels?"

"The sort that involve old families with long memories and extensive records." Madge's voice dropped to a conspiratorial whisper. "Mother has access to genealogical societies, magical registries going back centuries. She can trace bloodlines through methods most people don't know exist."

Eliza's pulse quickened. "She looked into my bloodline?"

"Extensively. I heard her telling Father that your magical signature suggested 'interesting possibilities.'"

The room felt suddenly airless. Lady Windermere apparently knew more about Eliza's heritage than Eliza herself did. "How much do your mum and dad know about my past?"

"More than they're telling you. Mother spent considerable money on those inquiries."

Fear and hope warred in Eliza's chest. If the Windermeres had access to records that could explain her heritage, her abilities, the gaps in her memory...

Eliza stood to leave. "I should go and 'ave a chat with Lady Windermere. Maybe you can get dressed, and we'll start lessons in an hour."

* * *

Eliza found Lady Windermere knitting in the morning room, surrounded by neat balls of yarn.

"Lady Windermere. Might I have a word?"

"Of course." Her sharp eyes seemed to assess Eliza's expression, or perhaps she'd caught the overly stressed *h*.

"Madge said you can access records. That you looked into me before offering the job."

"I did. Quite thoroughly." Lady Windermere put down her needles.

"And if it ain't too impertinent, ma'am, what did you find?"

"That you're not what you appear to be, Miss Clarke. Your magical signature suggests a bloodline far more significant than a rag-and-bone man's adopted daughter should possess."

"Then you know something about where I come from?"

"I know enough to intrigue me. The church records, which were sealed, state they found you in a pool of unregistered shadows. From there, I cannot say, but it is likely the nuns may have instructed your parents to keep them hidden. The church is at loggerheads with the Magisterium, Miss Clarke. They do not believe that using children in tournaments is in line with God's teachings."

Eliza gasped. The church had records? "So, so... it were the nuns who told my parents to... keep my abilities hidden?"

"I would say that it is likely."

"But why would the Clarkes have adopted me? I was just another mouth to feed."

"Ah, yes. The church pays families a small stipend to adopt children. Enough to feed and clothe you."

Or enough to pay for a daughter's laudanum draught and a father's gin habit, Eliza thought.

"Many families in the poorer districts adopt older children to put them to work. I take it you worked as a sweep's assistant?"

"Yes, ma'am. Until I was eleven and too big to fit up the chimney. Then I worked in the laundry."

"Ah, such a terrible life for a child." Lady Windermere pulled a string above the side table. A distant bell tinkled. "May I interest you in tea?"

Eliza bristled. Lady Windermere seemed kind, but apparently, she thought that tea would rid her of the distasteful matter of discussing poor folk's problems. "No, thank you, ma'am. May I ask what else you know?"

"What specific questions are you hoping to have answered?"

The words tumbled out before Eliza could stop them. "Everything. Who I really am. Where my abilities come from. What 'appened to my birth family."

Lady Windermere raised a brow. "You ask dangerous questions."

"Maybe. But I've lived with uncertainty my whole life, 'aven't I? I'm tired of it."

Lady Windermere nodded slowly. "I understand the need for answers. But you must understand—the sort of research required is delicate. And potentially hazardous for all involved."

"Hazardous how?"

"Some bloodlines carry political implications. Others have been deliberately obscured for good reason. There are names that appear in no official records, families whose histories have been... edited."

"You mean got rid of."

"Exactly. If your lineage is one of those, investigating it could draw attention we'd all prefer to avoid."

"How much attention we talking about?"

"The sort that involves midnight visits from Imperial officials. The sort that makes children disappear into government programs." Lady Windermere's eyes held grim knowledge. "The sort that turns governess positions into death sentences."

Fear crystallized in Eliza's stomach. But beneath it, determination burned brighter. "I need to know, ma'am."

The butler entered the room, carrying a silver tray with a teapot and one cup. He set the tray down at Lady Windermere's side, bowed, and then retreated to the door.

"Very well," Lady Windermere said, pouring tea. "But I set the conditions. You cannot access these records directly—they're held by families and institutions that don't allow outsiders. I can make discreet inquiries through established contacts, but it will take time. And you must be prepared for the possibility that some answers will raise more questions."

"Got it. I mean, I understand."

"Do you? Because once we start down this path, there's no turning back. Knowledge changes everything, Miss Clarke. Are you certain you're ready for that?"

Eliza thought of shadows that moved without her permission, of nightmares and a lifetime of living as half a person. "I'm definitely ready."

"Then tell me what you want to know specifically, and I'll see what can be discovered."

"My birth name. Who my blood family are. What 'appened to them."

Lady Windermere nodded, already reaching for a fountain pen and parchment. "It may take weeks. Possibly months. These inquiries must be made carefully."

"I can wait. I ain't going nowhere."

But even as she spoke the words, unease shivered through her. If she couldn't get Madge to control her power, how long before the Magisterium showed up at the door? How long before she was out on the streets again?

"There's something else," Lady Windermere said, not looking up from her notes. "If what I suspect about your heritage proves true, you and Madge may be more connected than simple governess and student."

"Connected how?"

"Some bloodlines complement each other. Light and shadow, for instance, often appear in linked families. Partners in power rather than simple opposites."

Eliza gasped. "You think we're related?"

"It's within the realm of possibility. Your magical signatures are... similar? If there is a family connection, it will be a thread. A thread that's been buried since the India purges." She waved a hand as if to brush off the idea. "This could all be supposition, of course. Perhaps I will know more after I make a few more inquiries."

A comfortable silence settled between them. Outside, London continued its daily bustle—carriages rolling past, servants calling to each other, the distant chime of church bells marking the hour.

"I should go prepare some lessons," Eliza said.

"Of course. And Miss Clarke? Thank you. For giving us hope."

* * *

Later that evening, Eliza climbed the main staircase, her conversation with Lady Windermere still echoing in her mind. Connected bloodlines. India. Threads buried in violence and secrets.

She knocked softly on Madge's door. "May I come in?"

"Please do," Madge said in a high-pitched voice.

Eliza stepped inside and froze. Madge sat on her bed, back against the headboard, hands clenched in her lap. Light bled between her fingers—no longer the gentle golden glow of yesterday, but something hungrier, brighter, like the amber flame that flares before a fire roars.

"I can't make it stop." Tears streaked down Madge's face. "It started a few minutes ago. I was thinking about the man with the silver streak. And the power just... erupted."

The air around the girl shimmered with energy. The wallpaper bore new scorch marks, and the mirror on her dressing table had cracked down the center.

"Every time I try to calm down, it gets worse," Madge said— quiet and shaking.

Eliza approached slowly. Heat radiated from Madge's skin, magic pressing against her like a physical weight. "We have to get you grounded, miss."

"I don't know what that is."

"I'll teach you." Eliza settled on the bed's edge, careful not to touch. "Close your eyes. Breathe along with me, right?"

Madge obeyed, but light still pulsed around her fingers. "It's not working."

"Focus on my voice. Nothing else except that, alright?" Eliza kept her tone steady despite the magical storm building around them. "Feel the mattress under you. The pillows at your back. The air in your throat."

The light dimmed. Then Madge's eyes snapped open.

"I saw it again. The arena. Children fighting while adults watch from golden boxes." The power flared brighter. "You were there, with burned skin. And the man with silver streaks in his hair—he was smiling."

The light exploded outward.

Eliza stumbled back, pushed by a wall of air.

China figurines on the mantel shattered. The window glass spider-webbed with cracks. Books tumbled from shelves as magical energy lashed through the room like living lightning.

Eliza threw herself forward, wrapping her arms around the terrified girl. Her shadows rose instinctively, darkness meeting blazing light.

The magical storm collapsed in an instant.

Madge sagged against her, sobbing. "I'm sorry. I'm so sorry. I destroyed everything."

"You destroyed nothing that matters." As Eliza held the trembling girl, her heart refused to still, thudding like a spooked horse's hooves against her ribs. Around them, the room had settled into silence, though her body had yet to understand that the danger had passed.

The demonstration had shaken her more than she dared admit. The raw power, the visions of arenas and burned skin—what exactly had she got herself into?

"Miss Clarke?" Madge's voice wobbled. "Will you stay until I fall asleep? The dreams are worse when I'm alone."

"Of course I will."

Eliza tucked the girl beneath her covers, smoothing curls away from her porcelain face. Within minutes, Madge's breathing deepened into sleep.

But Eliza remained by the window long after, staring out at

London's gaslit streets.

What on earth had made her think she was qualified for this? A working-class woman with no formal training, no understanding of magical theory, no experience with power that could reshape reality itself. She'd walked into this position thinking she could help a gifted child learn control.

Instead, she'd found herself drowning in prophecies and bloodline mysteries and forces that could perhaps level houses.

Her adoptive mother's voice echoed in her memory: "Don't you be gettin' too big for your boots, luv. They'll cut off your blood supply and you'll end up losin' yer feet."

Too big for her boots. That's exactly what she was. She'd convinced herself she belonged in this world of the magical elite and ancient secrets, when the truth was simpler—she was a governess from the East End, nothing more.

4 THE WORLD BEYOND MAYFAIR

"We need books," Madge announced over breakfast, stabbing her eggs with her fork. "I've read everything in father's library."

"Surely the house collection is sufficient for your studies?" Lady Windermere asked.

"Mother, I've read everything *twice*. Miss Clarke says I need to understand theoretical foundations before we work on control." Madge's bottom lip jutted out. "Chamblins has an excellent magical texts section. Everyone knows that."

Eliza nearly choked on her tea. Chamblins. The most exclusive bookshop in London. Where ladies in silk counted browsing as entertainment and shopkeepers treated working-class customers like contagions.

"An excellent idea," Lady Windermere said. "I'll ask for the carriage to be brought around."

"Actually." Madge's eyes sparkled with mischief, "I'd prefer to walk. It's such a lovely morning, and it's hardly a mile."

"That is not a good idea," Lady Windermere said. "To be on the streets with your... gift. No, I will not allow it."

"Rot and rubbish," Lord Windermere said. "We can't keep the girl locked up. She can walk through Kensington Gardens. Miss Clarke can accompany her."

Eliza stifled a protest. They should send a servant instead, or order books by catalog. But Madge was watching her with pleading eyes, and she heard her own voice saying, "Of course. Educational outings are important."

An hour later, they stepped into London's gray October morning. The chill bit through their coats, and low clouds promised rain before afternoon.

The difference between Mayfair and the East End was like comparing a Sunday roast to a bowl of gruel. In Mayfair, even the air seemed cleaner—ward spells filtered out the worst of the coal smoke, leaving only the artificial scents of rose perfume drifting from bulbs on top of gas lamps. Carriages glided past with supernatural smoothness, their wheels spell-treated to reduce noise. Every surface gleamed with preservation charms that cost more than most East End families earned in a year.

A passing woman wearing a garland of glittering pearls glanced at Eliza's hem—too plain, too rain-stained—then at her face, pausing a breath too long. Not quite frowning, but assessing. Eliza knew that look. Not East End curiosity, but West End calculation. Who are you? What are you doing here? And perhaps: what are you, exactly?

"Miss Clarke?" Madge touched her arm. "Are you feeling unwell?"

"I'm alright." She forced her shoulders straight. "Which way we going to Chamblins?"

They walked through Kensington Gardens and into Knightsbridge. Shop windows displayed goods that gleamed like jewels—scarves that shimmered with embedded enchantments, jewelry that pulsed with protective wards, perfumes guaranteed to enhance natural beauty through subtle magical influence.

Everything here was designed to remind people like her that they didn't belong.

A group of ladies emerged from a millinery shop, their laughter bright as crystal bells. Their dresses whispered against each other—fabric so fine it moved like water, colors so rich they seemed lit from within. One caught sight of Eliza and murmured something to her companions. They all turned to stare.

Eliza felt a flush of warmth on her neck. She knew what they saw—a working woman in clothes that marked her station as clearly as a branded letter. Her dress was clean but obviously mended. Her boots were practical but worn. Her gloves hid the unmanicured hands but couldn't disguise the fact that they'd been darned multiple times.

"Ignore them," Madge said quietly. "They're peacocks preening for each other."

But ignoring them proved impossible when they followed the same path toward Chamblins. Their conversation carried on the morning air—comments about "proper supervision" and "letting standards slip" and "the sort of person one finds in service these days."

"We should go another way, miss," Eliza suggested.

"Absolutely not." Steel threaded Madge's voice. "We have every right to walk wherever we please. I am a *Windermere*."

At the corner of Brompton Road, they passed a tea shop where elegantly dressed women sat behind floor-to-ceiling windows, observing the people passing by. One raised her lorgnette to study Eliza more closely. Another leaned forward to whisper behind her fan.

The scrutiny made Eliza's skin crawl.

"Miss Clarke." Madge stopped walking. "You're hunching."

"I am not."

"You are. Your shoulders are up around your ears, and you're staring at the pavement like it holds the secrets of the universe." Madge's tone was matter-of-fact. "Stop it."

"Easy for you to say. You belong 'ere."

"Do I?" Madge gestured at a flower seller on the street corner. The woman's spindly fingers wove light into daisies, power flowing like water between her fingers. "Look at her. Do you think she belongs?"

Eliza watched the practitioner work. Working-class, perhaps, judging by her plain dress, weathered skin, and the fact that she was a flower seller.

"Now look around," Madge continued. "How many people are actually paying attention to her?"

It was true. Passers-by ignored the woman entirely, treating the flower girls as no less interesting than a street sweeper clearing rubbish from the gutters.

"They don't see her power," Madge said. "They don't see her at all. She acts like she belongs here, so she does."

"I'm assuming you have a point, miss?"

"My point is that belonging isn't about blood or birth. It's about confidence." Madge straightened her spine. "So stop apologizing for existing and walk like you own the street."

The words stung because they were true. She had been apologizing—for her clothes, her accent, her very presence in spaces not designed for her.

But she was here on business. Legitimate business.

She lifted her chin and kept walking.

* * *

Chamblins occupied a corner building that radiated literary authority. Its windows displayed volumes bound in leather so supple it looked like skin. Gilt letters proclaimed titles in languages she recognized—English, French, Latin—and others she didn't. A discreet placard announced: "Magical Texts Authorized Dealer Inquire Within."

The doorman assessed them as they approached. His eyes cataloged Madge's quality dress and obvious breeding, then moved to Eliza. She felt the familiar calculation—servant or companion? Family or employee? Worth acknowledging or safe to ignore?

"Good morning," Madge said with perfect aristocratic authority. "We require magical theory texts. Advanced material."

The doorman's posture shifted. Whatever he'd been thinking about Eliza became irrelevant when faced with a customer who clearly had money to spend.

"Of course, miss. Third floor, east wing."

The interior was a cathedral of learning. Shelves stretched to vaulted ceilings, accessible by ladders that moved on hidden tracks. The air smelled of leather and vellum. Magical lights provided perfect illumination without heat or flicker.

And everywhere, people who belonged.

Men in academic robes browsed theoretical texts with scholarly intensity. Well-dressed women selected fashionable novels, their jewelry catching the magical light. Serious-faced individuals in expensive suits examined policy documents with the careful attention of those accustomed to authority.

All of them looked like they'd been born here.

"This way," Madge said, heading for a brass-gated lift.

The operator was a short, stout man with a monocle whose uniform was of better quality than anything in Eliza's wardrobe. He assessed them with what appeared to be professional discretion, then operated levers that sent them smoothly upward.

"Third floor, magical studies," he announced.

The doors opened onto paradise.

Books lined every wall from floor to ceiling—treatises on theoretical magic, practical guides to power development, historical texts about bloodline abilities. But it wasn't just the volumes that took her breath away.

Magic danced through the air like a living thing. A woman in silk gloves gestured lazily, sending three leather-bound tomes spinning slowly above her palm as she examined their covers. Nearby, a gentleman flicked his wrist and watched pages flutter through the air, turning themselves as he read without ever touching the book. Quills wrote notes by themselves, guided by invisible hands, while other customers browsed with books floating at eye level, pages turning at the reader's silent command.

The scent of preserved knowledge mixed with the sharp ozone of active magic—preservation spells, levitation charms, enchantments that made text glow faintly for easier reading. Even the ladders moved on their own, gliding along brass tracks in response to whispered requests.

This was what money and registration bought—the casual use of magic for convenience, comfort, luxury. A world where power served pleasure rather than survival.

A thin man with ink-stained fingers looked in their direction. He gave a cursory glance at Eliza, then smiled at Madge. "How may I assist you, miss?"

"Foundational texts on magical theory," Madge said. "Particular emphasis on power control and bloodline studies."

His eyebrows rose. "Advanced material for someone your age."

"I'm a fast learner."

He led them through sections organized by subject and magical school. Eliza found herself overwhelmed by the sheer volume of knowledge surrounding them. Entire shelves devoted to ward crafting. Dozens of volumes on healing magic. A locked case containing books that hummed with contained power.

"These might suit," the assistant said, pulling several volumes from a high shelf. "Theoretical Foundations of Magical Practice by Lord Ashford. Bloodline Abilities and Their Development by Dame Margaret Sinclair. And perhaps this—" He hesitated, then selected a slimmer volume. "Shadow Magic: Historical Perspectives by an anonymous author."

Eliza's pulse jumped. "Shadow Magic?"

"Academic interest only, of course. The practical applications are strictly regulated." His smile was diplomatic. "But the theoretical foundations are fascinating from a scholarly perspective."

Madge caught her eye. "We'll take all three."

While the assistant calculated prices, Madge perused a countertop selection of bargain books. Eliza noticed a small sign that said, "Latest shadow magic texts can be found in Aisle 3."

Aisle three was just two aisles over. Eliza was dead sure that there wouldn't be any books she could afford, but it was worth a quick look. "You stay right 'ere, Miss Madge. I'll be back in a jiffy."

She wandered deeper into the stacks. Hidden alcoves revealed specialized collections—books on rare abilities, historical accounts of magical bloodlines, theoretical works that pushed the boundaries of accepted practice.

In one shadowed corner, she found a section that made her breath catch.

Imperial Policies and Procedures.

The volumes were bound in official blue leather, their spines marked with government seals. She recognized several titles from overheard conversations among servants: *Registration Requirements for Magical Citizens. Protocols for Ability Assessment. Guidelines for Exceptional Individuals.*

Her hand moved toward them without conscious thought.

"Fascinating reading."

She spun. A woman in a black mourning dress stood behind her—middle-aged, with owl-like eyes that missed nothing.

"What's that now, ma'am?"

"Imperial policy texts. Not light entertainment, but essential for understanding how our government manages magical citizens." The woman's smile was thin. "Are you researching for academic purposes?"

The question felt loaded. "Just curious, that's all."

"Curiosity can be dangerous where Imperial policies are concerned." The woman stepped closer, and Eliza caught the scent of orange blossom eau de Cologne mixed with something sharper. Magic. "Particularly for those with personal stakes in the matter."

"I don't know what you mean."

"I think you do." The woman's gaze flicked to the shadows pooling around Eliza's feet. "Perhaps you should be more careful about controlling involuntary manifestations. Some people notice things others miss."

Fear coiled in her stomach as Eliza realized she'd given herself away. She tried to rein in her shadows, but they writhed around her boots, dark tendrils seeking escape. "That's just the bad lighting, ain't it."

"Shadow-worker blood runs thin these days," she whispered. "Most lines were extinguished years ago. Such a tragedy."

Eliza sucked in a breath. "That's got nothing to do with me."

"Of course not." The woman gave her a small, horrible smile. "The massacre in Delhi was quite thorough. The one in Calcutta was even more so. Imperial efficiency at its finest."

Eliza's knees buckled. Delhi. Calcutta. The fragments of her nightmares—jasmine gardens burning, hands pulling her from fiery turmoil.

"You're mistaken, ma'am," Eliza said, her voice choking as if she were breathing soot.

"Am I?" The woman's gaze dropped again to the shadows at Eliza's feet. "Such distinctive manifestations. The old bloodlines always had particular... signatures."

Heat crawled up Eliza's neck. Around them, other customers browsed with casual indifference, unaware of the predator circling in their midst.

"What do you want, then? I ain't got nothing of value."

"Nothing at all. I'm simply... observing. The Empire has such interest in lost bloodlines these days. Particularly ones thought to be extinct." The woman's fingers traced air circles—binding spells, Eliza realized with growing horror. She was preparing to magically restrain her while pretending to have a casual conversation.

The woman's spell created a miniature whirlwind in the air. "Perhaps you would be so kind as to produce your registration papers?"

"Miss Clarke?" Madge appeared between the stacks, voice bright with artificial cheer. "Mother's expecting us back for lunch."

The woman smiled. "How lovely. Your charge, I presume?"

"Yes," Madge said. "I am Madge Windermere, and I do not appreciate you harassing my employee."

The woman's finger paused, breaking the spell. "Windermere. I do apologize. Do give your parents my regards. Lady Beatrice Ashworth. They'll remember the name."

She melted back into the stacks, leaving a hint of darkness.

"What was that about?" Madge whispered.

"Trouble." Eliza grabbed the girl's arm. "Let's get out of here, miss. Right now."

Eliza's hands shook as she grabbed their books from the counter, coins scattering as she fumbled with her purse. The assistant's curious stare burned into her back. Every second felt like an eternity; the woman could return, could call for guards, could expose her right here among the leather-bound volumes and polite society.

"Hurry," she whispered to Madge, steering her toward the exit. Her shadows writhed with panic, and she fought to keep them from betraying her further.

They pushed through the heavy doors into the murky London afternoon, and only then did Eliza allow herself to breathe.

The London streets felt different now—hostile where they'd been merely unwelcoming before. Every glance from passing strangers seemed charged with suspicion. Every shadow looked deeper than it should.

"Did she see your shadows?" Madge asked quietly as they walked.

Eliza's hands trembled inside her gloves. "She saw a bit too much, miss."

A carriage rolled past—black lacquer with brass fittings that gleamed too brightly. Through the spelled windows, she glimpsed a figure in Imperial blue watching them with interest that curdled her stomach.

31

"We're being followed," she said.

Madge glanced back. "The carriage?"

"Among others." A man in a bowler hat had been behind them since Chamblins, maintaining a casual distance. Another lurked near the corner ahead, reading a newspaper that never seemed to turn pages.

"What do we do? Walk faster?"

Before Eliza could answer, tendrils of deep green ivy exploded from every doorway.

Not natural tendrils of plant magic—this was wrong, hungry, reaching for them with grasping threads that felt like ice and malice. Her shadows recoiled in recognition, shrieking warnings she felt in her bones.

"Run!" She grabbed Madge's hand and bolted.

Behind them, shouts erupted. Footsteps pounded on cobblestones. The black carriage wheeled around, blazing with pursuit magic.

They plunged into the maze of Knightsbridge's side streets, their breath misting in the cold air as Eliza's heart raced. The ivy followed—not alive, but something else entirely.

"This way!" Madge pulled her toward a narrow alley.

Light blazed around the girl like armor, pushing back the unnatural growths. But for every tendril her power destroyed, three more took its place.

They burst onto a main thoroughfare, and the ivy suddenly vanished. Pulled back as if by invisible chains, retreating to whatever hellish source had spawned them.

"What were those?" Madge gasped.

"I don't know." It seemed like she had no answers for any of it.

The stress of the chase caught up with her. Her shadows erupted without warning, boiling up from the cobblestones, wrapping around lampposts and shop signs. People scattered. Carriages wheeled away from the spreading darkness.

Footsteps pounded behind them. Imperial blue flashed between the fleeing civilians.

"There!" A voice barked. "Magical disturbance, northwest corner!"

A man stepped from the crowd—tall, thirty or so, with silver threading his dark hair. His uniform bore Imperial insignia. When he stepped into view, Eliza's heart stopped.

She knew that face. Knew the scar ghosting along his jaw like frozen lightning. When he moved toward them, her shadows writhed in recognition.

His gray eyes swept the scene, then found hers. Something flickered there—surprise, perhaps recognition. She could swear his pupils dilated slightly before he controlled the reaction.

"Stand down," he called to his approaching team. "I've got this."

A crystal device appeared in his hands. He swept it toward them, but she caught the way his thumb shifted across the device's surface—a subtle adjustment that looked like routine operation but felt like deliberate sabotage.

The detector remained silent.

"Clear," he announced. His team retreated.

"Your name?" he asked Eliza.

"Miss Eliza Clarke."

"Clarke. Hmmm. Not Windermere?"

Madge gasped. "I am Madge Windermere. But how did you know my name, sir?"

He ignored her question and instead kept his gaze on Eliza. "You are not a Windermere?"

"No, sir," Eliza said. Why was he being so insistent? It was clear from her dress that she was not upper crust. "I am Miss Madge Windermere's governess."

He studied her for a long moment, close enough that she could smell steel and danger on his skin. His gaze dropped to her mouth for just a heartbeat before meeting her eyes again. "Careful," he said quietly. "London's getting more dangerous for people like you."

Then he was gone, melting back into the crowd.

"That was the man I saw in my dream," Madge said. "But he didn't feel scary. And he helped us."

"Did he? Or was he just doing his job?" Eliza's pulse quickened. He *had* helped them—she was sure of it. How was it possible that Madge recognized him too?

They walked across Kensington Gardens in tense silence, the damp October air seeping through their coats as Eliza wondered about the stranger with silver-streaked hair who'd looked at her like he'd seen a ghost.

"We should get home," Madge said quietly.

As they continued into Mayfair, Eliza fought to keep her shadows contained while scanning every face for signs of pursuit. By the time they reached the Windermere mansion, her nerves were stretched thin as gossamer.

"They know," Eliza said as they approached the house.

"Know what?"

"What I am. What I can do. My shadows moved, and he saw, he did."

Madge was quiet for several steps. Then, "Perhaps we both need to contain our energy, Miss Clarke."

"I think it might be a bit late for that, miss. They know who you are, which means that they know who I am."

5 THE WINDERMERE SECRET

Inside the drawing room, Lady Windermere rang for tea, her hand steady despite the slight tremor in her voice moments before. Lord Windermere settled into his leather chair, pipe already between his teeth.

"Now then," Lady Windermere said as the door closed behind the maid. "What exactly did this woman say?"

Eliza recounted the encounter—Lady Ashworth's questions, her knowledge of the massacres, the way she'd recognized the shadow magic. Eliza left out the part about the Magisterium encounter, not wanting to distress Lady Windermere further.

Madge looked at Eliza and scrunched her brow. She opened her mouth to say something, but Eliza shook her head slightly. *Don't.*

"Ashworth." Lord Windermere struck a match. "I know the name. Genealogical society."

"But that doesn't mean anything," Lady Windermere said quickly. "There are at least a dozen Windermere families in London. Cousins, distant relations. She can't possibly know which branch we are."

"She knew," Madge said quietly. "When I told her my name, she knew exactly who I was. She asked me to give you her regards."

Lady Windermere waved a dismissive hand. "Social pleasantries, darling. Nothing more."

"Charlotte." Lord Windermere's voice growled with caution.

"No, Harold. I refuse to panic over one woman's curiosity." Lady Windermere's teacup rattled against its saucer as she set it down. "Tomorrow I'll make a few calls. Lady Pemberton always knows what's being whispered in drawing rooms. If there's genuine cause for concern, I'll hear it through the proper channels."

She smoothed her skirt with hands that trembled slightly. "Until then, we carry on as we always have."

But Eliza noticed how Lady Windermere avoided meeting anyone's eyes.

* * *

That night, Eliza woke to the house screaming.

But it wasn't human voices. The walls shrieked as magic tore through them like claws. Spelled mirrors cracked in their frames. Light fittings died with piercing pops.

She rolled from bed as another wave of power slammed through the mansion. The floorboards beneath her feet vibrated with energy.

Madge.

Eliza yanked on her wrapper and ran barefoot through corridors that pulsed with unstable magic. Servants pressed themselves against walls, terror stark on their faces. A maid sobbed into her hands. The butler stood frozen, staring into space.

"Where is she?" Eliza asked.

"Bedroom," the butler rasped. "Please, miss. Make it stop."

Another scream—this one human. Lady Windermere's voice, raw with panic.

Eliza sprinted down the hall as the chandelier above her head exploded in a shower of crystal. Tiny fragments rained down, slicing through her wrapper, drawing blood from her shoulders.

Madge's bedroom door hung askew, hinges melted from their frames. Inside was devastation. Every piece of furniture lay in splinters. The wallpaper had burned away, leaving charred patterns on the plaster. Windows had blown outward, letting in London's sooty dawn air.

Madge stood in the center of it all.

Magic light coiled around her like living flame—not the gentle golden light from yesterday, but something white-hot and furious.

It pulsed with her heartbeat, sending cracks lancing across the ceiling. Her nightdress whipped around her legs, caught in currents of raw magic.

Lady Windermere knelt near the door, hands pressed to a bleeding gash on her forehead. "I tried to wake her," she gasped. "She was having nightmares, and when I touched her—"

The power lashed out. Eliza dove sideways as a tendril of burning light carved through the air where her head had been.

"Madge!" She crawled closer, glass biting into her palms. "Madge, wake up!"

The girl's eyes were open but unseeing. Lost in whatever vision held her captive.

"Don't touch her," Lady Windermere sobbed. "Every time someone touches her, it gets worse."

The magic pulsed brighter. Eliza staggered as alien power crashed against her defenses. Her shadows writhed in panic, darkness scattering like startled birds.

She reached for Madge anyway.

The moment her fingers brushed the girl's wrist, the world exploded.

Light and shadow crashed together like opposing armies. Madge's burning power met Eliza's darkness, and for one terrifying instant, they fought for dominance. Heat seared through Eliza's veins. Cold bit deep enough to crack bones.

Then something shifted. Instead of fighting, the magic danced; darkness wrapped around brilliance, cooling the burning edges. The chaotic storm found balance and sputtered to nothing.

Madge collapsed. Eliza caught her before she hit the glass-strewn floor, gathering the trembling girl against her chest. Around them, the room settled into silence.

"Bloody hell." Lord Windermere stood in the doorway, face gray with shock. "Again?"

Lady Windermere pushed herself upright, blood still trickling down her face. "Yes. She had another dream."

Eliza gestured around the destroyed room. "And when she dreams, this 'appens?"

Lord Windermere stepped carefully through the debris. "Not always this severe. But yes. Every episode has been worse than the last. During them, she doesn't awaken, as if she is in a devil's trance."

Eliza looked down at Madge's pale face, at the dark circles under her eyes. "What does she see?"

"Blood," Lady Windermere whispered. "Always blood. On black stone, under starlight. She wakes up screaming about sacrifice and death and—" She stopped, eyes widening as she took in the darkness still clinging to Eliza's feet. "And shadow magic."

The silence stretched. Around them, servants whispered in the hallway—fragments about curses and demons and children who shouldn't exist.

"We need to talk," Lord Windermere said. "All of us. But first..." He looked at his daughter's unconscious form. "First, we need to get her back to bed."

They straightened the four-poster bed, replaced the mattress, and settled Madge onto it. The girl looked fragile against white linens, her breathing shallow.

Eliza stared at Madge's sleeping form. Even unconscious, energy sparked around the girl's fingers—faint traces of devastating power.

"Tell me everything," she said. "About 'er dreams. About 'er magic."

Lord Windermere and his wife exchanged a look weighted with secrets.

"Not here," he said. "My study is warded. We can speak freely there."

Minutes later, they gathered in Lord Windermere's study. Parents on the window seat, Eliza in the desk chair. Dawn light filtered through the curtains, but the room felt shrouded in shadow.

"The dreams started the night she turned twelve," Lady Windermere began. "We thought it was magical adolescence— children often have power surges during growth periods. But she described things. Specific things."

"Like what?"

"Dragons forged from ice." Lady Windermere's hands twisted in her lap. "Places she's never been. People she's never met. All of it drenched in blood and shadow."

Lord Windermere's voice was heavy with dread. "The Imperial Tournaments—that is what she imagines. Young girls of her kind, compelled to enter into some corrupted mockery of training in arms."

"The Empire doesn't just recruit talented children," Lady Windermere said, tears streaming down her cheeks. "They harvest them. Use them to fuel their devilish war machine."

Eliza's blood froze. "And the things Madge sees?"

"This is going to sound a little unorthodox," Lord Windermere said. "It's like she's tapping into something beyond the grave."

A memory surfaced in Eliza's mind—the woman with coal black hair and a blue circle chalked on her forehead, darkness consuming her like ghoulish vapor. The taste of terror. The smell of jasmine. The certainty that all-consuming darkness and whispers from the grave haunted more than just Madge's dreams. It haunted her own.

"We won't let them take her," Lady Windermere said fiercely. "We won't let them turn her into a weapon."

Lord Windermere sighed heavily. "We can't hide this much longer. Unless we do something, they will come for her."

Outside, church bells began to ring. Not the gentle chimes of morning service, but frantic clanging. Then came the wail of steam whistles. Magical sirens shrieking across the city.

Eliza moved to the window. Her breath caught.

London burned with golden light. St. Paul's great dome was cracked like an eggshell. Street lamps blazed like miniature suns.

Lord and Lady Windermere joined Eliza at the window.

"Dear God," Lord Windermere said. "Her magic—it didn't stop in the house."

More sirens wailed. In the distance, Eliza could see an Imperial carriage making its way toward the mansion. "How long do we 'ave?"

"Minutes." Lord Windermere was already moving, pulling documents from a hidden drawer. "Maybe less."

"Maybe I should take Madge and run then," Eliza said.

"But to where?" Lady Windermere's sob was barely audible.

"The back alleys of Whitechapel. I'll take care of 'er. Keep 'er safe until this all dies down."

"But why would you risk everything for my daughter?"

Eliza thought of the man who had lifted her from smoke and screams as a young child in India, of the stranger's voice that had whispered, "*run*." Someone had risked everything to save a child they barely knew. But before she could formulate a response to Lady Windermere's questions, a powerful magic blast pressed against her.

Then there was the unmistakable sound of the front door exploding inward. A thunderous crash echoed through the hallways as wood splintered into shards. Voices drifted up the stairwell—commands barked in clipped military tones, heavy boots thundering through the entrance hall below. Doors kicked open. Furniture overturned. The sounds of a house about to be torn apart.

"We're too late." Lord Windermere's face was ashen. "They're here. They're going to take her."

Eliza's shadows stirred with protective fury. "Not if I 'ave anything to say about it."

Lord Windermere grabbed her arm. "No. Do not show them your power. They will kill you as surely as they purged the Shadowbinders. And if you are dead..."

But Eliza was already moving toward the door, toward Madge, toward a fight she might not survive.

6 THE IMPERIAL RESPONSE

Heavy boots echoed on marble floors. Multiple sets, moving in synchrony like they were headed to battle. Voices barked orders in the clipped tones of those accustomed to immediate obedience.

"Imperial Magisterium! This house is under martial investigation! All residents will present themselves for immediate assessment!"

The footsteps had reached the bottom of the stairs now, accompanied by the hum of active magical shielding and the metallic click of weapons being readied.

Madge's voice came from the end of the hall. "They're here, aren't they?"

"Yes." Eliza didn't lie. "But we're going to face this together, right?"

"Together." Madge's smile was heartbreaking in its trust as she walked toward Eliza in her nightdress. "I'd like that."

Four Battle Mages climbed the stairs, weapons drawn, breaking into groups of two as they reached the top. Behind them, two figures in midnight-blue coats followed.

The woman was a sword wrapped in velvet. Her raven-colored hair pinned beneath a military cap adorned with iced lightning. Her eyes were the color of Thames fog and held all its warmth.

But it was the man next to her that stopped Eliza's heart.

Tall and chiseled, with a pale scar tracing his jaw—the only thing soft about him. It was the man from the street. He now wore a dress uniform, which bore more silver than the others, threads that formed patterns she recognized from her nightmares. When he stepped forward, her shadows bent toward him like iron filings drawn to a magnet.

She stared at his brass nameplate: Major David Thorne. She knew that name. When she met his gaze, there was mutual recognition of their encounter in Knightsbridge. But the way he stared, not at her, but at her forehead—as if she had an angry, infected pimple there that he could not keep from staring at. Something deeper flickered there too—an echo of an older meeting.

But where?

"Lord and Lady Windermere." The raven-haired woman's voice carried the warmth of winter wind through trees. "By order of Her Majesty's Imperial Magisterium, you will surrender all unregistered magical persons within this household."

Her words came wrapped in compulsion magic—subtle threads that tried to slip past mental defenses and demand obedience.

Lady Windermere swayed slightly before catching herself. "Surely we might discuss—"

"There is nothing to discuss." Thorne's voice sounded like it could cut bone. His attention fixed on Eliza in an unsettling way, as if he was sizing up a battlefield opponent. "The magical disturbance that emanated from this location constitutes a threat to Imperial stability. All responsible parties will be detained."

Why was this man talking about detention when he had let them go on the street? "Detained? But—"

"Do not speak," he said. "It is better that you do not."

Eliza bit her tongue, struggling to keep her retort contained. But his words—they were soft. Not a warning perhaps, but a suggestion. Was he protecting her? It made no sense.

The raven-haired woman moved toward Madge with fluid steps that made no sound. In her hands, she held the same crystal that Thorne held on the street. It was fused with metal, carved with runes that shifted when she wasn't looking directly at them. It pulsed with light the color of candle flame, and every pulse sent needles of pain through her skull.

Eliza pulled her shadows in tight, to a pinprick behind her brow. *Hide,* she said to her shadows, though the thought surprised her. She did not know if she could hide her magic, or what made her think she could.

The woman held the device at waist level, pointing it toward Eliza. "Magical resonance detector. It measures power levels."

Miraculously, the device swept silently past Eliza, and she stifled a gasp. Her thoughts of hiding her magic had worked, though she had no idea how or why. But the moment the device came within three feet of Madge, it screamed.

The sound was like nails on glass amplified a thousand times. The crystal sphere blazed with light so brilliant it turned the hall white.

"Impossible," The raven-haired woman said. "The readings are off the scale."

"What does that mean?" Lord Windermere asked, though terror in his voice suggested he already knew.

"It means your daughter possesses power at levels we haven't seen since the old bloodlines." Thorne's voice held respect. Or hunger. "Power that requires immediate specialized handling."

Had that been a note of disappointment in his voice? Regret? Eliza wanted to demand answers, demand an explanation for his vacillating behavior, demand that they be released this instant. Madge was just a *child.*

But as she stared at Thorne's silver-flecked gray eyes, she thought she definitely saw a warning there. A slight, almost imperceptible shake of his head. The same warning she'd given to Madge in the drawing room the previous evening: *Don't.*

But who was he protecting? And from what?

"You mean the Tournament." Madge's voice was calm despite the weapons trained on her.

Thorne's eyebrows rose. "You know about the Tournament?"

"I know it's where powerful children go to die for Imperial glory. I know most of them don't survive. And I know that's where you're taking me."

"The Tournament is an opportunity for exceptionally gifted individuals to serve the Empire at the highest levels." His tone suggested he was reciting official policy. "It's considered a great honor."

"It's a death sentence, that's what it is," Eliza yelled before she could stop herself.

Every weapon swung toward her. Their attention was a physical pressure, but it was Thorne's gaze that gave her goosebumps. Was that disappointment in his eyes? No, it was sadness, she was sure of it. She had seen sadness in his eyes before.

A fragment of memory flashed before her eyes. In it, Thorne was much younger. Age had not yet carved weary lines onto his face. In this memory, his eyes were full of tears. He was saying goodbye, and she was crying too.

"And you are?" the raven-haired woman demanded, snapping Eliza from her memory.

"Eliza Clarke. Madge's governess."

"Tell me, Miss *Eliza Clarke*," she asked. "What were you doing when this manifestation occurred? We detected two magical signatures from this house."

The question was a trap. Answer truthfully and reveal herself as an illegal practitioner. Lie, and the entire family could be whisked away for interrogation—which, according to East End gossip, meant death for anyone without sufficient magical power to withstand the interrogation methods.

She looked at the Windermeres' pale faces. If the gossip was true, her lie would doom them all.

She had to tell the truth.

"I was containing my magic, weren't I."

Silence fell. Even the other Battle Mages stilled, weapons humming with barely restrained power.

Thorne placed a hand over his mouth, as if shocked into quiet.

"Containing it how?" the raven-haired woman asked. Her voice was soft, deadly.

"With me shadows."

The admission was as good as signing her own death warrant.

"Show me," she commanded.

Eliza allowed her shadows to loosen just enough to make the detector shriek. As soon as it did, she withdrew her power again.

The raven-haired woman's eyes widened, while the other Mages shifted closer, their weapons emitting high-pitched whirrs.

The woman held up a hand, and the whirring ceased. "Well. That does complicate things. Mages, prepare both subjects for transport."

"Both subjects?" Lady Windermere gasped.

"That is the law. Miss Windermere will be enrolled in the Tournament. Miss Clarke..." Her smile was full of danger. "Miss Clarke presents a different sort of opportunity."

Opportunity? The word made her stomach turn. "What sort of opportunity's that then?" Eliza asked.

"The sort reserved for Shadow magicians. They can be quite... useful in the tournament."

Useful? Not valuable, not powerful, but *useful*. The way a hammer was useful. The way fish bait was useful.

Her knees threatened to give way as the implications solidified. They wanted her as fodder for the arena. A shadow magician thrown to the lions while spectators cheered for blood.

Before anyone could respond, Madge stepped forward. Light blazed around her like armor, power responding to her determination.

"If you want me to participate in your Tournament," she said, her young voice carrying surprising authority, "she comes with me. As my governess. My attendant. Whatever title makes it acceptable to your bureaucracy."

Eliza stared at Madge in disbelief. The girl was defending her— a near-stranger, a governess she'd met yesterday—and she clearly understood the deadly implications hidden behind the word "useful." Although she was but a little girl, Madge had seen straight through the Empire's polite threats.

The raven-haired woman's laugh was shrill enough to break glass. "You're hardly in a position to make demands, child."

Thorne said nothing. He stood still, his calculating gaze flicking back and forth as if he were watching a tennis match.

"Aren't I?" Madge's eyes blazed, and every light in the room flared brighter. "How many other candidates do you have who can reshape half of London with a nightmare?"

The Battle Mages exchanged glances. She'd struck home.

"Furthermore," Madge continued, pressing her advantage, "Miss Clarke demonstrated tonight that she can contain my abilities when they become uncontrolled. Unless you want me accidentally killing random people?"

As if to demonstrate, she let a tendril of power escape. Light lashed across the room, leaving a smoking gouge in the wall where it struck.

The Battle Mages hummed their weapons again.

"Hold your fire," Thorne said, raising a hand in a 'stop' gesture. "The girl has a point. Uncontrolled manifestations of this magnitude could be... problematic in a Tournament setting."

"Regulations prohibit personal advisors, sir," the raven-haired woman said.

"I am well aware of the regulations, *Sergeant*. Regulations allow attendants. Support staff whose job is to ensure contestant welfare." His voice carried a tone of authority. "I'll personally vouch for Miss Clarke's suitability."

Eliza took a breath. Vouch for her? Why? She could only know this man from one place: The East End. And she was certain she had not encountered him in any official capacity before that business yesterday. Had she seen him slipping into the brothel her mum used to scrub? Maybe he'd tossed a farthing to the little scrap in the doorway, waiting for her mum to be done. But if that were true, why speak for her now, unless he had some other dodgy game in mind? That had to be it. He'd likely taken her for a strumpet, now that she was of age. Well, she'd slapped off enough grabby paws in her time to know how to deal with the likes of him. If he tried any funny business—he'd rue it.

The raven-haired woman stared at Thorne, clearly trying to determine whether he was serious. "And if they turn her away at the gate?"

Thorne glared at the woman. "Then I'll explain what happens when a light-worker of this caliber loses control in close quarters with our other investments. I will also explain what happens to enlisted personnel when my orders are questioned."

The silence stretched.

The woman nodded. "Yes, sir. Very well." She turned her attention to Eliza and Madge. "But understand—you're both under Imperial custody now. Any attempt to flee, any hint of sedition, any uncontrolled manifestations, and the accommodations end. Permanently."

"Understood," Madge said before Eliza could speak.

As the Battle Mages filed down the stairs to wait in the corridor, the Windermere family gathered around their daughter in a desperate embrace. Tears flowed freely, along with whispered words of love and hollow promises that everything would be all right.

"Miss Clarke?" Madge hugged Eliza, face streaked with tears. "Thank you. For choosing to protect my family even when it meant revealing yourself."

"Thank you for making sure we stay together. That was very clever negotiating."

"I had a feeling we needed to stay together," Madge whispered. "You were in my dreams again."

"All good stuff I 'ope."

Madge shook her head. "We were about to be devoured by a monster."

7 ENTER THE BATTLE MAGE

When Major David Thorne spoke, shadows writhed at Eliza's feet in terror and want. The combination should have been impossible.

"The Imperial carriage is waiting," he said.

Eliza helped Madge into the plush interior. The carriage reeked of old leather and weapon oil. Brass fixtures were polished to mirror brightness that threw back distorted reflections of their pale faces. She settled beside Madge on red velvet seats, hyperaware of the man across from them who radiated energy like heat from a forge.

She caught the lemon-lavender scent clinging to him. Saw how his uniform bore no wrinkles, no stains, yet his hands told different stories. Scars ghosted across knuckles. Calluses marked his palms. When he shifted in his seat, she glimpsed more scars beneath his collar—silver lines that hinted at battles fought and barely survived.

He was younger than she'd initially thought—perhaps mid-twenties, with a weariness that aged him beyond his years. Along with the silver streak in his hair, it was his warm gray eyes, glinting with silver, that quickened her pulse.

She averted her eyes, smoothed her skirt, and gazed out of the window.

The carriage wheels found every rut in London's cobblestones, springs creaking under tons of reinforced armor plating. Each jolt sent her shoulder brushing against Madge's, the girl's warmth a stark contrast to the cold dread pooling in Eliza's stomach. Through shimmering spelled windows, she watched familiar neighborhoods blur past—the smoky tenements of her childhood, markets where she'd learned to stretch pennies into meals, churches where she'd prayed for answers that never came.

I know you. The certainty blazed through her mind like a chimney fire.

"We met before, 'ave we? Before the street the other day, I mean."

He considered the question, his eyes holding hers with uncomfortable intensity. The way he studied her made her hold her breath. It was not the casual assessment of a soldier cataloging threats, but something hungrier. More personal. His gaze traced the line of her jaw, the defiant tilt of her chin, as if memorizing details for reasons he couldn't voice.

Something shifted in his expression—surprise, perhaps, or confusion—as if her face triggered memories. "Possibly. You tell me."

Eliza bristled at the non-answer. Not "no." Not a denial. Just doubt wrapped in aristocratic dismissal. She was a hair's breadth away from slapping his perfectly sculpted face.

Heat crawled up her neck as she returned to the unwelcome thought that he might have been a brothel visitor. "I've been a governess since I was fourteen. Full-time. A respectable position, I'll 'ave you know."

His mouth curved in something that wasn't quite a smile— more like a lion about to bare its teeth. "I'm sure you *did* have a respectable position, Miss Clarke."

The emphasis on "did" made heat flare in her chest. But beneath his mocking tone, she caught something else. Genuine interest. As if her respectability mattered to him personally rather than professionally.

But this man was infuriating with his non-answers and aristocratic assumptions. The manner in which he looked her up and down, scrunching his mouth, suggested he was fighting some internal battle—assessment? Interest? She couldn't tell.

Rain began to spatter against the spelled windows as London's sprawl gave way to countryside that looked deceptively peaceful despite the gathering storm. Villages huddled around their churches like children seeking protection from wolves. Ancient forests pressed close to the road, trees twisted into shapes that suggested they'd grown around magical influences rather than natural ones. The air felt different here: thinner, charged with power that stirred her shadows.

The carriage lurched as they turned onto rougher roads, wheels finding the packed earth that led east into Essex. The change was immediate and jarring—air that tasted cleaner but emptier, stripped of the magical protections that blanketed the city like a warm wrapper. Ward boundaries snapped past with audible cracks, each one taking them further from civilization and deeper into Imperial countryside.

"Where exactly we going?" Eliza asked, fighting to keep her voice even though fear threaded her pulse like poison.

"Blackstone Fortress. An hour east." His gaze flicked to her mouth, then away with deliberate control. "You'll find it... educational."

His way of saying "educational" sent a shudder down her spine. "And what exactly does this 'education' consist of then?"

Something almost like amusement crossed his expression again—gallows humor that came from watching people break under pressure, no doubt. "You ask dangerous questions, Miss Clarke."

"I find that information keeps me alive."

"Does it?" The space between them was so narrow she could feel heat radiating from his skin. This close, she could count the silver threads weaving through his dark hair. Could watch the careful way he controlled his breathing, as if every reaction was cataloged and contained. "Most people find that ignorance serves them better in places like Blackstone."

"You could 'ave just locked me up," Eliza said, studying the tension that corded his jaw. "From what I 'eard back there, you don't 'ave to listen to what a child asks for. Yet you wanted this arrangement." She tilted her head, noting how his breathing changed when she leaned forward. "Why?"

For a moment, raw pain bled through his professional façade, before the mask slipped back into place. "Terrified children perform poorly under stress."

"I reckon you have your own reasons for wanting a Shadow-worker under close observation."

His fingers stilled against his thigh. "A Shadow-worker." He leaned back, but his gaze never left her face. "Is that what you are?"

"It's what the woman in charge of your party reckons I am."

He raised an eyebrow. "The woman in charge?"

"Back at the 'ouse when you broke in."

He chuckled, a sound with no humor in it. "First, we do not, as you put it, 'break in.' We are allowed to present ourselves in any Crown property, including private residences. And second, what my team leader may or may not think is irrelevant. That said, if the Empire finds out you are anything more than that, you'll be going somewhere else entirely." His voice dropped to a whisper that prickled her skin. "A place from which one does not return."

"If I'm anything *more*? What do you mean, sir?"

He held her gaze and smiled—an expression that promised secrets and danger in equal measure. "Tell me about your family, Miss Clarke. Your parents. Who are they?"

So that's how it was going to be. Ask questions without answering any. She wasn't about to give him ammunition to use against her at a later date. "Just ordinary folk."

"And they are..." he paused, stroking his chin, as if he was about to ask a delicate question. "Not related to the Windermeres?"

"No," she said, wondering why he was repeating the same question from their previous encounter. What on earth could make this man think that she was anything but a pauper from the East End?

"Just tell me straight, sir," Eliza said. "I feel like you're repeating the same question over and over, when I've been clear me name is Clarke. And to be honest, I don't like the way you're lookin' at me, sir."

"How I'm *looking* at you? Hmm. I apologize if I have offended you. The straight answer is that you remind me of a young lady I once knew."

Eliza choked back a laugh. "I can assure you, I ain't no lady. And I never 'ave been."

Thorne nodded, then looked out of the window. His eyes had

a distant look, as though fixed upon some memory leagues away. Still, she was thankful that his gaze was no longer on her.

"Are you okay?" she asked Madge.

Madge nodded. "Yes." She dropped her voice to a whisper. "A little scared."

Eliza placed her arm around Madge's shoulders and drew her close. She planted a small kiss on the top of her head and whispered back, "I'll take care of you, Miss Madge, don't you worry."

The landscape outside grew wilder as they traveled deeper into Imperial territory, passing a stone marker for Epping. The horses' hooves struck sparks from the road—flames that died as quickly as they appeared, suggesting the ground was infused with old magic.

Through the spelled glass, she glimpsed their escort. Four mounted Imperial Guards flanked them, faces hidden behind magical masks that gleamed like polished bone. Their movements were too fluid, too synchronized—like marionettes operated by the same hand.

"Expecting a spot o' trouble?" she asked.

"Always. Magical prisoners have a tendency toward dramatic escape attempts. It's considered good form to be prepared."

One of the guards turned his masked face toward the carriage, and her blood chilled. No human could move that smoothly, that silently. Whatever rode with them wasn't entirely alive.

"Revenants," Thorne said, noting her stare. "Warriors enhanced by Imperial magic. They don't tire, don't question orders, don't feel sympathy for their charges. They simply work until they drop."

"Charming," she said. But it was anything but. "And who might these warriors be, then? Poor sods who couldn't pay their debts? Workhouse folk dragged from one sort of chains into another?"

He didn't answer. Instead, he stared at her with weary intensity, like she was an impertinent child asking one too many questions.

Beside her, Madge had gone pale, staring out at the dead guards with the wide-eyed stare of a child realizing monsters were real.

"It's alright, miss," Eliza murmured, taking the girl's hand. Her shadows rose instinctively, wrapping around Madge's power like a dark bandage. "They ain't troubling you while I'm 'ere."

The promise was foolish—she didn't know what she could do against Imperial revenants. But the words calmed Madge, and that mattered more than logic.

Across from them, Thorne watched the interplay of shadow and light with an expression she couldn't read. When their powers harmonized, his breathing changed. Became deeper. More controlled. As if he was witnessing something significant.

"Major Thorne," Madge said suddenly, her voice small. "Are you going to hurt us?"

He flinched as though the question was loaded with spikes. "I'm going to try very hard not to. But I can't promise others will share that sentiment."

"Others?"

"The Tournament has many instructors. Many people with different ideas about how exceptional abilities should be... developed." Each word seemed to cost him something.

Rain drummed harder against the carriage roof. Forests pressed closer to the road, their branches dripping with rain, trees whose bark gleamed with an oily sheen that suggested corruption rather than health. The air itself felt heavier here, thick with magic that tasted of copper and decay.

They passed through villages that looked prosperous from a distance but wrong up close. Too quiet. Too empty. Windows that reflected nothing, even in full daylight. People who moved with the meticulousness of cogs in a clock.

"Pacification zones," Thorne said, following her gaze. "Areas where magical influence has been... concentrated."

"Concentrated how?"

"Imperial policy toward unregistered magical practitioners has become increasingly efficient over the years." His tone suggested this efficiency came at a cost. "Practitioners' skills have been contained and developed.

A prickling sensation ran down her spine. "Developed into what?"

"Into whatever the Empire requires." The neutrality in his tone felt forced. "The Imperial Magisterium serves the Crown's interests."

"How diplomatically phrased. They're going to try and weaponize Madge, then."

Madge shifted in her seat and mumbled. "I'd like to see them try."

"Miss Clarke—" Thorne protested.

Eliza jabbed a finger at him. "And you're going to help 'em do it."

"You don't understand the situation."

"Then out with it then."

"I can't." He leaned forward and whispered, "There are things about the Tournament—about what really happens to exceptional children—that I cannot discuss in present company."

The emphasis was slight but unmistakable. He couldn't speak freely with Madge listening. But his eyes held a message meant for Eliza alone: something darker than she could imagine was waiting for them.

"However," he continued, "there are those within the system who work to mitigate the worst aspects of Imperial policy."

"Mitigate. What's that mean then?"

His eyes met hers directly, and she saw desperation there. "You're missing the point, Miss Clarke. What I'm trying to say is that you can't defeat the Empire alone."

Her shadows settled as she understood the meaning of his words; the admission was laden with implications neither dared voice openly. He was telling her something important—that he wasn't entirely the Empire's creature, that allies might exist within the system. Was that why he had tried to protect her? Or was it because of that recognition—not just the one in his eyes, but the one her shadows felt.

The carriage began to slow, wheels crunching over gravel now instead of packed earth. Through rain-streaked windows, massive stone walls rose from the gathering dusk like something carved from a nightmare.

8 BLACKSTONE FORTRESS

Blackstone Fortress squatted against the horizon—a structure designed to break spirits before bodies ever saw the inside. Its walls absorbed light rather than reflecting it, creating the impression of a building made from shadow and despair.

The fortress sprawled across the landscape as if it were built for giants. Black stone rose in tiers, each level more forbidding than the last. Gothic spires twisted skyward, their peaks lost in gathering clouds that seemed to cling to the structure as if the air had been tainted. Gargoyles perched on every corner, their stone eyes following the carriage's approach with malevolent gazes that instilled a deep sense of unease in Eliza.

As they rolled through gates that closed with the finality of a cell door slamming shut, the sound echoed off stone walls with unnatural resonance. The iron portcullis descended behind them with grinding finality, each bar as thick as her waist and inscribed with runes that glowed red in the darkness.

The fortress contained dozens of interconnected buildings whose purpose she could only guess at. Courtyards where torches burned with flames stretched between them. The architecture defied logic, as if Westminster Abbey had been built with a workhouse in mind. Ancient towers connected to flat buildings via covered walkways that looked like they'd been carved from single pieces of stone.

Her stomach tied up in knots when she saw the children. They moved through the courtyards in identical clothes—dark brown uniforms that marked them as property rather than people. Even from this distance, she saw how they moved. Too carefully. Too quietly. Like animals that had learned to fear their handlers.

A group huddled near the main entrance, flanked by guards in Imperial blue. Three children, maybe four—it was hard to tell with how they pressed together for comfort, their clothes sodden from the rain. A spindle-thin boy, nearly swallowed by his oversized coat, clutched a soggy bible in his hands. A girl with auburn hair as unruly as street-cat fur clutched a torn doll, its fabric dark with moisture.

"Fresh meat," a revenant yelled with casual cruelty as their carriage passed. "These ones won't last a week."

The children flinched at the words, shoulders hunching as if expecting blows. The youngest—a girl with dark skin and saucer eyes—stood straighter than the others. Defiance blazed in her gaze, although tears tracked down her cheeks.

An open carriage rolled past them, with one passenger—a boy, perhaps thirteen or fourteen, his hands shackled with restraints that glowed with suppression magic. Even contained, power radiated from him in waves. His eyes held the flat emptiness of someone who'd already given up hope.

"Fire-shaper," Thorne said quietly. "Burned down half his village when his abilities manifested. The Magisterium considers him a priority acquisition."

"He's a child, not an acquisition."

"Here, he's both."

The carriage stopped before a two-story, rectangular building. The structure managed to look both old and new, with ancient stones fitted with modern conveniences in ways that suggested the fortress had been built over something much older. Gas lamps flickered alongside magical torches, their light creating an unsettling blend of shadow and illumination.

Massive doors dominated the entrance, carved from wood so dark it looked black. Iron bands reinforced every joint, inscribed with warding runes that pulsed like a slow heartbeat. The handles were shaped like serpents, their eyes gleaming with embedded gems.

Above the doors, a motto was carved into the stone in Latin: *Vis Per Dolorem*—Strength Through Pain.

The courtyard was a masterpiece of intimidation. Black granite flagstones stretched in perfect symmetry. Fountains dotted the space, but instead of water, they bubbled with liquid that glowed blue. The alchemical compound filled the air with a clean spring scent and a sense of calm, which was all too wrong in this place of fear. The sound was wrong too, more like bubbling tar than flowing water.

Guards stood at attention along the walls. Each wore the same bone-white masks as the revenants. Their stillness was absolute.

Thorne stepped out into the drizzle first, offering his hand to Eliza. Despite the chill in the air, his calloused hand was warm. She felt the same recognition that had blazed between them at the Windermere house.

I know those hands, her mind whispered. *I've felt them before.*

But when? Where? And why did touching him feel like coming home and walking into danger at the same time? The answers weren't forthcoming, and it was as frustrating as hunting for a dropped pin on a sawdust floor.

As her feet touched the wet flagstones, magic surged upward through the soles of her boots. The ward array strengthened, sending a tingle of energy through her. For a moment, her shadows writhed in response, before she willed them to hide from the probing magic.

"Processing begins immediately," Thorne said, his voice carrying undertones she couldn't interpret. "Miss Windermere will be assigned to junior dormitories. Miss Clarke, you'll be housed in attendant quarters with appropriate movement restrictions."

A new group of arrivals was being herded through a side entrance—older children, teenagers whose abilities had probably manifested violently. They moved in shackles, heads down, but Eliza caught glimpses of power still sparking around their forms.

One girl looked up as they passed, and Eliza's breath caught. She couldn't be more than sixteen, but her eyes held the burdens of someone much older. Burn scars traced up her neck, and when she turned her head, light leaked from between her lips like she'd swallowed the sun.

Their eyes met for one brief moment. The girl's lips moved in what might have been words: *Help us.*

Then the guards shoved her forward, and she disappeared into the fortress's depths.

"Welcome to Blackstone Fortress," Thorne said. "Try not to let them break you in the first week."

Around them, the fortress seemed to settle into a night watch rhythm. Guards changed positions. Sentries spread out to patrol the walls like predators claiming territory. Somewhere in the distance, beneath the sounds of settling stone and shifting guards, she could hear gears turning—the fortress was alive with hidden machinery, mechanical precision managing every aspect of this place.

And somewhere in the darkness, she could hear children whispering to each other—not just crying, but sharing stories of homes they'd never see again, making promises to survive another day.

It was as if she could, inexplicably, hear every word. And they were perhaps the most honest sounds she'd heard since their departure from London.

And it told her everything about what they were truly facing.

The sound of metal stirred her from her thoughts. The serpent handles turned without anyone touching them. The doors swung open on silent hinges, revealing a corridor that stretched into darkness beyond the reach of any light.

The children's cries pierced straight through her. Madge would surely become one of them. Broken. Hopeless.

Unless she found a way to protect her.

Yesterday, she'd believed she would find answers to the gaps in her past. And yesterday, she'd believed she would help Madge control her light outbursts. Now she wasn't sure either of them would make it to morning.

9 ORIENTATION

The registration hall sprawled before them—all marble columns and echoing footsteps. Eliza's boots clicked against polished stone as they approached the mahogany desk where a skeletal man in a navy uniform sat surrounded by ledgers thick as tombstones.

Behind wire-rimmed spectacles, his beady eyes assessed them. Everything about him suggested a lifetime spent shuffling papers—from his precisely knotted tie to the way he gripped his fountain pen.

"Names," he said without looking up from his ledger.

"Margaret Elizabeth Windermere," Madge said, chin lifted with aristocratic authority though her voice shook.

The clerk's pen scratched across parchment. "Age twelve. Light manipulation, unprecedented power levels." He glanced at Thorne. "Priority classification?"

"Confirmed. Direct Tournament entry."

The clerk made another note, then turned his attention to Eliza. His gaze lingered on her patched sleeves, her mended gloves. The assessment was swift and dismissive.

"A pauper. Name?"

"Eliza Clarke." Her voice came out steadier than she felt.

"Relationship to the contestant?"

"Miss Windermere's governess. I serve as her attendant."

"Attendant," he said, shuffling papers. "On whose authority?"

"Mine," Thorne said.

"Magical abilities?"

She was about to answer, but Thorne's hand settled on her shoulder. His touch burned through fabric, fingers pressing with deliberate weight.

"Minor shadow manipulation," he said. "Nothing worth documenting."

The clerk's pen stopped. "Any shadow work requires documentation—"

"She's simple-minded. Her shadows are weak and unpredictable. Barely worth recording."

Simple-minded? Fire erupted in her chest. How dare he brand her deficient? She jerked forward to protest, but his grip tightened.

"I see." The clerk nodded with patronizing understanding. "Show me these... weak abilities," he said slowly, enunciating each word. "Perhaps create a simple shadow ball. Can you do that?"

Panic slammed into her ribs. Around her feet, shadows exploded with wild energy, responding to the tempest storming inside her. Too much movement. Too obvious.

Thorne stepped closer. The darkness stilled as if he'd whispered commands to it directly. "It's a waste of time. Perhaps a simple demonstration?"

Understanding struck like lightning. He wasn't branding her— he was shielding her. Hiding deadly power behind a mask of weakness.

Eliza forced a tendril of shadow across the floor—pathetic, trembling, like a poisoned rat. The darkness obeyed her charade, moving with deliberate clumsiness.

"Pathetic," the clerk spat, stamping her papers with red ink. "Standard attendant classification."

The irony burned. If only he knew what prowled beneath her skin.

"Processing complete," the clerk said. "Report to Orientation Hall B for facility introduction."

As they left the registration desk, Thorne's hand remained on her shoulder. To anyone watching, it looked casual. But his fingers traced deliberate circles against her back—each touch sparking electricity down her spine.

Trust me, the caress whispered.

The orientation hall buzzed with nervous energy. Twenty-odd children clustered in small groups, their faces bearing the hollow look of those who'd lost everything. Some still wore the fine clothes they'd arrived in, now wrinkled and stained. Others had already been issued fortress uniforms—drab wool that marked them as property. To their left, a cluster of older women stood by. Attendants, Eliza guessed.

Madge found a seat near the back. Eliza settled beside her and patted her thigh. *It'll be okay,* the gesture said.

A man in a pressed navy-blue uniform strode to the podium. He held his clipboard like armor against disorder.

"You have been selected for the Tournament," he announced in a voice that carried no warmth. "The highest honor available to magical citizens. Only the exceptional are chosen. Only the worthy survive."

As he glanced around the room, he crinkled his nose and covered it with a handkerchief, as if he were faced with an open street sewer. "You will receive detailed schedules, dormitory assignments, and facility regulations. Adherence is mandatory."

A ginger-haired boy near the front raised his hand. He couldn't be older than eleven, his face still soft with childhood. "What about our families? When can we write to them?"

The instructor's expression didn't change. "Personal correspondence is forbidden during training."

The boy's face crumpled, but he made no sound. Smart child— he was learning the rules quickly.

"Combat magic, tactical deployment, psychological conditioning," the instructor continued. "You will learn to fight, to kill, to die if necessary for the greater good."

A collective gasp filled the room, followed by the sounds of children's chatter. "Kill? Did he say..." "Die?" "What did he mean by..."

Eliza had heard the rumors, of course. But to hear it stated as fact? Her mind seemed to grind to a halt, unable to process the new reality unfolding around her.

Next to her, Madge paled. Light spilled from her fingertips.

"Quiet!" the instructor bellowed.

The room snapped into silence, as if the instructor had used magic to hold every tongue.

"Attendants, you will serve at our discretion. You will see your charges through to final selection. Your charges' success or failure reflects directly on your competence. Failure carries severe consequences."

Consequences? Did that mean dismissal, or death? She went to raise her hand but thought better of it. A room full of children was no place to bring up the specific punishments the Empire had in mind. It didn't really matter to her what the consequences were anyway. She would not fail Madge—of that, she was certain.

A girl with a headful of straw-colored ringlets raised her hand. "What happens to those who don't make the final selection?"

The instructor's smile was thin. "They serve the Empire in other capacities. Permanent capacities."

A cold brick settled in Eliza's stomach. She'd heard whispers in the East End about children who entered government programs and never returned. About families who received letters saying their sons and daughters had "found new purpose in service."

The instructor's words suggested that most of the children in this room wouldn't be coming home either.

"Schedules and attendant assignments will be distributed shortly. Report to your assigned dormitories."

As the children filed out, Thorne appeared at Eliza's elbow. "Walk with me," he murmured.

They followed a corridor lined with portraits of previous Tournament winners. Sally Smith, 1873; James Garner, 1874; Eloise Stepney, 1875... They could have been portraits of veteran workhouse inmates, with their hollow eyes, vacant smiles, and dignity carved away. But these were children, not adults. And workhouse children lasted months, not years, before becoming phantoms in flesh. She could hardly bear the thought. This couldn't be Madge's fate. Wouldn't be Madge's fate. She simply would not let it. Somehow she would find a way to ensure that Madge's portrait was not the next to hang on the wall.

"They're all dead, aren't they?" Eliza asked. "The winners."

"Worse." Thorne stopped before a painting of a girl wearing a jeweled tiara. Her eyes held sadness, as if she were staring at an abused horse instead of an artist.

"They live. But not as themselves," he said.

"How many survive?"

"Define survival."

Her stomach dropped. The non-answer was answer enough.

As Thorne guided her away from the crowd—presumably to her quarters or perhaps more interrogation—she began to plot their escape, noting every corridor, every window, every passage that might lead to a door.

They reached a narrow staircase spiraling into blackness. The walls pressed close, carved with symbols that burned her eyes.

"Where are we going?"

"This is not the time for questions." His voice bounced off stone, rough with secrets.

Eliza gritted her teeth, realizing this was not the time for backtalk. If she remained compliant on the outside, perhaps she could trick him into complacency—even honesty.

They climbed in silence. Her shadows stretched toward him with each step, hungry and desperate. The pull between them grew savage in the confined space—her pulse hammering, her skin electric wherever his presence touched. What was it about this man? Every part of her soul wanted to hate him for what he had done, yet her shadows wanted to wrap themselves around him. She thought of how her shadows had erupted in Kensington, wrapping around lampposts and shop signs as if looking for something to strangle.

She knew that wasn't her shadows' purpose here. If only she understood her magic more... could read what they were trying to tell her. She had so much to learn, she realized. And here, in this place, with Madge's life in danger—she vowed to learn as much as she could. But then again, she had no teacher, no one to explain to her what her power could do, what it all meant.

She said a prayer as they continued up the stairs. *Please let the light shine on my magic, so that I can see within it, learn from it, use it to get us out of here.*

At the top, iron hinges groaned. A circular chamber opened before them, bathed in blood-orange light. Windows overlooked the fortress grounds.

Thorne drew her into an alcove—stone walls pressing close,

intimate as a changing booth curtained off from view. "One of the few places free from prying ears. The shadow magic you demonstrated. That wasn't your full capability."

An interrogation, then. She'd been spot on about that. "How would you know?" she asked, narrowing her eyes.

"Because I've seen what you can do. On the street."

In the dying light, something blazed in his eyes that stripped her bare. It wasn't a professional assessment—it was something that reached inside her chest and squeezed. But then again, perhaps this was a trick. Pretend to be her friend and trick her into honesty.

She averted her gaze to the window, refusing to give anything away with her eyes. If he was trying to read her, twig what she was thinking, she wasn't going to make it easy for him. Outside, evening mist devoured the fortress walls. Somewhere in the distance, a tawny owl hooted through the gathering dark.

"You recognize me, don't you?" he asked.

Her breath caught. "You look familiar, sir. But we saw each other yesterday, didn't we."

He exhaled hard, frustration bleeding through his composure. "If I'm to protect you here, you must be truthful. I know you, Miss Eliza Clarke. I wasn't sure at first. To be honest, I'm still not completely sure, although I swear I saw..." His gaze flicked to her forehead before he met her eyes. "You came from India."

A gasp tore from her throat. How could he possibly know? Had Lady Windermere told him? Had he spoken to the Clarkes?

"Sir, I don't believe my past concerns you."

Fire sparked in his eyes. "Either you are she, or you are not. It is a simple question. Were you ever in India? Were you adopted?"

Her hands shook. Her mouth went dry. The words wouldn't come.

He paced the narrow space. Minutes stretched. She watched him think, watched shadows play across his angular face.

Finally, he said, "I understand your fear. You don't trust me." His voice gentled, but steel remained underneath. "But if you are who I think you are, then I'm the only person in this fortress you can trust. The only person who can help you survive."

Heat exploded in her chest. "I survived in the East End, sir. If you think for one minute that I cannot survive this fortress, then you are clearly mistaken." She lifted her chin, defiance blazing through her fear. "Now, if you please, I would like to be escorted to my quarters."

10 THE SYSTEM'S GRIP

The following morning, the bell clanged, dragging Eliza from restless sleep.

She dressed in her damp brown uniform, cold fingers fumbling with buttons while her mind churned through yesterday's revelations. The Tournament winners live, but not as themselves. The words had burned themselves into her thoughts.

Before breakfast, she knocked on Madge's door. When the door opened, Eliza saw how immaculate the room was. Bed made with perfect corners, dirty clothes neatly folded on the blanket, slippers placed together underneath.

"You tidied already," Eliza said.

Madge scrunched her mouth into a frown. "I felt bad about you having to clean up after me. It isn't right."

Eliza knelt. "Thank you, Miss Madge. It's not that I ain't grateful, but you have to play their game, alright? That means letting me act as your attendant. We don't know what they'll do if they think I ain't useful."

Madge nodded and dropped her gaze to the floor. "Okay." She pointed at the neat pile on the bed. "Perhaps you could mend the hole in the seam of my blouse? I suppose they missed it when they handed out the garments."

Eliza stood up and smiled. "As you say, miss. I'll 'ave it done in a jiffy."

In the dining hall, they joined the stream of attendants and charges collecting their breakfast—thick porridge, fresh bread, and preserved fruit. Apparently, the Empire spared no expense when it came to their "investments." Whispered conversations drifted from nearby tables, fragments of fear disguised as information.

"Training schedules posted today," someone murmured.

"Advanced combat starts tomorrow."

Eliza sat down at the attendant's table while Madge went to the front of the dining hall and joined her fellow candidates.

Around her, other attendants ate in silence, faces blank with the careful neutrality of survival.

Minutes later, the bell rang, signaling the end of the meal. Around them, attendants and candidates began gathering their belongings.

After breakfast, Eliza was herded into the east wing with the rest of the attendants for a "daily briefing." The instructor was the same skeletal man from orientation, his voice carrying the enthusiasm of someone reading at a funeral service.

"The Tournament operates in three phases," he announced, consulting papers adorned with red wax seals. "Elimination trials reduce candidate numbers to manageable levels. Advanced training shapes survivors into useful assets. Final assessment determines Imperial placement."

Not people. Not children. Just "assets," resources to be allocated like ammunition or rations.

"Elimination follows established protocols. Random pairing ensures fairness. Combat continues until requirements are met. Questions?"

Eliza had a thousand of them. But she kept quiet.

A woman near the back raised her trembling hand. "What about attendants whose charges don't, uh, make it all the way to the end?"

Eliza bristled. That was the question she hadn't wanted to ask at orientation. Even now, she wasn't sure she was ready to hear the answer. She wasn't sure the children were ready to hear it, either.

"Your job is to ensure your charges stay healthy, motivated, and alive. Continued employment depends on this, and this alone."

The vague statement was confusing, but no one bothered to ask for clarification. It left a thread of hope that such attendants would be simply sacked rather than face an unimaginable fate.

Eliza filed out with the others, relieved that the children seemed to have settled, with less fear in their eyes. In the corridor, she nearly collided with a figure in Imperial blue.

"Miss Clarke."

Major Thorne stood before her, crisp and controlled as always. But something in his eyes made her pulse skip—the same intensity he'd shown her during their secret chat after orientation.

"Major." She stepped aside, but the corridor was narrow. Too narrow. His presence filled the space, making her acutely aware of his height, the controlled power in his movements.

"How are you settling in?"

Was that concern in his voice? She studied his face, searching for cracks in his professional facade. "As well as can be expected in a place where you're torturing children."

"The trials serve a purpose."

"Do they?" She tilted her head, emboldened by anger. "What purpose does watching twelve-year-olds fight each other serve, then?"

He gave a sideways glance at the walls, widening his eyes slightly. "Preparation. The Empire has enemies, Miss Clarke. Threats that require exceptional responses."

Eliza tried to decipher his body language, but only wondered why the dickens he was jerking his head at the wall. Did he have some kind of tic? "So you break children to turn 'em into weapons."

"I ensure they survive long enough to make a difference." His voice dropped, barely audible above the echo of boots in adjoining corridors. "And in some cases, I ensure they *survive*. Do you take my meaning?"

Suddenly, it registered. It was as if she could see inside his mind. He didn't have a tic. He was telling her that the walls were listening. What had he said the previous evening? Something about the circular room being one of the few places to speak freely.

His eyes drifted to her forehead, and he gasped. Not a loud exclamation of surprise, but more of a slight parting of his lips, a widening of his eyes, a catch of his breath.

She instinctively touched her forehead, feeling for a bug, a speck of dirt, something that would explain his unsettling gaze.

Before she could ask him what he was looking at, other attendants rounded the corner. Thorne stepped back, distance returning to his expression.

"Good day, Miss Clarke."

He walked away, leaving her standing in the corridor with questions buzzing in her skull like angry wasps. What had she seen in his eyes? Why did his presence make her shadows want to reach toward him?

She fought the urge to follow him.

The thought made her stomach churn. This man was her captor. Madge's captor. He watched children fight and called it necessary. Whatever brief moment of vulnerability she'd glimpsed didn't change what he represented. Didn't change the fact that he was a riddle wrapped in an Imperial uniform.

But as she continued toward the attendant quarters, she couldn't shake the memory of pain in his expression. The way he'd said "in some cases, I ensure they *survive*," like he was talking about her, about Madge.

Stop, she told herself firmly. He's manipulating you. Making you see what he wants you to see.

But the certainty felt slippery. That wasn't what he was doing, was it? Whatever game he was playing, she would figure out how to stay one move ahead.

Madge's survival depended on it.

* * *

The observation gallery overlooked the training yards; it was a theater box designed for watching gladiatorial sport. Eliza pressed against the wood barrier, her breath misting in the chilly air as she watched children learn to kill.

Below, Madge moved through combat forms that looked like a cross between shin-kicking and bare-knuckle boxing. Her instructor barked commands while she channeled light into rough blade shapes, spears of radiance that were supposed to slice the log in front of her but instead scattered upon impact.

"Focus the energy!" the instructor shouted. "Light scattered is light wasted. You're not making pretty patterns—you're forging weapons!"

Madge's face was blank as she obeyed, but Eliza caught the tremor in her arms.

Other children worked through similar exercises. A boy no taller than a beer barrel tried to hurl fire at practice targets shaped like human silhouettes. Twin girls shaped water into razor-edged disks that were supposed to shatter stone barriers.

"You useless wretches! Again! Again! We will be out here until sundown unless you lot learn control! Again!"

The children's breaths came in ragged gasps. Blades of light faltered, fireballs dimmed, and water disks splashed harmlessly to the ground as fatigue set in. Madge's last attempt at throwing a light blade finally worked, chipping into the wood block with a thwunk. The fire-worker successfully hit a target, but the water girls struggled to shape disks until they could barely summon water at all.

After another round of admonishment, the children filed out in ragged lines. They tried to march in formation but stumbled over each other's feet. Eliza caught glimpses of the fear they tried to hide—the way eyes darted toward escape routes that didn't exist.

They were still children underneath the conditioning. Still scared, still hoping for a rescue that would never come.

When attendants were dismissed, Eliza made her way to Madge's room.

Madge stood to greet her. "Miss Clarke." Relief flooded her voice as she collapsed back down onto the bed. "I was afraid they wouldn't let me see you."

"Why wouldn't they?"

"Because I've been struggling," Madge whispered. "With the combat training. The instructor says I'm too hesitant, too concerned with collateral damage."

"Good."

Madge's eyes widened. "Good? But Miss Clarke, they'll eliminate me if I don't improve. They made that very clear."

"And they'll destroy you if you do improve." Eliza leaned forward, keeping her voice low. "Tell me what you're feeling, Miss Madge. Really feeling."

"Scared." The admission came out broken. "Scared and angry

and so terribly alone. Some of the children enjoy the training. The twins chattered about how they can't wait to drown us all."

"But you're not enjoying it."

"No. When I shape light into weapons, all I can think about is what they're meant to do. Who they're meant to hurt." Tears leaked down her cheeks. "I keep remembering stories about children who went to places like this and never came home."

"And what do you think 'appened to them?"

"I think they stopped being children." Madge's voice turned fierce. "I think they became something else. Something that kills without question, that follows orders without conscience."

Her statements were too large, too complex for someone so young to carry.

"Listen to me carefully," Eliza said. "You think you 'ave to choose between being a monster and being eliminated. But there's another option, ain't there."

"What option?"

"You give 'em what they want to see while keeping who you really are safe up in your noggin.'" Eliza tapped her temple. "Make them think they're winning, Miss Madge, but don't let yourself think they're winning."

Madge's brow furrowed. "I don't understand."

"You listen 'ere. Learn their combat forms. Master their techniques. Excel at their training." Eliza's voice turned urgent. "But when you do it, remember why. Not because you want to kill, but because you want to live long enough to escape."

"You think we can escape?"

The hope in Madge's voice was heartbreaking. Eliza thought of Major Thorne's strange words, his hints about fates worse than death. Was he planning something? Could he be trusted?

"I reckon," she said, "that survival requires patience." She tapped her chest. "You stay strong in 'ere, while giving 'em what they need to see, you know?"

Madge nodded slowly. "Pretend to be what they want while staying who I really am inside."

"Exactly. It's harder than it sounds though. The longer you're 'ere, the more tempting it becomes to just give in."

Tears welled in Madge's eyes. "But you'll help me stay strong?

I don't think I'm strong enough to do it alone."

"Every day I'm able." Eliza squeezed Madge's hands again. "Promise me something, Miss Madge. Promise that no matter what 'appens in the trials, no matter what they make you do, you'll hold on to the part of yourself that knows right from wrong."

"I promise." Madge's voice was stronger now, determination replacing despair. "And Miss Clarke? Thank you. For not abandoning me."

11 MIDNIGHT WARNINGS

Two days later

Eliza pressed her back against the door, breathing hard, creating little puffs of white mist in the chilly air. Her room was barely larger than a coffin—a narrow cot, a washstand, and walls that seemed to press closer with each passing day. The stone walls must be three feet thick, but she could still hear them.

Children crying.

The sound carved through her. Somewhere in this fortress of nightmares, Madge was curled on a similar cot, listening to the same hopeless sobs. She wondered if Madge was waking up with the same nightmares, the ones that had light exploding out of her at the Windermere mansion. But here, the walls had layers of wards and charms, probably designed to keep magic in check. She was tempted to throw her shadows at the walls, just to see if the wards would repel her magic. But she also didn't want to hear the pounding of Imperial boots headed toward her door.

"I'm here, Miss Madge," she whispered. "I won't leave you."

But the walls were thick stone, and even if she screamed the words, her voice would carry no further than the iron bars that caged her window.

She sank onto the cot, springs creaking under her weight. The mattress was thin enough to feel every wire beneath the fabric. Her shadows writhed restlessly around her feet, responding to the terror that crawled through her veins.

Three days. They'd been here three days, and already she could feel the fortress grinding away at her humanity. The way guards looked through her like she didn't exist. The exactness of meal times and inspections. The constant weight of being watched, cataloged, assessed for usefulness.

The constant weight of Thorne studying her from across courtyards, through doorways, in corridors where their paths crossed. Always watching. Always waiting for something she couldn't name. For her to break? To confess? Would admitting she was an Indian orphan change everything—elevate her from attendant to participant, or mark her for elimination entirely? Both possibilities sent shivers through her. Either outcome would shatter her promise to protect Madge, leaving the girl alone in this nightmare with no one to care whether she lived or died.

Eliza drew her knees to her chest, arms wrapped tight around her shins. The position made her feel smaller, younger. Like the frightened child she'd been when the church found her on its doorstep, grime under her fingernails and the smell of the sea on her hair.

Don't think about that now.

A knock at the door disrupted her spiral into despair.

Eliza's head snapped up. Visiting hours had ended at sunset. The attendant quarters were supposed to be secured until dawn, locked down tight as any prison cell.

Another knock. Deliberate. Patient.

Her shadows stirred. Someone stood outside her door—someone whose presence made her magic hum with recognition.

"Who's there?" she asked, but she already knew.

Silence.

Then the lock clicked open. The door swung inward. A figure stepped from darkness like he'd been carved from it. Major Thorne filled the doorway, his military coat buttoned to his throat, brass gleaming in the room's gaslight.

But there was something wrong with the light around him. It bent strangely, creating shadows where none should exist. His face was half-hidden in darkness that moved independently of the flickering flames.

"Miss Clarke." His voice was soft as lamb's wool.

"What you doing 'ere?" She didn't move from the cot, didn't trust her legs to hold her if she stood. "Visiting hours—"

"Don't apply to me." He stepped inside, closing the door behind him. "I need to speak with you."

She clenched her fist, ready to strike. There was only one reason a man might visit a woman's quarters late at night, and if he was after a tumble, he had another thing coming. "About what?"

His gaze met hers in the dim light. The strands of silver light in his gray eyes flickered. "Have you had time to consider our conversation?"

Heat flashed across her cheeks. "I ain't got the foggiest clue what you mean."

He glanced pointedly at her feet. "Let's not play games, Miss Clarke."

She glanced down. Her shadows had spread, pooling across the floor like spilled ink. They reached toward him with hungry tendrils, as if drawn by some invisible force.

She jerked her feet back, trying to contain the darkness, but it only made them writhe more violently.

"Stop." His voice sliced through her terror. "Fighting it makes it worse."

"Fighting what?"

"The part of you that recognizes who I am."

He took another step closer, and the shadows beneath her bed surged toward him with unmistakable hunger. "I've seen the way you look at me these last few days. You feel it. The pull. The way your magic responds to mine. I am certain that your name is Elizabeth. Tell me that I am wrong."

She did feel it. A tugging sensation in her chest, like something vital was trying to break free. Her shadows danced around his boots, caressing leather with movements that felt almost sensual. But she bristled at the feeling. This man had imprisoned her. Imprisoned Madge. Whoever he was, whatever he was, she would not submit to him.

"Like I keep sayin', Major. Me name is Eliza Clarke." But as she said the words, they sounded wrong, like the name wasn't hers at all. She wondered for a hair of a second if the name Elizabeth would sound like truth. But, no, that wasn't her name. This man was playing mind games. "My magic is responding to fear and manipulation by you."

He crouched beside the cot, bringing his face level with hers. "Let's not indulge in trifles, Elizabeth. Let's not do this."

"My name is *not* Elizabeth, sir. You are confusing me with Madge, whose middle name is—"

He slammed his fist on the mattress. "Stop with this nonsense!"

Eliza opened her mouth to protest. But a memory surfaced. The woman she saw in her dreams, standing in the distance across a meadow of flowers. "Stop, Elizabeth! Come home this instant!" The name belonged to Eliza in a way that made no sense.

Then she felt Thorne's presence close in. "I'm here to help. You need to listen very carefully."

Help? She almost burst out laughing. Who was this monster who was pretending to be her friend? Despite her attempts to feel nothing, his proximity caused her heart to race. Heat radiated from his skin, warming the air between them. She caught traces of his scent—lemon soap and summer mornings.

Before he spoke, he emitted light as thin as gossamer. It flowed around them both in a barely perceptible cocoon.

"To ward off listening ears," he whispered. "It will not last long. I must be quick with what I have to say." He leaned in close, so close that she saw his long black eyelashes and tiny sparkles of silver in his eyes. "In the coming trials. You must not use your full power."

"My full power?" A laugh escaped her throat. "I can barely control what I 'ave. These shadows move without me permission, don't they. I ain't a clue what full power's s'posed to mean."

"That's what makes you dangerous." His gaze held hers with uncomfortable intensity. "True Shadowbinders don't control darkness—they become it."

Shadowbinder. The word was preposterous. "I ain't no Shadowbinder." Shadowbinders were the stories of fable, of dead gods, eradicated in the India massacre when she was a child. She was a street magician in comparison. How could he possibly accuse her of being a Shadowbinder when all she could do was throw shadows from her shoes in random directions? Besides...

"The Shadowbinder bloodlines were got rid of decades ago."

"Were they?"

"I'm nobody," she whispered. "Just a governess from the East End."

"Governesses from the East End don't make shadows dance." He gestured to the darkness writhing around them. "And they do not do this."

Warm white threads flowed from his legs and synchronized with her shadows, curling in the same directions, swirling together like the spiraled layers of a Chelsea bun. Was this a trick? As she studied his hypnotic eyes, she realized it had to be. This man was setting her up for something. Was this part of the Tournament? Making attendants believe they were as powerful as their charges?

Unbidden, the memory of that night at the Windermere mansion crashed over her—Madge's power exploding outward, windows shattering for blocks. The way Eliza's shadows had risen to meet that blazing light, cooling it to manageable levels.

"That night was different. Madge needed me 'elp. I couldn't control it, I just, just..."

Just what? Threw shadows out in random directions? Or had she thrown them in the direction of Madge's light? The understanding came suddenly. This man *was* using manipulation magic on her. But why?

"You provided the perfect balance to her light." His voice carried strange weight. "Using abilities you claim not to understand."

"What do you want from me?" she asked, realizing it was a ridiculous question. "I am not interested in you. If you want me, you're going to 'ave to force me, sir, because..."

He stared at the shadows billowing around her feet, then shook his head. "That's not what this is about, Elizabeth."

"Stop calling me that. Me name is Eliza." He probably relished the idea of her dying in the arena from some monstrous attack, while she stared, confusion on her face, realizing too late she'd been fooled by his manipulations into believing she could survive. "You want me dead."

"I want you to survive." An odd pain flickered in his eyes,

which didn't seem to match the man. "And surviving as an Imperial weapon is not survival at all."

"Weapons? Everyone keeps 'arping on about that, but I don't even know what that means."

"Broken creatures who've forgotten they were ever human."

Terror hollowed out her chest. "Madge—"

"Will be one of them if you can't protect her." He leaned closer, and she caught desperation in his expression. "But protection requires subtlety. If you reveal what you truly are, they'll destroy you."

Eliza threw her hands in the air in exasperation. "Then tell me what I am."

His eyes glistened. "You're hope. The hope that not everything good in this world has been destroyed."

Hope? No one had ever called her that. Least of all herself.

He stood. Magic rippled around him as he prepared to leave.

"Wait." She reached toward him without thinking. "You still ain't told me nothing useful. How am I s'posed to protect her if I don't understand—"

"The power comes from lightness, not darkness. It's the opposite of what you would logically think." He paused at the door, hand on the lock. "True Shadowbinding was designed to hide from those who would hunt it. Your ancestors survived centuries by being invisible to magical detection. Don't throw that advantage away."

The words made no sense, but they resonated in her bones like truth.

He placed a hand on the door handle. "Watch the trials. Learn from them. You'll need that knowledge to surprise your attackers. But remember to not show your full power until it is time."

"Attackers? Until it's time? I do not understand, Major—"

"Quiet!" He raised a hand just as the thin threads of light disintegrated. He placed a finger on his lips. *Shhh.*

"As I was saying, Miss Clarke. I suggest you do a better job of attending to Miss Windermere's needs; otherwise, your time here will be very short."

He exited the room, closed the door, and turned the lock.

Eliza's pulse raced. She tried to process what had just

happened. He'd appeared from nowhere, filled her cell with his presence, and left her with more questions than answers.

Yet something had shifted. The terror that had clawed at her throat since their arrival had eased to manageable levels. She no longer felt like a fox trying to escape the hunt.

Shadow isn't the absence of light—it's where light chooses to rest.

She didn't understand the words, but her power seemed to. The darkness pooled peacefully around her feet, no longer hungry or desperate. It felt... content. Like it had found something it had been searching for.

The power comes from lightness, not darkness.

A shiver ran through her that was unrelated to the fortress's chill. Something about his presence had calmed her magic in ways she couldn't explain. The way he moved through shadows, like they welcomed him. The strange bend of light around his face.

The oddly familiar feeling wasn't because of his features, though.

It was because of his light.

The realization hit her like a slap. She'd felt that particular quality of illumination before—warm and golden and impossibly safe. But where? When?

Fragments of memory teased at the edges of her consciousness. Strong arms lifting her from pandemonium. A voice whispering comfort in a language she almost remembered. And light—so much light that it burned away the darkness trying to consume her.

Arms of light.

Her heart fluttered as the pieces clicked into place. The rescue from India. The hands that had pulled her from a wall of screams and jasmine gardens burning in the night.

She'd always assumed her savior was a stranger. Some Imperial soldier doing his duty, delivering an orphaned child to safety before disappearing back into history.

But what if it wasn't a stranger at all?

What if she'd been staring into the face of her rescuer for days without recognizing him?

The thought should have been impossible. Thorne was too young to have been in India sixteen years ago. Too polished to have been the battle-scarred soldier who'd risked his life to save a terrified child.

Yet her shadows knew his light. Responded to it with a recognition that bypassed conscious thought.

Thorne's words echoed in the darkness of her cell.

"Governesses from the East End don't make shadows dance..."

Eliza curled back onto the narrow cot, pulling the thin blanket to her chin.

Major Thorne was connected to her past in a way neither of them could, or would, acknowledge. Tomorrow, she'd get to the bottom of it, if it was the last thing she did.

12 DANGEROUS GAMES

The bell clanged at dawn. Eliza jerked awake, cursing the bell for dragging her from sleep. If she heard it one more time, she'd march out into the corridor and rip it from the wall.

Around her, metal doors banged open. Boots thundered against flagstones, each footfall echoing off walls.

"All attendants report to the east corridor! Now!" A male voice bellowed. "Early breakfast today. Chop, chop!"

She stumbled from bed, yanking on her clothes, teeth chattering from the morning chill. Coarse weave chafed against her skin, designed for endurance rather than comfort. Everything in this place valued function over humanity.

The hallway swarmed with women in identical mud-brown dresses—other attendants, their faces blank with exhaustion or terror. Every face looked haggard, desperate. Some women looked seasoned, moving with the careful efficiency of survival. Others appeared fresh from their first night, eyes wide with the understanding that yesterday hadn't been a nightmare.

Eliza joined the procession of women in mud-brown, flowing toward the dining room. She passed a brass plaque, half-buried in dust, its engraved names still legible—Brigadier Timothy Johnson, Chaplain Paul Potts, men long dead in wars fought over opium, rubies, and someone else's god.

An attendant with dead eyes shoved past her. "Move faster, or you'll miss breakfast. Trust me, you don't want to miss breakfast."

The threat carried weight. Missing meals here meant more than hunger—it meant losing whatever small privileges kept attendants functional.

The fortress corridors stretched endlessly, lit by gas flames that flared against the frigid drafts whistling through ancient stonework. Iron locks studded every door—heavy mechanisms riveted by some long-dead armorer in Her Majesty's service, designed to keep secrets buried and prisoners contained. Everything felt calculated to disorient, to make escape impossible even if someone found an unlocked door.

The dining hall hummed with uneasy restraint. Overhead, wrought-iron chandeliers hung like cages, their gas jets hissing softly as flames danced against sooty glass globes.

Eliza scanned the candidates' section until she found Madge. The girl sat hunched over a bowl of porridge, dark circles shadowing her eyes. She'd grown thinner in just three days, her uniform hanging loose on her small frame.

Their eyes met across the room. Madge offered a brave smile, and Eliza nodded back, hoping it conveyed more reassurance than she felt.

"Looking at the livestock?"

Eliza turned. A fair-headed woman with sallow skin and yellow eyes slid onto the bench beside her. Her mud-brown dress was identical to Eliza's, but it looked shabbier, like perhaps it had been worn by a thousand attendants before her.

"Livestock?"

"The children. That's what they are, really. Trained and harvested. As if they were prize calves destined for the colonial cavalry." The woman's voice carried no emotion, as if she was discussing the weather. "You been here a couple days now, right?"

"Three."

She nodded. "Same here. We've probably got another week. Attendants don't last long here, I heard."

"Why?"

"The trials."

The implication horrified Eliza. She glanced around the dining hall, noting how some attendants sat alone, isolated from the others. How guards watched certain women with particular interest from their positions along walls where iron torch brackets threw harsh shadows across stone blocks. And weren't one or two attendants missing? She couldn't be sure.

The dining hall doors opened with a groan of hinges. Major Thorne strode in, his military coat pristine against the institutional drabness, his boots so polished they caught the gaslight like mirrors. He moved through the space like he owned every flagstone, every beam, every soul within these walls.

"The hierarchy's simple enough," the woman said, stirring lumpy porridge with her wood spoon. "Candidates at the top— they're the product. Instructors below them—they shape the product. Battle Mages like Thorne oversee everything. They treat attendants like old benches. You know, sit on one for a bit 'til it makes you uncomfortable, then toss it out and get a new one."

Eliza's shadows stirred restlessly around her feet. She forced them still. "Major Thorne seems... a bit different from the other mages though."

The woman cackled. "Different? That's one way to put it. The man's got a reputation for being thorough. Efficient. Doesn't care for loose ends."

"Loose ends?"

"Attendants who get too attached to their charges. Who start thinking they can change how things work here." Her gaze fixed on Eliza. "Word of advice—keep your head down, do your job, and don't mistake professional interest for personal kindness."

Thorne's gaze swept the room. When his eyes found Eliza's, they lingered for a heartbeat longer than necessary.

A flush spread across her chest, unwelcome and embarrassing. She dipped her head, hoping no one would notice her shame.

Thorne approached the instructors' table at the front of the hall, where brass fixtures gleamed against wood darkened by years of lamp smoke. He nodded to colleagues who straightened at his presence. He seemed to command respect through competence rather than fear—though Eliza suspected the distinction was academic for most people here.

"Miss Clarke." His voice carried over the dining hall with casual authority. "A word."

Every head in the room turned toward her. The fair-headed

woman's eyebrows rose with interest. The other attendants stared with mixtures of curiosity and pity.

Eliza stood, legs steadier than she'd expected. Walking across the dining hall felt like interrupting a church service, her footsteps echoing against flagstones. When she reached Thorne, he gestured toward an alcove near windows barred with iron thick as a man's wrist.

"Privately," he said.

They moved to the shadowed corner, which was far enough from the tables to avoid being overheard. The proximity made her acutely aware of his presence, the way shadows seemed to bend around him.

"How did you sleep?" he asked.

Was that a trick question? She was tempted to respond with a snarky *Oh, how would you expect on a thin bed made of rocks?* But she decided against it, thinking that Thorne probably had a special basement chamber for attendants who challenged him publicly. "Poorly. Me accommodation ain't exactly Claridge's."

"Comfort isn't the priority here." His gaze flicked to the candidates' table, where children pushed food around their plates with listless exhaustion. "How's Miss Windermere adjusting?"

Seriously? He was pretending to care. What sort of game was he playing? She lowered her voice so that only he could hear. "About as well as any twelve-year-old ripped from 'er family and tossed into a gladiator camp."

A muscle twitched in his jaw. "The Tournament isn't gladiatorial. It has purpose."

"Purpose." She let the word hang between them for a moment. "That what you call it when children are told one of 'em has to die in training exercises?"

His eyes narrowed. "You heard about that?"

"Word travels fast 'ere." She met his gaze directly, refusing to be intimidated.

He leaned in close, and her heart skipped a beat. "They do not actually die, Miss Clarke. You of all souls in this place ought to know that truth already."

More riddles. Was he talking about the revenants? Or something else? Either way, this man was infuriating. She felt sure he was toying with her now, tricking her into something. But what?

"What if we refuse to join in then?"

"Refuse?" His laugh held no humor. "There is no 'refuse,' Miss Clarke. There is only participation, willing or forced."

"So we 'ave a choice."

He was so close now, near enough that she saw the way gaslight caught the silver threads in his dark hair, close enough to catch the scent of lemon and lavender and something darker that clung to his uniform. If this was any other place, any other time, any other man, she'd brace for a kiss. But not only did she detest this man, there was no passion in his eyes either. Just coldness, calculation, predation.

"Tell me, Miss Clarke, did you possess the luxury of choice when we came for Miss Windermere?"

The question stung because it was accurate. They'd all been swept along by forces beyond their control.

"So we bow our 'eads, play your brutal games, and pray we ain't the ones chosen for the gallows or the front lines in some corner of the Empire?"

"We navigate their games," he said. "And look for moments of leverage." His gaze held hers. "Smart players learn the rules. Exceptional players find ways to change them."

"And which are you?"

"I'll let you be the judge of that. The question is, which are you?"

Before she could answer, a commotion erupted at the candidates' table. A boy with curls the color of August hay was arguing with one of the guards, his voice rising with each word.

"I said I'm not hungry! I want to see my sister!"

The guard's response was swift and brutal. His hand connected with the boy's face with a sound that echoed off vaulted stone ceilings like a gunshot. The child crumpled against the scarred oak bench, blood streaming from his nose and spattering across the wood.

Silence fell. Every candidate stared at their plates, shoulders hunched with the knowledge that they were one wrong word away from similar treatment. Gas flames hissed in their brackets, the only sound in a hall suddenly thick with fear.

Eliza took a step toward the boy before Thorne's hand closed around her wrist.

"Don't." His grip was firm but not painful. "Interfering will make it worse for him."

"Someone 'as to—"

"Someone has to think *strategically*." His thumb brushed against her pulse point, a gesture so brief she might have imagined it. "Emotional reactions get people killed here."

Her first instinct was to argue, but the boy was already being dragged from the hall by two guards. His cries echoed until an iron door slammed with the decisiveness of a judge's gavel, cutting off the sound.

"Lesson one," Thorne said quietly. "Pick your battles carefully. Not every injustice can be fought directly."

She tried to yank her arm away, but his grip remained solid. "I'm tired of your riddles, Major Thorne. If you don't mind an' all, I'd like to return to me breakfast."

He placed a hand in her pocket and dropped something there. She went to reach for it, to see what it was, but he grasped her hand and shook his head.

"Later," he said. "Live long enough to effect change, Elizabeth."

How he said her name weakened her at the knees. But was it her name, really? Yet it seemed to fit, to sound right, at least on his lips.

The breakfast bell rang, signaling the end of the meal. Attendants and candidates began shoveling what remained of their breakfasts into their mouths.

She looked at her wrist. "If you please..."

He released his grasp and walked away without another word, leaving her standing with a feeling of emptiness and a strange, warm sensation in her pocket. The brief encounter had felt like a chess match where she didn't know the rules, let alone the stakes.

Back at the attendants' table, the fair-headed woman was waiting with a knowing look.

"Interesting conversation?" she asked.

"As professional as whispers in a brothel."

"Of course it was." Her smile was razor-thin. "Word of advice?

You aren't the first attendant Major Thorne has shown a personal interest in. That makes you either very unlucky or very dangerous."

"Which d'you think?"

"I think," the woman said, gathering her empty bowl, "that you'd better sort out which one you want to be before someone else decides for you."

The next few hours passed in a blur of orientation and regulations. Attendants were expected to maintain their candidates' physical and emotional well-being in the arena while staying invisible to the instructional staff.

Eliza raised her hand. "Attendants will be in the arena?" She thought of the light knives, the spinning water disks, the furious balls of fire that the children threw. "How will we be protected from the, uh, assaults?"

The instructor smiled devilishly. "You'll be provided with shields."

* * *

As Eliza made her way through the fortress corridors toward the candidates' quarters, her fingers slipped into her pocket and found the object Thorne had given her. Something small and hard—a stone, perhaps, or a piece of metal. Her instincts screamed to pull it out and examine it, but guards stood at every intersection, their eyes tracking movement with predatory focus. Whatever Thorne had given her, it was meant for her alone. She forced her hand away from her pocket and kept walking, the mystery burning against her hip with each step.

Madge looked smaller than ever in her tournament uniform— dark blue fabric that marked her as a junior candidate. Her eyes held a brittle brightness that suggested she was holding herself together through sheer will.

"How you managing then?" Eliza asked, settling into a chair whose wooden seat had been worn smooth by countless desperate conversations.

"I'm fine." The words tumbled out, too bright. "Everything's fine. The other candidates are nice enough. The instructors are very... thorough."

"Miss Madge." Eliza leaned forward, voice gentle. "You don't 'ave to pretend with me."

Tears spilled down her cheeks as she reached for Eliza's hands.

"I'm scared," she whispered. "The things they're teaching us... the things they want us to do... I don't think I can—"

"You can." Eliza squeezed her hands. "Whatever they ask of you, you can survive it. You're stronger than you know."

"But what if I'm not? What if I fail and they—" Madge's voice broke. "What if I never see Mama and Papa again?"

The question hung between them. Eliza wanted to promise everything would be fine, that she'd find a way to get them both out of this nightmare. But lies wouldn't help either of them survive.

"I don't know what's going to 'appen," she said instead. "But I know I ain't leaving you. Whatever comes next, we're in it together."

Madge nodded, wiping her eyes with the back of her hand. She looked like the brave, intelligent girl Eliza had met in the Windermere drawing room. But then shadows returned to her expression and tears welled in her eyes.

"Miss Clarke? I dreamed about blood again. But this time, I saw myself alone. You weren't here. You were gone, and I was alone. I think something's going to happen to you in the arena."

Eliza gripped Madge's hands tighter. "Don't you worry about me, Miss Madge. I'll 'ave a shield, remember? You worry about you."

The room felt smaller suddenly, the iron-barred windows pressing closer.

"I don't know if I can." Madge's voice was as light as leaves rustling.

Before Eliza could respond, boots thundered in the corridor outside. The heavy oak door burst open, slamming against stone with enough force to rattle the iron hinges.

"Visiting hours are concluded." A guard with sergeant's stripes filled the doorway, his weathered face carved from granite and indifference. "All attendants to the east corridor immediately."

"But we still 'ave ten minutes—" Eliza started.

"Now."

The word cut through her protest. Imperial scheduling had shifted, and that couldn't mean anything good.

Eliza squeezed Madge's hands one final time. "Remember what

I said about being strong."

"Miss Clarke." The girl's eyes were too wide, too bright. "The blood in my dreams—it was on stone. Black stone, just like—"

"Move!"

The guard's command severed the connection between them. Eliza was swept into the stream of brown-clad women flowing toward whatever fresh hell awaited.

13 THE CULLING BEGINS

The east corridor hummed with tension thick enough to choke on. Attendants pressed against walls that wept moisture in the morning chill, their faces reflecting the gaslight like pale ghosts. Whispered conversations died as uniformed figures appeared from the shadows.

"Attention!" The drillmaster's voice crashed over them. He stood at the corridor's end—a man built like a siege engine, his scarred face bearing the marks of magical combat that had gone badly wrong. His left eye was gone, the socket sealed with puckered scar tissue.

"First practical assessment begins in one hour." Each word dropped into the silence like a stone into still water. "Four candidates. One must die for three to survive."

Eliza's world tilted sideways.

The woman beside her made a sound like air from a tea kettle about to boil. Someone else whispered "no" over and over, a prayer to a god who'd abandoned this place.

One must die.

Not fail. Not be eliminated. Die.

"Partnerships," the drillmaster continued, consulting a brass-bound ledger with pages yellowed by age and stained with reddish-brown smears. "Miss Windermere—light, with Mr. Jones—shadow. Miss Brooks—fire, with Miss Clarke—shadow."

The rest of the group sighed in relief. Their names hadn't been called this time, but they soon would be. It was at that moment that Eliza realized her purpose as an attendant was not to assist Madge, but to serve as cannon fodder, a bait dog, a Christian to the lions.

The drillmaster gestured toward a rack of battered equipment. "Attendants, select your shields."

Eliza approached the weapons rack with growing dread. Dented metal shields hung from iron hooks, their surfaces scarred by previous battles. She hefted one, running her fingers along the cold steel rim.

No magic. No protective wards. Just crude iron that might stop a sword, but would crumble against fire magic or light blades.

Jones examined his shield with mounting horror, turning it over frantically, searching for hidden enchantments that didn't exist.

"There's no magic on these," he said, his voice rising with panic. "Surely they wouldn't send us in without proper protection."

But looking at the drillmaster's satisfied expression, Eliza knew better. They absolutely would send attendants into magical combat with nothing but scrap metal for defense.

"Standard issue protection," the drillmaster said with cold amusement. "Any questions?"

Eliza strapped the useless shield to her arm, its weight a mockery of safety.

The full reality of the drillmaster's words hit her then. Blood roared in her ears. Madge's prophetic dreams crashed over her with new meaning—blood on black stone, children screaming, the nightmare that had woken her from sleep.

The girl had seen this coming.

"Candidates will be prepared in holding chambers. Attendants will observe and provide tactical guidance within permitted parameters." The drillmaster's smile revealed a set of haphazard, rotting teeth. "Assessment begins when arena doors seal."

Eliza stood frozen, her mind struggling to process what she'd just heard.

The rumor was true. They were going to force children and attendants to murder each other. And call it "assessment."

"Miss Clarke." Major Thorne appeared beside her like fog

given form. "You look surprised."

"Surprised?" The word came out as a croak. "You're throwing us in there to die."

He stepped closer. "This is unavoidable."

"Madge is twelve!"

"And I assume you want her to live?"

The question landed like a fist to her chest. Of course she wanted Madge to live. But not like this. Not by becoming a killer before she'd even had her thirteenth birthday.

"There 'as to be another way—"

"There isn't." His gaze dropped to her pocket, where the stone pulsed warmly. "The arena doors seal in forty-seven minutes. Use that time to prepare her."

"But 'ow can I possibly do that?" she asked.

He leaned in and patted her pocket. "You're a smart woman, Miss Clarke. You'll sort out how to protect her."

Protection. He was telling her the stone was a ward stone. But she had no training with such things.

He walked away before she could ask him to explain, ask him what she had to do to conjure protection, ask him how he expected a governess to know what to do with a lifeless rock. She was left standing alone with a horror that sat in her stomach like sour milk. Her heart thudded erratically, as if he'd cast a magic spell over her.

Damn this man! Damn him to hell!

She had less than an hour to prepare a child for murder.

* * *

The holding chambers were carved from the fortress's deepest levels, where stone creaked under the weight of the tonnage above. Iron doors lined the corridor like crypts, each one containing a child whose life would be measured in minutes.

Eliza found Madge in the third chamber, curled on a stone bench. The girl had wrapped her arms around her knees, making herself as small as possible while her whole body trembled.

"Miss Clarke." Relief flooded Madge's voice, but her eyes remained wide with the glassy brightness of shock. "They said— one of us has to..."

"I know what they said." Eliza knelt beside her, gripping the girl's shoulders with hands that she willed not to tremble. She wouldn't let Madge see her fear. Wouldn't let this place strip away the last pretense of protection. "But you're gonna survive, you 'ear me?"

"The Shadow-worker—I've seen him in the training yard. He's older. Stronger." Tears cut tracks down Madge's cheeks. "His magic feels like drowning in cold water."

"Your light buggered up half of Mayfair." Eliza's voice turned fierce. "Shadow magic withers against power like yours. You've felt what 'appens when your abilities respond to emotion."

"I can't kill someone," she whispered. "I won't become a monster."

"Then find another way." Eliza pulled the girl closer, lowering her voice. "But you will come out of that arena alive."

"What if I can't control it? What if my power—"

"Then you let it loose. Better to be a living monster than a dead saint."

Madge's eyes widened at the blasphemy, but she nodded. In this place, survival trumped morality. The Empire had made sure of that.

"What about you?" Madge asked, glancing down at Eliza's battered shield. "What if you get killed? I don't know how to protect you, Miss Clarke. I don't know how..." Tears streamed down her face as her voice trailed off.

Eliza opened her pocket and lifted the stone just enough for Madge to see. She mouthed the words "Ward stone" in case there were prying ears. Then she lifted a finger to her mouth. *Don't let them know*, the gesture said. Of course, she wasn't about to let Madge know she had not the first clue how to use it, but she didn't need Madge distracted by Eliza's safety. Better that she thought Eliza had magical protection.

"It ain't your job to protect me. It's your job to survive," Eliza said loudly.

Thorne's words came to her, and she paused to consider if they were true words or if they were deception. He'd said that her shadows came from the light, and that the notion defied logic. It meant that Madge's light power came from dark. She wasn't completely sure, but felt somewhere deep inside that the words were rooted in truth. At the very least, they might give Madge focus. "Listen 'ere, Miss Madge. Your power comes from darkness, not light. Repeat it back, right now."

Madge scrunched her brow. "What? I don't understand..."

"You don't 'ave to understand; just repeat."

"Okay. My power comes from darkness, not light."

A key turned in the lock. The door swung open and a guard entered. "Time to go."

The corridor leading to the arena stretched like a throat designed to swallow hope. The Shadow-worker—Mr. Jones—shuffled ahead of them, his thin shoulders hunched with resignation. No one offered strategies or comfort.

Madge walked beside him, confusion clear on her pale face.

A girl fell into step beside Eliza. Her ginger hair caught the torchlight like burnished copper, and her lavender eyes glistened not with fear, but bloodlust. The fire magician.

"You're Miss Brooks?"

"And you're my partner." Miss Brooks's smile was sharp as broken glass. "Shadow magic, I'm told. Should make for an interesting combination."

"Fire magic?"

"I make things burn." Her eyes glittered with something between anticipation and madness. "Hot enough to melt stone when properly motivated."

Eliza's stomach clenched as she began to understand the implications. If they were partners, and Madge was partnered with the other Shadow-worker, that meant—

No. They wouldn't pit her against Madge. They couldn't.

The arena doors loomed ahead—iron-reinforced oak twice the height of a man, carved with symbols from around the Empire: two entwined dragons. Fairies in flight. Dueling ogres. Ward stones flanked the entrance, pulsing with containment magic. Once they were inside, Eliza felt certain the wards would seal them in until one was dead.

"Four enter." A ceremonial guard read from an official proclamation, his voice echoing off vaulted ceilings. "Three emerge. One dies. Begin when the doors seal."

The words were not a suggestion but an absolute requirement.

The arena was a circular pit of black stone, surrounded by tiered seating where instructors observed from safety. Torches burned in wall sconces, casting shadows that moved wrong, independent of any natural law.

This wasn't about efficiency. It was about breaking spirits. And if the dark gray sky and frigid temperature were any indication, sleet or snow was on the way.

Mr. Jones entered first, darkness already stirring around his feet like hungry smoke. Madge followed, confusion clear on her face as she stayed close to her assigned partner. She rubbed her hands together in an attempt to warm them up. Miss Brooks moved ahead with flame-like grace, heat already radiating from her skin.

Eliza stepped onto the black stone last, her shadows rising, defying every attempt at control. Above them, Major Thorne took his seat among the observers. Their eyes met for a brief moment. Was that regret in his expression, or just torchlight reflecting off features too controlled to reveal genuine emotion?

The doors slammed shut.

Ward magic blazed to life, creating a shimmering dome that turned the arena into a sealed tomb. No escape. No intervention. No mercy.

Just four people and the certainty that one would be dead within the hour.

"Well," Miss Brooks said, flames beginning to dance around her fingers. "I suppose we should begin."

Eliza watched the flames swirl around Miss Brooks's body as she coaxed them into life. It was then she saw the dent in the flames, about a foot from the stone in her pocket. Was the stone actually working? She couldn't be sure—it might be weak, might fail at any moment. David had given her no reason to trust him or his tokens. But something was deflecting the worst of the heat, warding off magic in such a subtle way that it might not be noticed from the stands.

She looked across the arena at Madge, whose face crumpled with terror.

"Miss Clarke?" she asked, her voice trembling. "What do we do?"

"You give it everything you got, you 'ear me, Miss Madge? You don't 'old back."

She prayed she was right about this. Just to be sure, she risked a glance at Thorne. Was that a small nod he gave her? Or was she merely imagining it? She would soon find out—of that, she was sure.

Mr. Jones stepped protectively in front of Madge, his shadow magic surging outward like a living tide. He understood the arithmetic. Two against two. Kill or be killed.

"Stay behind me," he told Madge, his voice hollow but determined.

Miss Brooks raised her hands, heat shimmering as fire began to coil around her fingers. "Well then, let's see who burns first."

The flames roared to life, blazing toward Mr. Jones. His shadows rose to protect him, darkness clashing against fire in a display that lit the arena like a hellish sunrise.

But the fire burned through his defenses as if they were kindling, forcing him back toward the arena's edge. Miss Brooks's power was too strong, too refined. Mr. Jones was outmatched.

"Madge!" Eliza called. "Your light! From the darkness, remember?"

Madge hesitated. Then light exploded from her hands.

The illumination was pure and brilliant enough to make everyone shield their eyes. It crashed into Miss Brooks's flames; they were perfectly matched, with fire and light dancing together in devastating harmony.

The light skirted around Eliza's around the stone in her pocket. The edge of her shield blazed with light, but she was unharmed.

What she should have done was given the stone to Madge before they went into the arena. Slipped it in her pocket when no one was looking. But it was too late now. A hundred pairs of eyes were upon them, and the only way for her to get near Madge was for Eliza to invoke her full shadow power, something that Thorne had warned her not to do.

Then Madge's power began to overwhelm everything else. She stood frozen at the arena's heart, terror feeding abilities that responded to emotion rather than conscious will. Light poured from her in waves that made every surface gleam like the sun, each pulse stronger than the last.

Miss Brooks tried to maintain control of her flames, but the light was too intense, too pure. It fed the fire until it blazed white hot, beyond anyone's ability to direct or contain.

Eliza held her shield high, focusing on the ward stone in her pocket, willing it to protect her from the heat, from the light. Her shadows responded to her emotions, rippling around her torso in soft waves and protecting her from the worst of the heat. Still, sweat covered her body, as if she were standing too close to a coal furnace.

Mr. Jones, caught between the two forces, had nowhere to retreat. His shadow magic offered no protection against fire this intense. It withered and vanished, leaving him exposed as super-heated air seared his flesh.

He opened his mouth and screamed.

14 BLOOD ON STONE

Silence stretched, thick and suffocating.

Thomas Jones lay crumpled on blackened stone; his body twisted at unnatural angles. The acrid stench of burned hair mixed with a sweet-sick smell of flesh cooked beyond recognition. Smoke curled from his fingertips where shadow magic had died with its wielder, leaving only a charred corpse and the memory of power that would never flow again.

But it was the absolute stillness that cut deepest. The sudden absence of everything that had made him human—breath, heartbeat, the desperate hope that had flickered in his eyes even as flames consumed him.

"No." The word escaped Madge's throat—a prayer to gods who'd long abandoned this cursed place. "No, no, no."

She stood frozen in the center of the arena, light still bleeding from her hands in weak pulses that painted the carnage in sickly gold. Her face had drained of color, leaving her looking like a discarded porcelain doll. The brilliant illumination that had fed Miss Brooks's flames now faded, responding to horror instead of terror.

Around them, the arena bore witness to what her power had helped create. Stone walls showed fresh scorch marks where fire had licked hungrily at ancient granite. The air itself still shimmered with residual heat that made breathing painful. Every surface gleamed with an oily luster that implied temperatures hot enough to melt metal.

"I didn't mean—" Madge stumbled backward, her foot catching on uneven stone. "I was trying to protect—he was going to kill us—"

Her words came out in broken fragments. Light leaked from her fingertips in erratic spurts, no longer the controlled illumination she'd managed during their lessons but something wild and grief-stricken. It painted shadows that seemed to reach toward Thomas's body with grasping fingers before recoiling in shame.

"You did what you had to do." Miss Brooks's voice carried the casual satisfaction of someone commenting on a dead rat rather than a child's death. She examined her fingernails, flinching in a way that suggested the fire magic had left them warm to the touch. "Survival requires sacrifice. You'll learn that lesson quickly enough."

Madge flinched as if she'd been slapped, then she doubled over and retched onto arena stone already stained with blood and worse things. Nothing came up but yellow, watery bile.

Her light exploded outward without warning.

"Madge!" Eliza threw herself forward, shadows rising instinctively to shield her from the blazing torrents that carved smoking gouges in stone walls. The ward dome above them groaned, magical barriers straining against forces that defied every safety protocol the Empire had established.

"Stay back!" Madge's head snapped up, tears cutting tracks through the grime that coated her cheeks. "Don't come near me. I'm dangerous. I'm a monster!"

The light around her hands shifted from gold to white-hot silver, each pulse strong enough to make everyone in the arena shield their eyes. This wasn't gentle illumination; this was primal power responding to emotional chaos rather than conscious will. The temperature spiked again as her abilities fed on grief and guilt, turning the arena into a furnace that made breathing an act of endurance.

Above them, the instructors leaned forward with renewed interest. Pens scratched across parchment as they observed the breakdown with the detached fascination of entomologists studying a rare butterfly on a pinboard. Whatever they were recording, it bore no relation to helping a traumatized child and had everything to do with cataloging her pain for future use.

"Fascinating," one of them said, his voice carrying clearly in the dome's acoustics. "Emotional manifestation at levels thirty percent beyond projected parameters."

They spoke about Madge like she was a stubborn horse to be trained rather than a young girl who'd just been forced to watch her partner burn alive. Their clinical detachment sent rage building in Eliza's chest like a physical pressure that demanded release.

Her shadows responded to the fury, hunger rising. Darkness boiled around her feet, reaching toward the observers with tendrils that tasted their fear and found it sweet. For one wild moment, she imagined letting her power loose—showing these monsters exactly what untrained shadow magic could do when motivated by righteous anger.

She fought for control, forcing the shadows down through sheer will. They resisted, straining against her like caged animals desperate for blood.

"You want to see what my power can do?" The words escaped her throat as a snarl. "Keep pushing her and you'll see alright."

"Miss Clarke. Control yourself."

Eliza spun. Major Thorne stood behind her, having entered the arena while her attention was fixed on Madge. His eyes held a mixture of warning and genuine concern.

"Control myself?" Laughter bubbled up from her chest, bitter and sharp enough to draw blood. "You forced Madge to become a murderer, and you want me to control myself?"

"I want you to think strategically." His voice dropped to a bare whisper, pitched low enough that she could barely catch the words. "Losing your temper helps no one. Least of all her."

He gestured toward Madge with a subtle tilt of his head, and Eliza followed his gaze to see the girl collapsing to her knees beside Thomas's body. Her small shoulders shook with silent sobs as she stared at what remained of her partner—what her light had helped transform from living boy to charred corpse in the span of heartbeats.

"I'm sorry," Madge whispered to the body, her voice so broken it barely qualified as sound. "I'm so sorry. I didn't want to hurt you. I just wanted to live."

The words sliced through Eliza's core. She forced her shadows down, swallowing her rage. Thorne was right—her anger wouldn't help Madge now. Nothing would, except getting her out of this arena before her guilt destroyed what remained of her sanity.

Madge buckled, almost crumpling to the floor. "I felt him die. When my light touched his shadows, they didn't fight at first. For just a second, they danced together like they were meant to be partners. Like we could have been friends instead of—"

Her voice cracked, then shattered completely. Light poured from her hands again, but gentler this time. Mournful rather than terrified.

"I felt the moment when his soul left his body." The admission hung in the air: a curse that would follow her forever. "It was warm at first. And then it just... went away. Like someone blew out a candle."

Eliza's breath caught in her throat. She'd heard of magical practitioners forming brief connections during combat, but for a twelve-year-old to experience death through that bond—the trauma would scar deeper than any physical wound.

Around them, the arena's machinery of death ground forward with mechanical efficiency. Guards entered through side passages, their movements as practiced as undertakers. They carried stretchers and buckets, mops, and coarse brushes—tools for hauling away bodies and scrubbing blood from stone. The sight of their casual competence made Eliza's stomach turn. How many children had they carried out? How many times had they mopped up blood?

"We need to leave," Thorne said. "Debrief is mandatory for all survivors."

Debrief. The word felt obscene when applied to children.

"Give us a bit," Eliza said without looking up from Madge's trembling form.

"You don't have a 'bit'." His voice carried urgency disguised as authority. "The longer Miss Windermere remains in this space, the more trauma becomes entrenched. Movement helps prevent psychological fixation."

Another clinical term for human suffering. But beneath his academic language, Eliza caught something else—a slight note of sadness.

Thorne stepped back, melting into the shadows near the arena wall as guards approached.

"Can you stand?" she asked Madge gently.

The girl nodded, though her legs shook as she pushed herself upright. Light still poured from her fingertips in steady streams. Her power had been fundamentally changed by what it had done, marked by death in ways that might never heal.

Miss Brooks sauntered past them toward the exit, spring in her step as if she'd just received a delightful birthday present rather than helping to murder a child. She paused beside Madge's trembling form, her smile thin and humorless.

"Don't feel guilty, Madge," she said with false kindness that dripped like honey over poison. "He woulda killed you if given the chance. They all would. That's what this place teaches—trust no one, kill before being killed, survival above all else."

"Get away from her," Eliza said through gritted teeth.

"Or what?" Miss Brooks's eyes glittered. "You'll fight me? Here? Now?" She gestured toward the guards and instructors watching from their elevated positions. "Go ahead. Give them another show. I'm sure they'd love to document what happens when a pathetic little Shadow-worker loses control."

Eliza clenched her hands into fists, shadows coiling around her knuckles. It would be so easy to let her power loose—to show this cow exactly what shadow magic could do with the right motivation.

But Madge needed her whole, not broken on the arena floor for the sake of revenge. And Thorne had warned her only to use her power when necessary. Could she have stopped Thomas's death? Perhaps, but at what cost? If they made her a full trial participant instead of an attendant, her time with Madge would be severed.

Miss Brooks laughed at her restraint, the sound bright and terrible as a death knell. "Smart choice."

She strolled away, leaving behind the sulfurous stink of spent fire.

Eliza knelt beside Madge, careful not to make contact. The girl's power still sparked unpredictably around her fingers. One wrong touch might trigger another explosion.

"Miss Madge. Look at me."

The girl's eyes remained fixed on Thomas's ruined face. "He had a sister. I heard one of the guards mention it during orientation. She's probably waiting for him to come home."

"She'll never know what 'appened," Eliza said quietly. "The Empire doesn't send bodies back to families. They just... disappear from the records."

"Because of me," Madge whispered. "His sister will spend her whole life wondering why he never came home, and it's because I killed him. My light fed the fire. My power burned him alive while I stood there and let it happen."

"You survived," Eliza said fiercely. "You chose life over death. That ain't a crime."

"Isn't it?" The question came out as a snarl that felt wrong from someone so young. "How do you know survival was worth this price?"

Eliza had no answer for that. How could she explain that survival was a form of honoring the dead? That living meant their sacrifices hadn't been meaningless? The words felt queer even in her own mind, pretty lies to cover ugly truths.

Around them, the arena's reset process continued. Servants hauled away Thomas's corpse like it was debris rather than the remains of someone's son.

They spread fresh sawdust across bloodstains, covering the evidence but never truly erasing it. New torches replaced the ones melted by magical fire, their flames dancing with cheerful oblivion. By noon, another group of children would enter this space. Another set of partnerships would be tested. Another life would be reduced to ash and educational value for Imperial observers.

How many more children? How many more "necessary" sacrifices?

The thought made Eliza's shadows writhe with helpless fury.

Two guards approached with indifference, their faces showing no emotion as they gestured toward the exit. "Debrief in ten minutes. Move along."

Madge rose on unsteady legs, her small form dwarfed by the arena's vast emptiness. She looked like a ghost already—pale and insubstantial, as if part of her had died alongside Thomas and might never fully return.

At the threshold, she stopped and turned back toward the center of the arena, toward the blackened patch where her partner had breathed his last.

"His name was Thomas," she whispered. "Thomas Jones. He was sixteen years old. He liked to read adventure stories when the guards weren't watching. He told me during orientation that he wanted to see the ocean someday."

Her words carved themselves into the stone walls, an epitaph for a boy who would have no grave, no mourners, no one to remember his dreams except the girl who'd helped destroy them.

"I killed him." The confession broke from her throat like blood from a wound. "I killed him."

She mouthed the words one final time, softer and more broken, until she was speaking without sound. The guilt was beginning its slow work of destroying everything bright and hopeful that had once lived in her heart.

The arena doors slammed shut behind them like a tomb sealing. But the real tomb was already inside Madge's chest, where innocence lay buried beneath the pressure of what could never be undone.

15 HOLLOW DAYS

The next morning, Eliza walked to Madge's room, her whole body aching from the hard mattress and the chill of the night. She rapped on Madge's door. No answer came, but she pushed inside anyway.

The smell hit her first—stale air and something sour: fear-sweat that hadn't been washed away. Madge sat curled on her narrow bed, knees drawn to her chest, staring at the stone wall with eyes that held no light. Her dark curls hung greasy and unwashed. Her uniform was wrinkled, stained with something that might have been yesterday's tears.

"You missed dinner last night," Eliza said, settling into the bedside chair. She'd been worried about Madge's absence, but attendants weren't allowed to see their charges after dinner, so all she could do was worry. And by the looks of Madge now, she'd been right to worry.

"I wasn't hungry," Madge mumbled.

Eliza studied the girl's blotchy cheeks, the way her small hands trembled where they gripped her knees. When had she got so thin?

"The breakfast bell just rang. We should get something to eat."

"Still not hungry." Madge's shoulders hunched inward, making her look even smaller.

Eliza's chest tightened. This wasn't grief—this was something deeper. A sort of breaking that might never heal. "You 'ave to eat."

"Why?" The question came out flat, but underneath it, Eliza

caught a note of something that made her body weaken as if drained of all energy. It wasn't defiance or sadness. It was emptiness.

"Because your body needs—"

"My body killed someone." Madge's voice cracked on the last word. "I felt him die, Miss Clarke."

She reached for Madge, intending to pull her close and promise everything would be all right. But she lowered her arms almost immediately. Something told her not to touch her yet, not when she was filled with emotion. Not when that emotion could spark a furious storm.

Eliza's shadows writhed around her feet, reacting to the helpless rage building in her chest. "Death can be really 'ard the first time you see it." She thought of all the death she'd seen and heard of in the East End. Consumption had swept through the workhouse like the plague. Cholera had taken two uncles and a cousin. Three babies that she knew of had died at the hands of parents, unable to feed another mouth. After a while, she'd got used to hearing of friends and family who didn't make it, of walking past the occasional body lying in an alley or doorway. But that wasn't going to help Madge. And she wasn't sure if she knew of any words that could help her right now.

"I keep seeing it," Madge whispered, tears streaming down her cheeks. "In my dreams. But now it's not just Thomas burning. It's me. Standing over his body, covered in blood, and I'm smiling." Her breath hitched. "I hate this monstrous magic. I'm never using it again."

Terror clawed up Eliza's throat. If Madge refused to use her power, she'd die in the arena.

"It ain't monstrous," she said fiercely. "What you're feelin' is relief at being alive. Relief that it weren't you on the slab. It's normal to feel like that."

In truth, she didn't know if it was normal, but that's how she felt every time she heard of yet another baby who'd been tossed in the sewers, or another child who'd died from "a sleep affliction," which Eliza now knew to mean a laudanum overdose.

"Then why does it feel like I'm a monster?" Madge finally looked at her, and the pain in those young eyes was devastating.

"Why is it okay to feel relief that it was him and not me? What sort of person thinks that?"

Eliza struggled to hold back her own tears. Here was a slip of a girl grappling with the sort of moral questions that broke grown men. And the Empire had done this to her. David Thorne had done this to her.

Her fingers found the small stone in her pocket—Thorne's mysterious gift. During the arena trial, when Miss Brooks's fire had lashed toward her, she'd felt the stone grow warm, deflecting the magical attack somehow. She didn't know exactly how the protection ward worked, but she knew what it could do.

She pulled it out, turning it over in her palm. It was such a small thing to carry so much hope. What if she was wrong? What if it only worked for her and not Madge? What if she was sending Madge to her death with nothing but false comfort?

But what choice did she have?

"Miss Madge." She reached for the girl's cold hands, pressing the stone into her palm. "Keep this with you. Put it in your pocket and don't let nobody see it."

Madge's fingers closed around the stone reflexively. "What is it?"

"My magic protection." Eliza squeezed her hands, trying to will some of her own strength into the fragile girl. "You won't need to fight to the death. It'll keep you safe. But you have to believe it'll work. Magic needs belief to be strong."

"How do you know?"

Because I felt it work. Because I'm desperate and you're dying inside and I can't bear to watch you break completely.

"Trust me," she said instead, reminding herself the walls had ears.

A spark flickered in Madge's eyes. Not hope, exactly, but something filling the emptiness that had been there a moment before. "Will it really?"

"Yes." Eliza prayed that was the truth. "Hide it well. And when the time comes, remember you don't 'ave to kill, right? You just have to protect y'self."

Madge slipped the stone into her uniform pocket. Then she looked up at Eliza with the ghost of her old determination.

"Now come." Eliza stood, gripping Madge's arm. "You're going to breakfast whether you want to or not."

She half-dragged, half-guided Madge through stone corridors toward the dining hall. Other attendants moved through the passages with the same purpose: brown figures shepherding broken children through another day of survival.

When they entered the dining hall, Eliza noticed the empty chairs dotting both sections like missing teeth. There were five gaps at the attendants' table and two missing from the candidates' section. It was as if they'd never existed at all.

Eliza guided Madge to her assigned table among the other candidates, then made her way to her seat. Around her, attendants ate in careful silence, each probably calculating their chances of survival with every bite.

Across the room, Madge stared at her porridge without lifting the spoon.

"Trouble with your charge?"

Eliza turned.

The woman next to her, a spindly woman with black fingernails, gestured toward Madge with her chin, her voice pitched low. "She don't look so good."

"She's grieving."

"Dangerous thing, grief." The woman's eyes were as empty as Madge's eyes had been this morning. "Makes them unpredictable. And unpredictable children..." She glanced meaningfully at the empty chairs.

Around them, other attendants nodded with the resigned understanding of people who'd learned not to get attached.

Footsteps approached. Major Thorne appeared beside her table, his presence like a change in air pressure, rousing her shadows despite her fury.

"Miss Clarke."

She took a bite of porridge, forcing herself to chew the tasteless paste. She stared intently at her bowl, ignoring his close presence, but her body betrayed her. Her pulse quickened, and something deep in her core responded to his nearness like a bee to nectar. She hated herself for the reaction.

"A word in private?"

"No." The word came out sharp enough to draw looks from nearby tables.

He moved closer. To her horror, her shadows fluttered toward him, drawn by whatever connection linked their powers.

"You'll be in the arena again next week," he said quietly. "There are things you need to know—"

The woman with the blackened fingers looked at Eliza with distaste. She was probably assuming, like many of the other attendants, that Eliza was drawing favors from the Major with unsavory acts of lust.

"I said no." She finally looked up at him, fixing him with a steely gaze. "Leave me alone."

Hurt flickered across his features for a brief second before he resumed his military bearing. The sight of his pain sent another unwanted flutter through her chest.

"As you wish." His voice carried a note of resignation.

He walked away, leaving her sitting with the certainty that she hated him. Hated him for forcing them to come here. Hated him for the impossible position he'd put her in. Hated him for making her feel anything at all when she should feel nothing but contempt.

Most of all, she hated herself for the way her shadows still yearned for his retreating form, seeking his light.

Across the room, Madge sat motionless, her breakfast untouched.

Please let the stone work, Eliza prayed silently. Please let it be enough.

Because if it wasn't, she would watch another child die. And this time, it would be the one that mattered most.

16 FRACTURES

It had been five days since Thomas Jones had died screaming, and Eliza's shadows refused to stay still.

She stood shivering outside the dormitories, waiting for the morning bell that would allow attendants their brief visits with their charges. Other women clustered nearby—figures in mud-brown clothing who'd learned to make themselves invisible in a place that devoured the conspicuous.

But invisibility required control Eliza no longer possessed.

Her shadows crept across the flagstones, drawn to every dark corner like hunting hounds following a scent. They moved with purpose outside her conscious will, reaching toward other attendants' feet, tasting the fear that clung to everyone in this cursed place.

Stop. She tried to pull them back, but they stretched further instead—thin tendrils of darkness that snaked between boots and under hems.

The woman beside her noticed. She shot Eliza a look that promised trouble if this continued.

A flush crept over Eliza's cheeks. She squeezed her eyes shut, willing herself to draw the shadows in. But they refused to cooperate. She was about to give up, to open her eyes and scream in frustration, when she saw a tiny pinprick of light in the darkness. Thorne's words came rushing back to her. *The power comes from lightness, not darkness.*

Golden threads began to sparkle from the pinprick of light. Warm light that pulsed like a heartbeat, connecting the threads to something expansive and luminous, yet hidden.

She reached for the threads with her mind, drawing them back into the circle of light, which now pulsed yellow. Her shadows snapped back like chastised dogs.

"Better."

The voice made her eyes fly open. Major Thorne leaned against the wall ten feet away, arms crossed over his chest. His expression held what looked like admiration.

"How long you been watching me?" she asked.

"Long enough." He pushed off from the wall with fluid grace. "Your control is improving."

"Is it?" She gestured toward the shadows still writhing around her feet. "Because it feels like everything's falling apart. Thanks to you."

He ignored the dig and stepped closer. "Control isn't about perfection. It's about recovery. When you lose your grip, how quickly can you find it again?"

"I don't understand," she said, her shadows stirring restlessly.

"Don't you?" he whispered. "Three days ago, you couldn't calm your power if your life depended on it. Yesterday, I watched you struggle to contain your shadows in the hall. Just now? It took you less than thirty seconds to rein in the magic."

Had he been watching her struggles from the shadows like some sort of magic accountant? Yes, that's exactly what he'd been doing. Watching her like some creepy back-street punter. The thought sent a hot blaze of anger slicing through her.

Her shadows responded instantly, surging outward in a wave of hungry darkness. They moved faster than thought, wrapping around Thorne's ankle and yanking hard.

His bum hit the flagstones with a hard thump, his perfect composure shattered. But the moment his control slipped, light exploded from his hands, a wild and blazing light that painted the corridor white-hot.

The gas lamps flared so bright their globes cracked. Stone walls reflected the brilliance until the entire space became a furnace of radiance that made everyone shield their eyes.

"Bloody hell," someone whispered.

Eliza stared in shock. Thorne—controlled, calculating Thorne—had lost his grip on his power just as completely as she had lost hers. The light pouring from his hands responded to anger and embarrassment.

He's just like me.

The realization struck her like a thunderbolt. His power responded to emotion the same way hers did. The same loss of control, the same struggle to contain abilities that wanted to break free. Why did that surprise her? She waited for him to yell at her, certain she had just made a terrible mistake.

"Sorry, Major," she said, reaching toward him. But she wasn't sorry, not really. She felt a growing sense of satisfaction that he had fallen on his arse.

"Don't." He pushed himself upright, light still sparking around his fingers. "Don't touch me when my power is active."

She stepped back in surprise, partly because of his harsh tone, partly because he wasn't yelling at her for tripping him up. "Why not?"

He stepped close and whispered, "Because I'm not sure either of us is ready for what happens when our magic dances together again."

His words rang true, and the strange thought of their powers mingling sent heat springing to her face. His closeness seemed to coat their surroundings in a warm, protective cocoon. Gone were the gray stone walls, the attendants' stares, the stink of mold and mildew in the corridors. And gone was her anger at him for everything he'd done. She knew he must be using compulsion magic. Knew it in her core. But she couldn't resist, almost welcoming the reprieve from grief and rage and hatred that haunted her every waking moment.

She stared at Thorne's hands, where golden light flickered.

Without closing her eyes, she saw it now. The threads of power that connected his light to every flame in the corridor. Warm energy that pulsed with his heartbeat, responsive to emotions he tried so hard to hide.

"I can see your light," she said.

His entire body went still. "What?"

"Even with me eyes open. Golden threads that connect to the gas lamps. Power that moves when you're angry." She scrunched her brow, studying the patterns that wove around him like Christmas lights twinkling through London smoke. "It's beautiful."

She clenched her teeth at the outburst. This man, this thing, was beautiful? No. He was her captor. A monster, a henchman, an Imperial goon. What was *wrong* with her?

"Eliza." Her name on his lips sounded like a prayer and curse combined. "When did you start seeing that?"

"A few days. It started the day after the first arena trial. I lay in bed at night thinking of your words about focusing on lightness instead of darkness." The admission felt dangerous, but she couldn't stop herself. "When I reach for your light, my shadows obey."

His expression held surprise, calculation, and underneath it all, hunger that prickled her skin with awareness.

"Show me," he said.

She didn't ask what he meant. Her shadows were already moving, reaching toward him with careful purpose. But instead of wrapping around his ankles like weapons, they danced with the light that surrounded him—darkness and radiance finding harmony instead of conflict.

The effect was breathtaking. Golden threads wove through living shadow, creating patterns that pulsed with shared power. Where light touched darkness, new possibilities bloomed—magic that belonged to both of them and neither.

"Elizabeth," he breathed. "I found you."

Before she could respond, Imperial Guards rounded the corner in full armor, weapons drawn and magic crackling around their hands.

Thorne's light vanished instantly, pulled inward with control that hinted at years of practice. But Eliza's shadows took longer to obey, and by the time she'd wrestled them into submission, suspicious eyes were upon her.

"Major Thorne," one of the guards said. "Sir. We detected a strong magical manifestation."

"Training exercise," Thorne replied without missing a beat.

"Miss Clarke's abilities require specialized instruction."

"In a corridor full of civilians, sir?"

"Where better to test control under pressure?" Thorne asked. "Unless you're questioning my judgment, corporal?"

"No, sir. Of course not, sir." But the corporal's gaze lingered on Eliza. "Will there be more... training exercises today?"

"That depends entirely on Miss Clarke's progress." Thorne's eyes found hers, holding secrets she was only beginning to understand. "Some lessons can't be rushed."

The guards dispersed with obvious reluctance, but the corporal remained behind, making notes in a brass-bound ledger.

"My office," Thorne whispered to Eliza. "One hour."

He left, leaving her standing alone with the knowledge that all her assumptions about her power—and him—were about to change.

17 RECOGNITION

On her way to Thorne's office, Eliza passed Madge heading toward the training yards.

Yesterday's visit had shown Madge emerging from the depths of despair, but seeing her here in the corridor, walking with purpose instead of shuffling like the condemned, drove home how far she'd come. Her spine was straight, shoulders squared. Another candidate said something, and Madge's mouth quirked upward. Eliza felt a flutter of hope.

"Miss Clarke." Madge's voice carried strength.

"How you feeling, miss?"

"Better." Madge's gloved hand patted her pocket. "Much better. I wanted to thank you again—for giving me hope when I had none left."

Eliza's shadows stirred with protective warmth. "The nightmares?"

"Gone. I slept through the night." Madge's smile was small but real. "For the first time since Thomas."

Relief settled in Eliza's chest. "Good. That's really good. Look, I 'ave to go see Thorne, but I'll see you when I'm done, alright?"

Madge nodded, then continued toward training, not with the shuffle of the broken, but the stride of someone walking toward battle with purpose. There was something odd about her movements, about the marked change in her demeanor. Had Eliza's words been that powerful? Had she really said the right thing? Or was there someone else whispering in her ear?

She shook the notion away and headed for Thorne's office. After climbing the stone stairwell, Eliza stood outside his door, nerves crackling beneath her skin.

She'd spent one hour pacing her room, replaying every moment in the corridor. The way his light had blazed when he fell. The hunger in his voice when he'd asked her to show him her power. The impossible harmony when their shadow and light had danced together.

But had it been the first time? Something nagged at her, a memory just out of reach.

She raised her hand to knock. Before her knuckles touched wood, the door swung open.

"You're early," Thorne said.

He'd changed from his military coat into shirtsleeves and a simple waistcoat, the formal barriers stripped away. Without the Imperial uniform, he looked younger. More human. Dangerous in entirely different ways.

"You said an hour."

"It's been fifty-three minutes." His mouth curved into a faint smile. "Eager to continue our lesson?"

Lesson. As if what had happened between them was something that could be taught from a textbook instead of magic that defied every rule she'd ever heard of.

"What exactly you planning to teach me?"

"Control." He stepped aside, gesturing her into the office. "Among other things."

Heat spiraled through her at the promise in those words. She hated how he affected her—this man who'd imprisoned them, who watched children die for sport. Her pulse quickened against her will. She clenched her hands, fighting the traitorous response.

The space was dominated by a massive desk carved from dark wood. Maps covered one wall—not of England but places she didn't recognize: New Zealand. Nigeria. Singapore. Territories marked with symbols in languages that were foreign to her eyes. A fireplace crackled against the evening chill, flames dancing in spiral patterns.

But it was the bookshelf that caught her attention. Volumes

bound in leather, blackened with age, their spines marked with titles in English and Latin. One lay open on a reading stand, its pages yellowed with age.

Thorne moved to the door, fingers tracing symbols carved into the wood. Light flowed from his touch, sealing them into privacy. "Ward against listening ears."

He followed her gaze to the bookshelf. "Shadowbinder histories. From before the purges."

"Purges?" She recognized the word from a conversation with Lord Windermere. She didn't know exactly what it meant to her, but she recognized the deep, stirring pain that came with hearing it.

"Sit." He gestured toward a chair near the fire. "We need to talk."

She remained standing, crossing her arms defensively. Every instinct screamed at her to leave. This man was her captor, her enemy. Yet something held her in place—something that made her pulse race and her shadows reach toward him of their own accord. The contradiction made her furious.

"About what?"

"About what you are. What I am. What happens when our kinds of magic find each other." He moved to the bookshelf, selecting a volume with careful reverence. "About why the Empire tried to erase your bloodline from existence."

"My bloodline?"

"Shadowbinder." He opened the book, pages rustling with age. "Something the Crown considered too dangerous to survive."

Somehow the word Shadowbinder fit, though she had no idea how or why. "I don't understand." She took a step back, her body warring with itself. Part of her wanted to flee. Part of her wanted to move closer.

"Don't you?" Thorne looked up from the book, and something in his expression made her catch her breath. Those gray eyes, sparkling again with silver, held depths that seemed achingly familiar.

"You've felt it," he continued. "The way your power responds to mine. The harmony instead of conflict."

"That don't mean nothing." But even as she said it, her

shadows stirred, reaching toward his chest like ravenous hands. She yanked them back, but not before catching the way his breath hitched at their touch.

"Stop doing that," she said.

"Doing what?"

"Whatever magic you're using on me," she said, unable to keep the snap from her voice. "I won't be manipulated by you."

"I'm not manipulating you." He closed the distance between them in three steps. Too close. She could smell him, an intoxicating lemon scent that drew her in, made her want to lean into him even as every rational thought screamed against it.

He said, "It means you're what they fear most. What they spent decades trying to erase."

"Stop." She pressed her palms against his chest, intending to push him away. Instead, his light responded to her touch, warm and golden, calling to her shadows with irresistible pull. For one moment, she imagined melting into his warmth.

She jerked her hands back as if burned. "What is this magic you're doing to me?"

His eyes darkened. "The magic isn't mine, Elizabeth. It's ours."

"That's not my name." But the protest sounded weak even to her own ears. When he said her name, something inside her chest fluttered.

"Isn't it?" He tilted his head, studying her with unnerving intensity. "Tell me, do you remember your dreams?"

The question caught her off guard. "What?"

"Your dreams. The ones where you scream about fire and burning jasmine." His voice was soft, almost hypnotic. "Do you remember what came after the flames?"

Her throat went dry. Those dreams had haunted her for years, but she'd never told anyone about them. "How could you know about all that?"

"Because you live in these walls. And the walls hear everything."

"You've been spying on me?" She could barely contain her rage. "While I'm sleeping? How dare you!"

He closed his eyes and let out a breath. When he opened his eyes, he said, "No. Not me. They monitor everything. You talk in your sleep."

She stepped backward, and she found herself pressed against the door, trapped between freedom and warmth.

He took a step toward her. "Tell me what you remember about the ship."

"I don't remember any ship." The lie slipped out easily. This man might know half her secrets, but she certainly wasn't going to let him know her whole self.

"Don't you?" His hand came up to brace against the door beside her head, close enough to feel the warmth radiating from his skin. "Try harder."

"I don't like how you're speakin' to me, Major Thorne." Her intent was to sound defiant, but her voice wavered. There was something about the way he looked at her, as if he could see straight through her defenses to the frightened child still cowering inside.

"What about the boy?" His voice was a scarce whisper. "Do you remember a boy who made light dance between his fingers? Who spent hours reading to you to keep the nightmares away?"

Her breath caught. The images were there, buried beneath years of deliberate forgetting. A cramped cabin. Salt air. The creak of timbers and the endless sound of waves against the hull. A boy telling her stories of Lightbinders and Shadowbinders. The memory formed as a hazy image, like a lantern's glow through fog.

"Don't be scared," the boy whispered, sitting cross-legged on the narrow bunk across from where she huddled in the corner. "Look."

Light bloomed between his small fingers, warm and golden, shaping itself into a butterfly that fluttered around the tiny cabin. It landed on her knee, and she gasped—she could feel its warmth through her torn dress, could see the delicate patterns of its threads shifting in the air.

"How?" she breathed, her voice hoarse from crying.

"Magic," he said, as if it were the most natural thing in the world. "Don't you remember?"

She shook her head. "I can't. Mine's bad."

"Magic isn't bad if you're a good person, Elizabeth. Watch."

He made the butterfly dissolve back into pure light, then held out his hand to her. "Trust me?"

After a long moment, she reached toward him with a trembling hand. The moment their hands touched, her shadows responded—not wild or angry, but gentle, laden with memory. They flowed around his light like silk ribbons, weaving through the golden radiance in patterns. She gasped with renewed wonder.

"See?" He smiled, and it transformed his whole face. "They're not bad. They're beautiful. They just needed something to dance with."

Together, they made magic fill the small cabin. Shadow horses galloping through fields of light. Dark birds soaring past golden suns. A castle made of intertwined radiance and darkness, where light princes and shadow princesses lived in perfect harmony.

"Who was the man that rescued me?" she asked when they finally let the magic fade, exhaustion making her eyelids heavy.

"My father," he said. "When they purged our school, he saved you."

She opened her mouth to answer, then stopped. All she could remember of the school was flames and screaming.

"Why?"

"Because you're special. Because of your golden third eye."

She didn't have a golden third eye, whatever that was. She was on the edge of asking him, but her eyelids were lead weights, and sleep beckoned like a siren.

David began to hum then, a soft melody that reminded her of her mother, singing in the gardens. Eliza looked at her friend through her sleepy vision, seeing the way his gray eyes sparkled with silver light...

Eliza shook the memory away and pushed against David Thorne's office door, willing herself to sink into the wood, to escape to the other side and away from this witchery. "No. Stop, please stop. I don't remember nothing."

"You're lying." He said it gently, without accusation, and somehow that made it worse. "Why are you lying to me? If we are to escape from this place, we must have trust."

Escape? Was this a ruse? "Because—" She stopped, choking on words she couldn't say. Because remembering hurt too much. Because if she admitted to those memories, she'd have to face what they meant. Because the boy in her dreams had been kind, and this man was a demon, and she couldn't reconcile the two.

"Because you're afraid." His free hand traced the air near her cheek, not quite touching but close enough to feel his power reaching for hers. "Afraid that if you remember, you won't be able to hate me anymore."

She turned her face away, but there was nowhere to go with the door at her back and his body caging her in.

"I don't understand what you want," she said, more breath than sound.

"I want you to see the truth." His thumb traced her cheekbone, the touch so light she might have imagined it. "Where were you born, Eliza?"

"London." Another lie, but easier than the alternative. Admitting she was born in India seemed like an admission that would feed into his black magic.

"Try again." His eyes searched her face. "What's the first thing you remember?"

"I don't—" She started to shake her head, but he caught her chin gently, holding her gaze. His touch sent flutters of excitement through her body.

"The first thing. Before London. What do you remember?"

The images crashed over her without warning. Running through jasmine gardens chasing shadows. Marble floors cool beneath bare feet. A woman with a blue, pulsating circle above her eyes, whispering in a language that felt like home. *"Meri chhoti rani, andhera tujhe kha nahi sakta."* My little queen, the darkness cannot devour you.

"Gardens," she whispered, the word torn from somewhere deep inside. "There were gardens. White flowers everywhere, and the air smelled like... like..."

"Like jasmine." His voice was soft, almost reverent. "What else?"

"My mother. She used to sing to me." Tears pricked Eliza's eyes, and she blinked them back furiously. "She had a mark on her forehead. Blue, like ink."

"What happened to her?"

"I don't know." The admission felt like the pain of a thousand bee stings. "I don't remember. There was fire, and screaming, and then—" She broke off, the memories too painful to voice.

"And then a man rescued you," he whispered. "He told you everything would be all right."

She stared at him, her heart leaping into her throat. "How d'you know that?" But it was a rhetorical question. She knew the answer. Of course she did. She'd known it from the second she laid eyes on David Thorne.

"Because my father was the one who pulled you from those flames." His hand dropped away from her face, and she immediately missed the warmth. "Because I was there when he brought you to our ship, covered in ash and blood, clutching my *Lightbinder* book like it was the most precious thing in the world."

She saw it suddenly—not just the rescue, but what came after. The narrow cabin that bobbed left and right with the waves. David—her friend from one of the school's upper forms—sitting cross-legged on a bunk, watching her with patient eyes.

"David," she said. His name was a dream and a nightmare combined.

Thorne went perfectly still. "You remember."

"I remember a boy." She backed against the door, her body trembling with the effort of fighting what she felt. "But that don't make you him. And even if it did, it don't change what you've become."

His eyes darkened. "What I've become? What exactly do you think I've become?"

"A monster." The word hung between them like a scythe. "You watch children die. You've kept me prisoner. You take part in this... this slaughter."

"To protect you." His words were tinged with desperation. "Every compromise, every horror I've witnessed, every child I couldn't save—it was all to keep you alive long enough to find a way out. Don't you see, Eliza? I had to be here to find you. I knew you were out there, and it was just a matter of time before you discovered your power. If I wasn't here, then they would have found you and destroyed you with a flick of the Queen's wrist."

Her voice turned bitter. "That sounds like an excuse for your part in this..." She waved a hand, trying to think of the right word.

"This death machine."

"You want to know about a death machine?" He moved to his desk, yanking out a leather portfolio. "Let me show you what would have happened to you at the Windermere residence if I hadn't intervened."

Before she could answer, he withdrew a document bearing the royal seal. Heavy parchment, official stamps, reeking with government approval for whatever lay inside.

"Read," he said.

She stepped over to the desk.

"Royal Decree 847," he said, his voice turning clinical as he read. "Signed by Her Majesty Queen Victoria, dated 15th March, 1851."

She should have slapped him. She should have screamed at him and told him she hated him, that she wasn't going to take his orders. But instead, she read.

> By Royal Proclamation and in the interest of Imperial Security, it is hereby decreed that all persons of Shadowbinder lineage, their children, descendants, and known associates, pose a clear and present danger to the stability of the Crown and the safety of Her Majesty's subjects.
>
> Having demonstrated abilities fundamentally incompatible with lawful society and having shown persistent resistance to proper Imperial guidance, said individuals shall be subject to immediate detention, interrogation, and elimination. This decree extends without exception to all children, regardless of age or demonstrated ability, all descendants to the third generation, and all persons found to be harboring, aiding, or associating with known Shadowbinder families.
>
> No appeals shall be heard. No mercy shall be granted. No exceptions shall be made for age, cooperation, loyalty to the Crown, or claims of ignorance.

The penalty for harboring, aiding, failing to report, or refusing to cooperate in the identification and elimination of Shadowbinder activities is immediate execution. All previous guarantees of protection, promises of amnesty, and assurances of safety are hereby revoked.

Let it be known that the patience of the Crown has been exhausted. By Her Majesty's Command, under the authority of Parliament, and by the Grace of Almighty God, let this be done swiftly and without quarter.

Eliza stepped back from the desk and gasped. Each phrase was crafted to strip away any hope, any possibility of mercy. She'd been seven years old when that decree was signed.

"How?" The word came out strangled. "How'd they know who they were?"

"Not *they*, Eliza. *You.* You, your family, and the other Shadowbinders." David's expression turned grim. "The census. For three decades, the Empire conducted magical lineage surveys in India under the guise of public health and safety. They claimed it was to track hereditary magical conditions, to provide better medical care, to ensure proper education for gifted children. But they were hunting. You see, they could never detect Shadowbinders through magical means. The third eye," he tapped his forehead, "can usually only be seen by other Shadowbinders. They had to use trickery. The Shadowbinder families registered willingly. Proudly, even. They saw cooperation as proof of their loyalty to the Crown."

"They trusted the system?"

"Completely. Parents brought their children to registration centers, answered detailed questions about their abilities, provided family histories going back generations. They were told it was for their own protection—that registered families would receive government support, special academic and occupational opportunities, legal protections. Every bit of information they provided was cataloged, cross-referenced, and ultimately used to hunt them down."

"The Shadowbinders thought they were gonna be protected. But they were signing their own death warrants."

"Exactly. Names, addresses, family trees, known associates, safe houses, magical signatures—everything the Empire needed for a systematic elimination." His voice turned bitter. "They even had detailed maps showing where to hit first, which families had the strongest abilities, which children posed the greatest potential threat."

She stared at the decree, her vision blurring. She sat down on the chair, knowing that if she stood for a moment longer, her knees would buckle. "My parents trusted them."

"Everyone did. The countrywide purges began simultaneously. Coordinated strikes at noon, when parents were working and separated from their children, when children would be in nurseries, in schools." His hands clenched into fists. "By sunset of the first day, ninety-nine percent of all known Shadowbinder bloodlines had been eliminated."

"Wait," Eliza said, David's words suddenly coming into focus. "You said they couldn't see the third eye, *usually*. What's that s'posed to mean? Usually?"

"It means it's hidden: as long as you control your power, they cannot see it."

He stared at her then, a long, penetrating, uncomfortable gaze that began with her eyes and then moved to her forehead. "There's a prophecy. About a powerful Shadowbinder who will unite the Empire and bring peace. It's said that this Shadowbinder will not have the blue third eye, but a golden ring, as if they are light and shadow combined. A *golden* ring. Sound familiar?"

She averted her gaze, trying to break free from his spell. "Well, that's just mythology, ain't it?"

"Mmmhmm," he said. "If that's what you choose to believe."

"What *I* choose to believe? What does it matter what *I* choose? *I* didn't choose none of this..." she waved a hand around the room. "So what does a stupid prophecy 'ave to do with me?"

He bit his lip then, as though he wanted to say more but was forcing himself to be quiet. He took in a deep breath and let out a slow, deep, breath. "I think perhaps you need to let this all sink in before I answer that question."

That was fine with Eliza, as she was in no mind for more of his riddles. But there was one question she couldn't let go of. "Fine. But you saved me." The words tasted strange on her tongue. "I mean, your father saved me. Why?"

"Because he was looking for a girl with long black hair and huge emerald eyes, holding *The Voyage of the Lightbinders*."

"But why? That don't explain why he chose to save me. Why not the other kids? Why just me?" In her mind's eye, she saw the dead children—dozens of them, lying in the schoolyard, in the gardens. What right did she have to be the only survivor?

"My father was, like me, a rebel who infiltrated the Magisterium. He couldn't save them all, Eliza. He wanted to, trust me. But with hundreds of Empire minions flooding the school, there was nothing he could do. But he chose to save you because I'd told him about my schoolfriend who had the golden mark." He tapped his forehead. "And he knew you were the prophesied Shadowbinder." His hand flew to his mouth then, as if he'd let slip a secret. "Sorry, I'm not sure you are ready to hear that."

"But I don't 'ave a mark." Surely he couldn't be talking about the tiny ring she'd spun in her mind? "I mean, I don't have an actual mark on me forehead."

"That's the thing, Eliza. No one is supposed to be able to see the mark of the Shadowbinder. That's why the Empire had so much trouble finding them. Because the marks were hidden, invisible. But *I* had seen your mark. You showed it to me. And my father made me tell him everything about you... what you looked like, how tall you were, what clothes you usually wore. That was the morning of the purge. He gave me very clear instructions. To lend you my *Lightbinder* book. He said I must insist on you having it and tell you to keep it with you all day, because your very life depended upon it—he needed to be able to quickly identify you in the crowd. I didn't understand at the time why he saved you. But I do now."

She studied his eyes, searching for the boy she remembered beneath the hard lines of the soldier. "But... I don't understand. Your father thought me worthy of saving, yet you brought me here?"

"I did. Eliza, it's more complicated than I know how to explain.

But I can tell you that I have spent my life searching for you." He clenched his hands into fists at his side. "Building my career, gaining influence, placing myself exactly where I'd have the best chance of finding you. When I finally found you, when I saw you again—"

The pain in his voice made her chest ache, even as fury blazed through her. The contradiction between savior and murderer was maddening—she wanted to reach out and throttle him, yet her heart fluttered at the same time.

"So instead you brought me 'ere. To this place where children die to serve the Crown and their attendants serve as cannon fodder."

"I brought you to the only place where I could protect you."

"Protect me?" Her laughter bordered on hysteria. "You threw me into arena trials!"

"I watched with a failsafe in place," he said. "The ward-stone I gave you—whoever's within its sphere of power cannot be killed. Not spared pain, not spared injury—but spared death."

"And if I'd dropped it? Or 'ow about if I'd given it to Madge?'"

"I know you gave it to Madge, Eliza. It's my family stone. I can sense it. I know where it is. But the second I saw you defenseless, then I would've intervened and blown my cover. But I couldn't do that while there was a chance to keep you alive without exposing us all. We are watched, Eliza. Every moment."

"You tricked us! Do you 'ave any idea what you put us through?"

"I did what I had to do to keep you alive!" The words exploded from him with enough force to make the windows rattle. Light blazed around his hands—not wild, but controlled and severe in its intensity. "Do *you* have any idea what it cost me to watch you suffer? To let Madge go through hell because showing favoritism would have exposed you and got you both killed?"

His face went pale, revealing desperation she hadn't seen before. The vulnerability in his eyes made something twist in her chest—something she absolutely did not want to feel.

"I've spent every day since you arrived hating myself," he said. "Watching you break a little more each time, knowing I was the cause. Knowing that everything you're going through is because I wasn't strong enough to find another way."

"Then why—"

"Because the alternative was execution. Haven't you been listening to me?"

His sudden anger stole her breath. She'd been saved only by his intervention. It was obvious he expected gratitude, but the knowledge only made her angrier. It meant she owed him something she didn't want to owe.

"So I should be grateful?" She laughed bitterly. "Thank you for keepin' me alive long enough to see kids die in front of me?"

"You think I wanted this?" His voice turned raw. "I had no *choice*, Eliza. Military service is not an option for my kind. It is mandatory. It was either here or at the frontlines in some godforsaken desert. I would be responsible for murdering by the tens of thousands: men and women, children. Here, yes, it's still murder, but..."

His voice trailed off. He took a deep breath. "You think I don't see dead children every time I close my eyes? Every child who doesn't make it out haunts me. But if I don't maintain my position, then I get sent to a distant land where I can't fight the rebel cause."

She could feel the anguish in his voice through the connection their powers shared, could feel his guilt and self-hatred as if it were her own. And that made everything worse, because it meant he wasn't the simple monster she needed him to be.

"How convenient," she said, but the words lacked their earlier venom. "More excuses for what you've done."

"Eliza, please—" He reached for her, and she flinched back. "You don't understand. I can't stop the Empire's madness. But you can."

"Don't," she snapped. "Don't you dare put this on me. I might be forced to stay 'ere in this nightmare, but I won't pretend to forgive you for creating it."

"I'm not asking for forgiveness!" He stepped back and threw his arms up. "For heaven's sake, Eliza!"

Her shadows writhed with her emotional turmoil. They reached toward him instinctively, seeking the light that called to them, and she had to fight to pull them back. Even her magic betrayed her when it came to this man.

The silence stretched between them.

"I've been planning our escape," he said quietly. "Building networks, calling in favors, preparing for the day I could get you away from here."

"Our escape?"

"You and me. And Madge. It's possible for us to secure a passage to America. New identities, enough money to start over somewhere the Empire can't reach. You can build your power, find others, sort out a way to stop this madness."

America. Freedom. A life where children weren't turned into weapons and power wasn't measured in body counts. The offer dangled before her like salvation, but accepting it would mean trusting him. And she wasn't sure she could survive that sort of trust.

"You're plannin' to come with us?" She wanted him to say *no*, sure that she never wanted to see this man ever again. But deep inside, she wanted him to say yes, to feel his light touching her, to—

She let out the scream that had been building up since she entered the room. It rattled the fixtures, moved the desk, shuddered the books so that they fell to the floor. She hated this man. Hated him for his magic and his riddles and his games.

But most of all, she hated him because she knew he was right. He was right about her childhood, right about her feelings for him, and right about the power she held inside her. She'd known it all along. The nebulous thing niggling at her senses for years, now had a name: Shadowbinder. It was like feeling an itch and finally finding the grass burr hidden in a hem.

He looked at her for what felt like a long time, and she saw something vulnerable flicker across his features—the ghost of the boy who'd made light dance for a frightened child.

"Do you *want* me to come with you?" he asked.

The question was loaded with the memory of childhood magic that had felt like home. She should say no. But her shadows stirred, reaching for him with unmistakable longing, and she knew her answer would be a lie.

"I dunno," she whispered. "I remember the boy who played shadow games with me. But I don't know the man who watches children die in arenas."

"Neither do I, sometimes." His voice turned gentle, and she heard an echo of the boy who'd sung her to sleep during storms. "But I know the man whose father saved you for a reason. And I know the man who would burn this entire fortress down if it meant keeping you safe."

"Prove it, then." The words escaped before she could stop them. If he was a trick magician, fooling her with lies, casting a spell of enchantment over her for sport, she had to know.

"What? You want me to burn this place down?"

"That's not what I mean. Prove that you're still the boy who made me shadows dance. Show me the magic we used to make together."

It was a spur-of-the-moment request. But at that moment, she saw fragments of a boy she used to know, and she was highly aware this could be trickery, a wolf dressed as a grandmother, pretending to be something he is not. But if he showed her his light—the way she remembered it, the way she used to feel it, laugh at it, play with it... only then would she know.

She thought he might refuse. But then light began to flow from his hands, something gentle and golden and achingly familiar. The same warm radiance that had filled a ship's cabin, that had turned her shadows into butterflies.

Her shadows responded, reaching toward his light like daisies seeking sun. When they touched, the office filled with patterns of impossible beauty—darkness and radiance weaving together, creating art from opposing forces.

It was exactly as she remembered. Exactly like coming home.

And that terrified her more than anything else in this place of horrors.

"David," she whispered, his name torn from somewhere deep inside her chest.

"Elizabeth." Her name sounded like want and promise combined.

Around them, shadows and light danced in patterns that expressed childhood innocence and adult desire, of a lifetime apart and the possibility of forever. But beneath the beauty lay the weight of everything between them—the dead, the betrayals, the impossible choice between love and justice.

At that moment, Eliza began to believe that some broken things could be made whole again.

She just wasn't sure she was ready for what that would cost her.

18 THE MISSING THIRD EYE

That night, Eliza lay shivering on the narrow bed, staring at the iron bars that striped her window with moonlight. Sleet fell outside, thick, wet drops of white that promised a frigid, wet morning.

Every time she closed her eyes, she saw David's face—not the hardened Major Thorne, but the boy who'd made butterflies from light. The boy who'd hummed her to sleep when nightmares came calling.

She pressed her palms against her closed lids, seeing those golden threads that pulsed behind her eyelids. The strange light that seemed to live inside her darkness, connecting her to something vast and warm. David had called her a Shadowbinder, and in her heart she knew it to be true, but what did that even mean?

Half-dreaming, she drifted back to the gardens of her childhood. Not the burning jasmine that haunted her nightmares, but something earlier. Peaceful. A woman's voice singing in Hindi, hands entwining hibiscus flowers into her hair.

The woman—her mother, she understood now—turned, sunlight catching the blue mark that hovered just above her brow. Not painted—floating. Pulsing with gentle radiance—a third eye opened to some other realm.

"My little queen," her mother whispered "Darkness is your friend."

Behind her, a man approached—tall, distinguished, with kind green eyes and curly brown hair. Her father. He knelt beside them.

"Show Papa," her mother urged.

Little Eliza giggled, reaching out with pudgy fingers. Shadows danced at her command, weaving through the jasmine blossoms, making patterns that sparkled with hidden light.

Both parents smiled, her mother's mark pulsing brighter with pride. "See, Leo Papa," her mother said. "She has the Golden Eye."

Eliza's eyes flew open. She stared at the barred windows, her heart racing. The memory felt real—too real. Leo Papa? That was her father's name? Her mind raced then, remembering Madge mentioning an Uncle Leonard. Surely... it couldn't be. Leonard was a common name, and perhaps, because she had a hazy memory of her father, she was getting the name wrong. Had her mother really said, "Leo Papa"? She wasn't certain; the memory was dissipating.

She sat up, pressing her fingertips to her forehead where the Shadowbinder mark should be. Nothing. Just skin and bone and the persistent ache of memory gaps.

Maybe David Thorne was wrong. Maybe she wasn't a true Shadowbinder at all, just some lesser magic-worker with delusions of grandeur. But if that were true, why had the Empire marked her for death in the purges?

The questions circled her mind like carrion crows, each one sharper than the last. She clutched her head, fury building at the endless mysteries that surrounded her existence. Her shadows stirred, reaching toward the walls with hungry tendrils.

Stop. The warning echoed in her mind. They were watching. Always watching. If they could hear her sleep-talking, they could probably sense her magical signature when it flared.

She forced her power inward, compressing it to a tight knot behind her ribs. The effort left her breathless, but the shadows obeyed. For now.

Madge. She had to think of Madge. Tomorrow would bring new trials and fresh horrors. And somewhere in this nightmare fortress, Madge was probably lying awake too, terrified of what dawn would bring.

Eliza had made a promise. Whatever else happened—whatever

David wanted from her, whatever he claimed about their childhood connection—she wouldn't abandon Madge. Wouldn't let him use their shared past to manipulate her into compliance.

Even if every fiber of her being yearned for his touch. Even if her traitorous heart raced when he said her name. Even if her shadows reached for his light like moths toward a flame.

The boy from the ship's cabin might have been kind, but David Thorne was still the man who had imprisoned her here. Still the one who'd thrown her into the arena trials. Still the enemy, no matter how her body betrayed her when he was near.

She just hoped her weakness wouldn't cost Madge everything when the trials resumed tomorrow.

Outside her window, the sleet continued to fall. Eliza pulled her thin blanket up to her chin and tried not to think about the warmth of David's hands, or the way his light had felt like coming home. And she tried not to think about why she was missing the mark of the Shadowbinder.

19 THE CONSTRUCT'S HUNGER

Dawn broke gray and merciless over Blackstone Fortress, but Eliza had been awake for hours.

Sleep had been impossible. Every time she'd closed her eyes, she'd seen David's face—not the controlled Major Thorne she'd known for weeks, but the boy from her memories. The friend who'd written her letters in secret code. The child who'd made shadow and light dance together in a ship's cabin.

The words picked at wounds she'd thought long healed. How was she supposed to feel? Grateful that his father had saved her? Furious that he'd lied for days? Heartbroken that her childhood friend had become her captor?

She dressed, chilled fingers struggling with buttons while her thoughts spiraled. Today was the second trial. Eliza would have to focus on keeping Madge alive when all she wanted was to run back to David's office and demand more answers.

Why didn't you tell me sooner? Why did you let me suffer in ignorance? Why do I still want to trust you after everything?

The questions had no good answers.

After breakfast, she made her way through stone corridors, darkness flowing around her feet in agitated streams. Other attendants avoided her gaze—word traveled fast in places like this, and everyone knew something had happened between her and the Major. They just didn't know what.

If only she knew herself.

The preparation chamber buzzed with tension. Six children huddled together—survivors of systematic culling disguised as "training trials." Three wielded fire magic, including Marcus and twin brothers who kept close together, their combined flames stronger than either could manage alone. Sarah shaped stone with her thoughts, the only earth magic that had survived the elimination round. James's water magic shimmered around him in nervous spirals, and Madge stood straighter than the rest despite being the youngest, light streaming from her fingertips in steady pulses.

Six children. Two attendants—Eliza and another woman whose hollow eyes spoke of a multitude of witnessed deaths. Eliza wondered who, of the six present, would die this round.

It was *not* going to be Madge—not while Eliza drew breath.

A guard read from his list. "Clarke with Windermere. Harris with the fire-wielder Marcus."

"What about us?" Sarah demanded, her voice shrill with panic. "Where are our attendants?"

The guard's gaze was as chilled as the morning air. "The most promising candidates receive the attendants. The rest of you will prove your worth alone."

James pressed himself against the wall. "That's not fair! How are we supposed to—"

"Fair?" The guard laughed. "Nothing about survival is fair, boy. Adapt or die."

Eliza nodded, relief flooding through her: she'd be with Madge. The other attendant—Harris—looked resigned as she trudged toward Marcus.

"The trial commences in five minutes," announced a voice that echoed off stone walls. "All magical restraints will be lifted upon commencement. Attendants, you will not be receiving shields for the trial. Your charges will act as your shields."

Or our charge's ward stones, thought Eliza. Madge had the protective stone in her pocket, and if Eliza had any chance of staying alive, she needed to stay close to Madge. She couldn't count on Thorne "intervening," whatever that meant.

Guards herded them toward the arena. Eliza walked beside Madge. Harris trailed behind with Marcus. When they crossed the threshold, their boots crunched on a fresh carpet of snow. The gusting wind blew thick flurries into the arena, blasting Eliza's face with an icy chill. A moment later, the ward stones along the walls hummed with containment magic, and the dome shimmered into place over the arena. Instantly, the temperature warmed from freezing to bearable.

A voice announced. "Let the trial commence. Those alive after eight minutes will move on to the next trial."

Before anyone could speak, before Eliza could make any sense of the announcement, the arena floor began to tremble. Deep beneath the black stone, something stirred.

The construct erupted from the arena's center in a geyser of impossible contradictions.

It was magnificent and horrifying—a dragon the size of a house, wrong in every conceivable way. Shadow and light writhed along its massive form, scales that gleamed like black diamonds bleeding radiance from their edges. Fire leaked from gaps between its armor, while wings of living darkness spread wide enough to eclipse the sky.

The group scattered.

Terror carved through Eliza's chest as she stared at the beast. Something about its movements, the way darkness and radiance warred across its scales, felt wrong yet familiar, as if she knew this magic, as if she recognized all magical signatures. The thought seemed impossible.

The beast's roar, a sound like worlds ending, shook dust from the ground and vibrated the dome.

Madge stumbled backward, light blazing around her hands. But instead of driving the creature away, her power seemed to feed it. The construct's burning eyes fixed on her with predatory hunger.

Eliza had to do something. But what? David had told her the power came from lightness, not darkness. One cryptic sentence—hardly guidance for a time like this.

But standing there, watching that monstrosity bear down on the children, all she felt was rage.

Madge's eyes were as wide as carriage wheels. She stepped backward, her mouth open in a silent scream. Her light intensified, snaking through the air toward the beast. The ward stone could protect her body from assault, but could it protect her from being drained of magic? She didn't think so. She bellowed over the roar of magic. "Madge! Don't feed it your fear!"

Madge's gaze snapped toward her, but she stood rooted in place, her light moving faster now toward the beast. Around them, the other children fought desperately. Marcus hurled fire at the construct, but its hide devoured the flames. The twins tried to douse it with water while buffeting it with wind, but their attacks had no visible effect.

James pressed himself against the arena wall, his water magic spiraling around him in chaotic patterns. He screamed, an ugly wail of terror that reverberated in the arena. It drew the construct's attention like blood in water.

The creature broke its spell on Madge. One moment, it crouched in the arena's center, feeding on her light; the next, it was airborne—wings of shadow and light carrying it toward the terrified boy.

James' scream cut off as talons of black fire pierced his chest. For one heartbeat, he hung suspended, a grisly look of horror on his face. Then his magic poured out—water and life force flowing into the construct's hungry form.

The creature grew larger. And from its throat came a sound that froze Eliza's blood. Not just a roar, but voices—dozens of them, screaming in harmonies which told of children who'd died in agony. She caught fragments of words, familiar cadences.

"Help us," one voice whispered, and she recognized Thomas Jones—the Shadow-worker Madge had helped kill in training.

Understanding crashed over her. That creature wasn't just a magical construct—it was a graveyard. Children who'd failed their trials, their abilities and souls harvested and bound into this abomination.

The creature turned its attention back to Madge. It spread its wings and took flight.

Eliza's vision blurred red. Her power erupted—darkness boiling up from every corner of the arena. She willed herself to remember David's words. *The power comes from lightness, not darkness.*

She shut her eyes tightly, looking for light within the maelstrom of her own fury.

Golden threads flickered through the black rage. Warmth pulsed with a familiar rhythm, connecting her to a vast and radiant light.

When she opened her eyes, her shadows moved with purpose instead of rage. They flowed toward Madge, wrapping around her ankles—not to restrain, but to guide. When the construct's claws swept toward her, Eliza's shadows pulled Madge sideways. When fire erupted from its maw, the darkness nudged her into a roll.

But she couldn't protect them all.

Sarah raised desperate stone barriers, walls of granite that should have been impenetrable. The construct's fire struck them, and they glowed, then cracked, then melted like candle wax. Sarah screamed as molten stone splashed across her arms, her earth magic failing her when she needed it most.

The beast's talons found her before she could raise another defense.

"Sarah!" Madge sobbed, light flaring wildly around her hands.

Marcus stepped forward, fury blazing in his eyes. "Die, you devil!" Fire erupted from his hands in torrents, flames hot enough to melt steel. For a moment, Eliza thought he might actually hurt the creature.

But the construct opened its maw and swallowed his fire whole, growing brighter as it fed. Marcus poured everything he had into the attack until exhaustion dropped him to his knees.

The creature's shadow-wrapped claws pierced his chest with a butcher's precision.

Eliza hugged Madge tightly, watching the horrific scene unfold, desperately looking for a weakness, something in the creature that she could aim for. Madge shook in her arms, and it was then that Eliza realized that they weren't going to last eight minutes. They weren't going to last another two minutes, unless she thought of something—and fast.

The twins were next. They worked together desperately. One brother called water while the other summoned wind. Together, they created steam clouds thick enough to blind. For precious seconds, the construct thrashed in confusion, unable to see its prey.

"We can do this!" one brother gasped to the other. "Keep

going!"

Eliza felt the warmth of Madge's ward stone. If they stayed in this position, tightly locked together in a hug, would it be enough? Could she rely on the word of David Thorne? She might have to, she realized. It was the only hope they had left. Even their combined magic: Madge's immature light power and Eliza's awakening Shadowbinder power, might not be enough to save them.

The beast lashed out with wings of living darkness, sweeping the arena floor next to the boys. They went down together, their combined scream cutting off with horrible finality.

"No!" Madge sobbed as each child fell. "Stop it! Please!"

Eliza's shadows lashed out in protective fury. But her power felt small, inadequate against something that had consumed so many.

Each death fed its growth, each scream strengthening its hunger. The beast now filled half the arena.

The other attendant lay crumpled near the wall, her chest rising and falling in shallow gasps. Still alive, but unconscious.

Desperation clawed at her thoughts. She couldn't fight this thing with her shadows. But what was shadow but the absence of light? If she could somehow obscure this thing's vision, cloak her and Madge in darkness, perhaps they could hide.

She reached for her shadows again. Darkness erupted around them, wrapping all three survivors in a shroud.

The creature roared in frustration, lashing out at empty air. But Eliza could feel the shroud already beginning to fray at the edges.

In the safety of shadow, Madge looked at the dying woman, then at Eliza, understanding dawning in her eyes. "I can't," she whispered, backing away from them both. "I can't go on."

"Madge—"

"No!" Tears streamed down her face. "I'm done! I have no energy left!"

"No." Eliza grabbed Madge's arm, yanking her back. "I promised to protect you. I meant it."

"You can't protect everyone!" Madge said, her voice breaking. "Look around! They're all dead. I won't let you die, too. You need to use your magic to protect yourself."

"We ain't going to die Madge. The stone, it's..." Her voice trailed off. She didn't know how to tell Madge that the stone might protect them from death, but not from maiming—that was if they could rely on the word of David Thorne—or that she couldn't just stand there and do nothing, or that her Shadowbinder magic could do more than protect, or one of the other million fragmented things racing through her head.

"We can both protect ourselves." Eliza's mind raced back to David's words, to what she'd learned about their opposing magics. "The power comes from darkness, not light. Remember what I told you."

Madge's head tilted—she'd heard. Eliza watched her close her eyes, saw her reach for something deep inside.

For one moment, Madge's light stuttered. Then it focused, becoming a spear of pure illumination that lanced toward the construct's heart.

The creature recoiled with a shriek that rattled the dome. Where Madge's focused light struck, scales cracked and bled darkness.

But the effort cost too much. Madge swayed on her feet, light guttering around her hands. The construct sensed weakness and pressed its advantage, wings spreading wide to block any escape.

"I can't," Madge gasped. "There's nothing left."

"You can't give up." She shook Madge's shoulders. "You can't give up, you 'ear me?"

The creature turned its burning gaze between them and the unconscious attendant, as if deciding which would make the more satisfying meal. It chose Madge.

Now was either the time to stand there and see if David Thorne's words had been truth. Or now was the time to honor her word to protect Madge, no matter what.

No choice. There had never been a choice.

As the construct lunged for Madge, Eliza threw herself protectively in front of her.

20 UNLEASHED

Madge's shriek tore through the air.

The sound shredded what remained of Eliza's control. All her attempts to find light within darkness, David's advice about balance—gone. Obliterated by the sight of Madge, about to be eviscerated while demons watched from the stands.

The construct's jaws stretched wide enough to swallow them both whole. In seconds, Eliza would be nothing but shredded meat, and Madge would be fuel for the beast that wore the faces of murdered innocents.

"No!"

The word erupted from Eliza's soul, carrying with it every ounce of rage she'd swallowed over twenty-three years of powerlessness. Every injustice she'd witnessed, every child she'd failed to save, every moment she'd stood by while the strong devoured the weak.

Power burst from her with the intensity of a star dying and a black hole being born.

Darkness poured from every pore of her skin—not shadows, but something deeper. Primal. Ancient. The void between stars given form, hungry and absolute and utterly without mercy. It boiled up from the arena floor, cascaded down from the ceiling, erupted from the walls themselves as if the fortress were bleeding night.

The construct froze mid-lunge.

The power emanating around her wasn't composed of the careful tendrils she'd used to guide Madge, or even the desperate whips that had struck uselessly against the beast's hide. This was darkness as a living force—intelligent, furious, and starved for vengeance.

The shadows didn't just move. They hunted.

Tendrils thick as tree trunks wrapped around the construct's limbs, squeezing with crushing force. The creature's guttural roar turned to pain as darkness invaded every crack in its unholy armor, worming between scales to find the softer flesh beneath.

The ward dome exploded, sending fragments of light spraying like fireworks.

"Stop!" a man screamed.

But Eliza ignored him. Ignored the other screams erupting from the spectators. She was pure instinct and protective fury, a force of nature given human form. The darkness obeyed her will like an extension of her body, flowing through the arena with apocalyptic fury.

The construct thrashed, trying to break free. Its fire blazed brighter, attempting to burn through the shadows that held it. But Eliza's darkness wasn't afraid of light—it devoured it, consumed it, turned the creature's own power against itself.

"Madge!" Eliza's voice carried inhuman resonance, as if the shadows themselves were speaking. "Get away from it!"

The girl scrambled backward, eyes wide with a mixture of shock and wonder. As if she was seeing something miraculous instead of monstrous.

The construct's struggles grew more desperate. It was gorged on the deaths of children, armored in their abilities. But Eliza's shadows weren't trying to overpower it.

They were trying to unmake it.

Darkness flowed into every joint, every gap, every weakness in the creature's form. Fire sputtered. Light dimmed. The harmonious contradictions that held the beast together started to tear apart.

"She's dissolving the binding matrix," another man yelled from the observation gallery.

"The construct's magical cohesion is failing!" another voice bellowed.

Eliza was sure this wasn't supposed to happen. The construct was meant to be invincible, a perfect fusion of opposing magics that could harvest power from any source.

But Eliza's darkness was older than the Empire's cleverness. Deeper than its minions' understanding. It was the silence after the last death rattle. It didn't fight the beast's magic—it simply told it how to cease to exist.

The creature's form began to blur at the edges. Scales fell away. The impossible fusion of shadow and light that comprised its hide started to separate, elements returning to their natural states.

"Deploy suppression fields!" a woman yelled. "Maximum power!"

Ward stones blazed to life around the arena, pouring magical energy as thick as London fog. But the suppression fields that could contain ordinary magic shattered against Eliza's power like waves against a mountain.

She wasn't using magic anymore.

She *was* magic.

Raw, unfiltered, and absolutely beyond their ability to control.

The construct's death-screech shook the fortress to its foundations. Windows exploded outward in cascades of glittering death. The ground beneath them cracked under pressure. The air seemed to fracture as the beast's stolen energies sought escape.

But instead of dispersing, the freed power flowed toward Eliza.

Fire and water. Earth and air. Light and shadow and the spark of life itself—all of it rushing toward her like rivers toward the sea. She should have been torn apart by the chaotic energies. Should have been consumed by forces that had never been meant to coexist.

Instead, she absorbed them.

Her body blazed with impossible radiance while darkness poured from her skin. Ice crystals formed in the surrounding air, only to melt in the flames. The very foundations of magical law bent and buckled under the pressure of what she was becoming.

"What is she?" someone bellowed from the stands above. "What in God's name is she?"

Eliza turned toward the fleeing crowd. When she spoke, her

voice carried the sounds of the undead and the promise of endings. It reverberated through the arena, rattling metal and pounding stone.

"I'm what you created when you murdered children for sport."

She raised her hand, and shadows erupted toward the observation gallery. They wrapped around the few remaining mages, lifting them from their feet.

The darkness squeezed. The mages' screams cut off with a wet crunch.

Pandemonium erupted throughout the arena.

Spectators fled for the exits, trampling each other in their desperation to escape. Guards poured in from every entrance, weapons crackling with suppression magic that proved utterly useless. She flung the guards to the edges of the arena.

She occupied the heart of it all, darkness flowing around her like a living storm. Energies of the dead blazed through her body, and with them came their memories.

James, terrified and alone, dreaming of parents who'd sold him to save themselves.

Marcus, whose flames had never been strong enough to satisfy his instructors.

The twins, who'd held each other as the construct tore them apart.

Sarah, who'd shaped her last barrier from stone and tears.

All of them flowing through Eliza's consciousness like ghosts seeking justice. Their power, their pain, their desperate desire for someone to remember that they'd existed—all of it became part of her.

And something else. The voices of a thousand trapped souls, calling to her from the distance. "Here," they said. "We are here."

"Eliza!" Madge's voice cut through the chaos. "You have to stop! You're going to bring down the whole fortress!"

Cracks spider-webbed across the arena walls. Rock foundations groaned under pressures they'd never been designed to bear.

She was going to tear herself apart. And take half of Blackstone Fortress with her.

But she couldn't stop. Wouldn't stop. Not when there were still devils wearing human faces, still children being fed to Imperial ambitions. The darkness had tasted blood, and it wanted more.

So much more.

Then the construct's final gift activated.

It hadn't been truly dead—just dormant, conserving energy while its stolen components scattered. Now, the beast's remaining essence charged.

Not at her body, but at her mind.

The psychic assault hit with the force of a battering ram, carrying with it the concentrated hatred of everyone who'd died to create the monster. Decades' worth of agony and despair, weaponized into a spear of pure malevolence.

Eliza's defenses, already strained by the energies flowing through her, shattered like glass.

The darkness exploded outward with uncontrolled fury, punching through the arena's walls like a fist through wallpaper, creating a whirlwind of intertwined light and shadow that reached toward the stars.

But the construct's essence wasn't finished. Having failed to destroy her mind, it turned to a cruder approach.

Physical assault.

What remained of the beast's form—nothing more than animated shadow and spite—rose from the arena floor like gas given malevolent purpose. It had no substance, no real power. But it had enough hate to dismember, to shred, to eviscerate.

And it was heading straight for her.

Eliza tried to summon her shadows, but the darkness no longer obeyed her will. The stolen energies had burned out her ability to control them, leaving her defenseless against the creature's final attack.

The construct struck like a frozen truncheon, driving into her chest with agonizing pain that radiated through her body. Blood frothed from her lips. The inexplicable power that had made her temporarily invincible began to drain away, returning to whatever darkness had spawned them.

The construct's essence wrapped around her, squeezing tighter with each heartbeat. It whispered in her ear with the voices of the undead twisted into malice. "Join us. Let the darkness take you."

The words carried seductive promise. No more pain. No more

watching innocents suffer. Just the cold peace of oblivion, the sweet surrender of giving up the fight.

For one moment, she almost accepted.

Then she heard Madge shout her name.

The girl was running toward her across the devastated arena, light leaking from her hands. "Get away from her!"

The construct's essence was inside Eliza's defenses, wrapped around her soul like a parasitic vine.

"I don't have enough," Madge sobbed. "Tell me what to do!"

What to do? She didn't know how to defeat this thing—it was engulfing her, blending with her, taking her thoughts and sharing its own. In an instant, she saw its weakness.

"Don't aim for the creature," Eliza said, her voice weak but clear. "Aim for me."

"What?" Madge's eyes went wide with horror. "I can't hurt you, Miss Clarke!"

"You won't hurt me. Light and shadow... work together."

Understanding blazed across Madge's face. She raised her hands, and threads of light began to flow—not attacking the construct's essence but flowing into Eliza herself.

The effect was immediate and devastating.

Light and shadow exploded through Eliza's body, finding the perfect balance. The construct's essence howled as opposing forces tore it apart from within, its hatred no match for the harmony it had never understood.

But the explosion of balanced power was too much, and Eliza felt herself dissolving, becoming one with the forces that flowed through her. Light and shadow, fire and ice, life and death—all of it merging into something that transcended human limitations.

As consciousness faded, she felt Madge's desperate love blazing through the haze. Felt the construct's death-screech as balance triumphed over hatred.

Then darkness claimed her—not the hungry void she'd wielded, but something softer. Peaceful.

The last thing she saw was light blazing down from above, wrapping her in radiance that felt like coming home.

21 INVISIBLE

Heat pressed against her skin, dragging her back from unconsciousness. Strong arms held her against a chest that rose and fell with labored breathing.

David.

She tried to speak, but her voice had vanished. Her body hung limp, muscles refusing every command.

"Stay still." His words rumbled against her ear. "We're almost out."

Out. She'd been dying—the construct's essence strangling her heart until darkness swallowed everything. But warmth wrapped around her now, holding her together when her body wanted to collapse.

She forced her eyes open.

Light blazed around them—not harsh, but flowing like liquid gold. Stone walls blurred past. Ancient passages twisted into shadows that hurt to track.

"What..." The word scraped out.

"Lightbinding." His grip tightened as they moved through corridors carved from living rock. "We're invisible."

Memory slammed back. The arena. The construct's death-screech. Power exploding through her core until she thought her body might disintegrate. Voices shouting from the galleries. Footsteps. People who wanted her dead.

She wriggled in his grip. David's arms held firm.

"Don't fight the illusion. It's keeping us alive."

Light pulsed with his heartbeat. She could feel it—not just see the radiance, but sense it flowing through her mind like molten gold. His power searching for hers, seeking the harmony they'd found as children.

Her shadows answered.

They rose from her skin like smoke, tentative at first, then bolder as they recognized his light. The same illumination that had danced with her darkness in a ship's cabin years ago. When shadow touched radiance, heat blazed through her.

His thoughts bled into her consciousness. Her body's dead weight in his arms. The strain of maintaining the draining illusion. A protectiveness that drove him forward despite exhaustion that should have toppled him to the ground.

She bled into him in return. The ache of absorption. The way the construct's stolen power had changed her. Whispers in her mind that told her things she couldn't grasp.

"I can hear them," she whispered. "The children the construct killed."

His step faltered. "What are they saying?"

"Help us." The words came out broken.

Their connection flared brighter. His guilt crashed over her—years of self-hatred for being born to the bloodline that destroyed hers. But underneath lay something else. Relief. Joy. The desperate happiness of a man who'd found what he'd spent half his life searching for.

They moved upward through passages older than the fortress above. Ancient stones fitted in perfect balance. The air grew fresher, carrying hints of fresh air and freedom.

"Almost there," David gasped. Blood ran from his nose; channeling his power was nearly destroying him. His whole body shook with exhaustion.

But he kept walking. Kept carrying her. Kept maintaining the illusion that stood between them and an execution squad.

The passage opened onto daylight. Snow swirled and spun like glittering confetti, the white fresh and clean against the gray and black of the world.

Yet, inexplicably, stars wheeled overhead as unconsciousness claimed her again.

* * *

She woke to a dark gray sky. The forest surrounded her, a tangle of snow and ice.

David still carried her, but his breathing had turned ragged. Each step sent tremors through his frame. Dried blood marked her cheek where it pressed against his shirt. Snow crusted the shoulders of his cloak.

They came out of the dense trees and into a glade. Rolling hills stretched around them, covered in dense woodland. Nothing like the barren lands surrounding Blackstone Fortress. Even the light felt different—golden amber instead of harsh white.

"How long..." she managed.

"Shh." His voice was barely audible, weak from hours of physical strain. "Almost there."

His illusion flickered around them. Whatever magic had hidden them was failing, each pulse weaker than the last.

They followed what might have been a deer path through ancient oaks. The snowfall slowed to a sprinkle now, lazy flakes fluttering outside David's light bubble. A stream chattered nearby, bright with ice crust.

She felt David stumble, catch himself against a massive oak, then sink to his knees with her in his arms. The magic concealing them died completely, leaving them exposed under the canopy.

"David." She forced herself to focus past the fog clouding her thoughts. "Let me down."

"Can't stop now." But his arms shook so violently he could barely hold her. His face held the ashen pallor of someone pushed to the brink of exhaustion.

"You have to." She slid from his embrace to the snow-crusted ground. "You'll kill yourself."

"Better than letting them take you again." His eyes held fierce determination, but she saw his power flickering like flame in the wind.

Pressure stirred behind her eyes—not pain, but something trying to push through from inside. She blinked, and the world shifted. Layered. Through the ordinary darkness, she glimpsed something else.

A cottage. Distant and hazy, but real. Light glowed in its windows—not David's golden radiance, but something older. Something safe.

"You rescued me," she said.

He said nothing. He just nodded, breathing in ragged gasps.

"I don't understand," she said, as a pressure formed in her skull. "You could have rescued me at the Windermere mansion. From the carriage, from the—"

The pressure intensified. She pressed fingertips to her forehead and felt it—a mark. Circular and small, hidden beneath skin but undeniably present. She felt it then, his pain, his regret, his sadness at not recognizing her sooner. "You didn't know it was me for sure."

He nodded.

He didn't need to speak, didn't need to explain. She understood. If he'd rescued her from the mansion, he could have thrown away his life, his career, his hard-earned foothold as a rebel disguised as a loyal Imperial officer. All for a girl who may or may not be his Elizabeth. Yet that opened up another train of thought, one she wasn't sure she had the energy to fully comprehend. Lady Windermere had been right all along. Somehow, Eliza was related to one of the most prestigious families in London.

The golden light behind her forehead pulsed. "This way."

David furrowed his brow, but exhaustion had stripped his ability to question. She helped him to his feet. Together they stumbled through woods, following a path through the snow that seemed to exist only when she needed it. The vision grew stronger, clearer, pulling her forward.

The cottage waited at the meandering path's end, tucked in a grove where ancient trees grew so thick their branches formed a natural roof. Not overt magic, but a misdirection that came from ancient skill. Built to fool the eye, not enchant it.

Light glowed warm and welcoming in the windows. Daylight had all but disappeared, blackness cloaking the forest.

They made their way down the path together, leaning on each other. Her shadows moved with strange purpose now, no longer hungry but somehow recognizing this place as sanctuary.

The cottage door opened at David's touch. He stepped inside

and snapped his fingers, kindling flames in the stone hearth.

She stepped across the threshold on unsteady legs, his hand steadying her elbow.

"Welcome home," he said.

22 THE COTTAGE

Warmth bloomed from the hearth David had just lit. Books lined every wall—not Imperial texts, but ancient volumes with weathered covers. Maps covered one section, marked with symbols that made her eyes water when she tried to focus.

But it was the feeling that stole her breath. It wasn't just a shelter. It was a sanctuary.

"What is this place?"

"My childhood home. I grew up here when my father was stationed in England."

Eliza glanced around. The place was cozy, lived-in, like a place from a fairytale with its thatched roof and stone walls. A soft cooing came from outside the walls, a sound she recognized from London. "Pigeons?"

"Homing pigeons." David said. "Three of them, outside in the aviary."

The cooing was a gentle balm, and apart from the rustling of trees, it was the only noise. She had grown up in a tenement with thin walls and the constant voices of neighbors screaming, yelling, moaning. What it would have been like to grow up in such peace.

A knot of guilt formed in her gut. She was safe in this storybook cottage, while Madge was imprisoned in the fortress. "Madge. Where is she?"

David's face went pale. "Still at the fortress."

Panic clawed up her throat. "We 'ave to go back—"

"She'll be fine." His voice carried strange conviction. "The trials are over. Nothing will happen to her now. Besides, we're both too weak. We need time to recover."

Eliza stared at him. Her newly awakened senses picked up something wrong. Where shadows should fall naturally across his face, there were gaps. Dark spaces that didn't belong, as if something was being hidden. He was lying. She knew it with absolute certainty.

Yet his words soothed the terror in her chest. Panic receded, replaced by odd reassurance she couldn't explain.

Eliza caught David's elbow as he swayed. "You're exhausted. Sit before you collapse."

He let her guide him to a chair beside the hearth. His legs buckled, and he slumped on the chair, the full cost of their escape written in every line of his body.

The cottage stretched larger inside than it had appeared from the path. Rooms branched off the main space, disappearing into shadows that suggested impossible depths. Her breath caught at the sense of safety, the bone-deep knowledge that nothing could touch them here.

David gestured weakly toward the kitchen. "There's food. Help yourself."

She found provisions in the pantry: fresh bread and cheese, preserved fruit. She prepared two plates and returned to the front room. "Fresh bread? Who knew we were coming?"

He chuckled. "Preservation magic. Costs a King's fortune but worth every penny for times like this."

As she bit through the crumbly crust and into the pillowy-soft delight, she had to agree.

They ate in silence, David slowly regaining color as food and rest restored him. When they'd finished, she made tea for both of them, settling into the chair across from his.

"We 'ave to talk about Madge," she said.

His jaw tightened. "There's nothing to discuss yet."

"She's alone in that place because of me."

"She's alive because of you." David leaned forward, firelight catching the chiseled planes of his face. "Your power, your sacrifice—it saved her life. But going back now would be suicide."

"So we abandon 'er?"

"We prepare." His voice turned to steel. "The moment you leave these wards, every magical sensor in the Empire will scream your location. In your current state, they'll destroy you before you can fight back."

"Then what d'you suggest?"

"Training. Planning. Becoming strong enough to succeed." He stood, moving to the bookshelves. "But first, you need to understand what you are."

He pulled down several volumes, their ancient leather bindings brittle and ragged. "Your heritage. Your people's history. Everything the Empire tried to erase."

Eliza opened the first book that David handed to her. Although foxed and yellowed, the pages were still legible. Illustrations showed figures wreathed in shadow, their faces marked with small blue circles between their brows. Like the mark she'd felt forming beneath her skin but had yet to see.

"The third eye," David said, noting her attention. "The source of true Shadowbinder power. Your parents probably had the mark."

Shivers raced down her spine. "What 'appened to my family?"

David's face darkened. "The massacres were surgical."

He didn't need to say more. "And the other Shadowbinder kids at our school?"

"My father's battalion was ordered to make sure none survived," he said hollowly, as if conjuring a painful memory.

"He saved me though. What 'appened to him?"

"He continued to rebel against the Empire for many years—from the inside. But the guilt over the purges destroyed him. He drank himself to death trying to forget the faces of the dead."

"Why did he give me away then? When we got to England?"

"He thought he was keeping you safe, temporarily. When he went back to the church a week later, you were gone. The nuns said you'd been adopted, and that was that. He tried to find you, but the records were sealed. On his deathbed, he made me promise to continue his search for you."

Eliza absorbed this, mind reeling. "So you think I really am the last Shadowbinder?"

"The last pureblood Shadowbinder. Yes." David leaned forward, urgency replacing exhaustion. "But not just any Shadowbinder. The prophesied Shadowbinder. Which is why you have to get stronger. Much stronger."

She heard his words, but they didn't fully register. Besides, it wasn't a question of what he thought she was, it was a question of time—time that Madge was running out of.

"How long will that take then?" She was thinking that a few days would suffice to gather her strength.

"Weeks. Maybe months." He must have seen her aghast expression because he quickly continued. "But Madge will survive. The Empire doesn't waste valuable assets."

The shadows around his face flickered again, but somehow his words still brought comfort. Was he using his light to influence her emotions?

"Are you using magical compulsion on me?" she asked.

He laughed. "This again. I can assure you; I am not. I have no such skills. If anyone was using compulsion magic, it would be you, I think."

At that, his face flushed, but she wasn't ready to decipher what that meant.

"Show me," she said, opening the first book. "Show me what I need to learn, then."

"The one you have in front of you is a general history." David pulled down more volumes. "This one covers breathing exercises to center your power. Meditation techniques to strengthen your connection to shadow. And this—" He held up a slimmer text. "Combat forms that turn darkness into weapons."

"The key," he explained, "is what I told you in the fortress. It is understanding that shadow isn't the absence of light. It's where light chooses to rest. The two forces aren't opposites—they're partners."

"Like us."

He met her eyes across the flickering firelight. "Like us."

For the next hour, they planned. David showed her maps of the fortress, detailing guard rotations and ward patterns. He explained the magical defenses she'd need to overcome, the skills she'd have to master.

"Tomorrow we start training," he said finally. "Physical conditioning, magical exercises, combat practice. Everything you'll need to match Imperial Battle Mages."

"And when I'm ready? What 'appens then?"

"When you're ready, we rescue Madge." His tone was sharp as a blade. "And then we make them pay for what they did to your people."

"How will I know when I'm strong enough?"

He ran a hand through his hair. "When you can maintain perfect control under extreme stress. When your power obeys your will instead of your emotions. Because without control, magic is nothing but destruction."

He gestured to the cottage around them. "These wards will hide your magical signature while you train. But the moment you step outside, the Imperial wards will sense you. If you're not ready—if you lose control like you did in the arena—they'll overwhelm you before you can save anyone."

"I understand."

"Do you?" His gray eyes held hers. "Because going back too soon won't just get you killed. It could get Madge killed, too."

The burden of his words settled on her shoulders. But underneath the fear, determination burned bright. She would get stronger. She would learn control. And she would make the Empire pay for every life they'd stolen.

"Teach me," she said. "Teach me everything you know."

David nodded. Shadows stirred with anticipation around her feet. The Empire had taken everything—family, childhood, innocence. Soon, she would take something back.

But as David's light began to shimmer, she saw how thready the strands were. Before she could ask him to help her, she needed to address his weak light, the exhaustion carved into his face, the tremor in his hands.

"You look like you're about to fall over," she said.

"I'm fine."

Her shadows wrapped around his wrist. "You nearly killed yourself getting me 'ere."

"Worth it." His eyes found hers. "You're worth all of it."

The words hit her harder than any blow. She'd thought herself to be alone in the world. But here was proof that someone had searched for her. Waited for her. Nearly died for her.

She moved closer. "Show me."

"Show you what?"

"Your light," she said simply.

David's hand cupped her face. "My lightbinding isn't strong right now. The best I'll be able to do is a gentle whisper."

"Show me a gentle whisper, then."

Golden radiance bloomed from his fingertips. Not the harsh illumination that had hidden them during their escape, but something softer. Warmth that sank through skin and muscle, easing aches from the construct's blows.

Her shadows rose in response, drawn to his light. When darkness touched gold, heat danced between them.

"I remember this," she said. "On the ship. Your light playing with my shadows."

"You were so small. So fierce." His other hand found her face, cradling her between his palms. "I knew even then that you were meant to be mine."

"Yours?"

"My partner. My equal. The other half of what we could become together." His voice was a lover's purr that sent shivers through her, caressing every inch of skin.

She reached for him, lips finding his in the golden glow of firelight and magic. He tasted of exhaustion and years of desperate searching. When her shadows mingled with his light, the cottage itself seemed to sigh with approval.

His hands tangled in her hair, pulling her closer. The kiss deepened, becoming something desperate and grateful and alive with the knowledge that they'd both survived to find each other again.

"Elizabeth." Her name was a prayer on his lips.

"I know." She pulled back just enough to meet his eyes. "I feel it too."

The connection between their powers pulsed stronger, drawing them together.

She stood, offering her hand. "Come with me."

David looked up at her—shadows and firelight playing across

her skin, power radiating from every inch of her—and nodded. His fingers laced through hers as she led him toward the cottage's inner rooms.

In the bedroom, moonlight streamed through windows, turning everything silver and soft. She turned to face him, her heart racing.

"Are you certain?" David's voice was rough with want and exhaustion and something deeper. Uncertainty flickered across his features. "You've been through so much. I don't want to—"

"David." She pressed her fingers to his lips, shadows curling around his wrist. Perhaps this wasn't compulsion magic, but whatever was happening between them was equally intoxicating. "D'you feel that?"

His breath caught as her shadows whispered across his skin. His light responded, golden warmth blooming to meet her darkness. Their connection pulsed with mutual recognition, mutual choice.

"Yes," he breathed.

"Then you know this is right." She let her shadows move gently over him, tracing the dried blood at his temple, the darkness beneath his eyes, the soft curve of his lips. "You must see... this means more to me than words."

His breath hitched. "Eliza..."

"You saved me." She stepped closer, her body going taut and loose all at once. "Now it's time I repay you, in whatever way I can."

Her fingers found the buttons of his shirt, working them free, feeling the electricity sparking between them. When the fabric fell away, she saw the bruises blooming across his ribs where exhaustion had made him stumble. His skin was checkered with scratches from branches he'd pushed through in the dark.

"All for me," she whispered.

"I'd do it again." His hands found her waist, pulling her closer. "Every time."

She rose on her toes to kiss him again, pouring desperate hope into their embrace. His light responded, warm and golden and gentle, wrapping around them both.

When they came together, it was with the inevitability of sunrise after the longest night. Her shadows and his light twined around them, creating something entirely new—not darkness or illumination, but the perfect balance between them.

She gasped as he pulled her closer, the heat of his skin burning away the last memory of stone cells and iron bars. His light responded to every touch, every breath, his power caressing her shadows with gentle reverence—never forcing, always asking permission. Her darkness wrapped around his radiance in return, protective rather than possessive, cherishing rather than consuming.

"I've been searching for you for so long," he gasped against her throat.

"I know," she replied, fingers curling into the muscle of his shoulders as sensation built between them. Even without her memories, some part of her had recognized him from their first meeting. Had known he was important in ways she couldn't name.

They moved together in the silver moonlight, her breath hitching as he whispered her name. Their magic pulsed in harmony with their bodies, creating waves of sensation that went deeper than the physical into something transcendent. The scratch of linen beneath her skin, the salt taste of his shoulder under her lips, the way he shuddered when her shadows traced the hollow of his throat.

When release crashed over them both, their combined power lit the cottage—warm and bright and utterly safe. She cried out, her magic flaring wild and unrestrained, and felt his light catch her darkness in a net of gold that held her together as she shattered and remade herself in his arms.

Afterward, she lay against his chest, listening to his heartbeat slow toward normal. His fingers traced lazy patterns on her bare skin, and she felt more at peace than she had since childhood.

"What 'appens now?" she asked.

"Now we heal." His arms tightened around her. "And then we take on the Empire."

She smiled against his chest, shadows purring with contentment around them both. The future stretched ahead—uncertain, dangerous, but worth fighting for.

23 BREAKING POINT

The next afternoon, Eliza paced the cottage like a caged wolf.

Each step seemed to carve a deeper groove into the ancient floorboards. Her shadows writhed around her, restless and hungry, responding to the fury that clawed at her ribs. Outside, afternoon light filtered through the windows.

She gripped a cast-iron pan, in half a mind to throw it through the window and hear the satisfying shatter of glass.

"I 'ave to go back." The words tore from her throat for the hundredth time. "I've studied the books. I'm stronger. And Madge is still there. Still trapped."

David sat by the roaring fire, perfectly still. He'd been watching her pace for hours, his eyes tracking her movements with patience. "No."

The single word felt like a slap. She spun toward him, darkness erupting outward in jagged tendrils.

"She's a defenseless child!"

"She's also alive." His voice had a tone of winter steel. "Which she'll remain as long as she's useful to them."

"Useful?" She tensed every muscle in her body as her anger rose. "You mean as long as they can torture 'er into becoming their weapon."

"Yes."

The casual admission shattered something inside her. This man who'd held her through the night, who'd whispered promises against her skin—gone. It wasn't him anymore.

"How can you be so calm when she's sufferin'?" she asked, her voice barely more than a gasp.

"Because emotion gets people killed." He leaned back, a stern, almost condescending expression on his face.

As if caring about a child's life was a weakness. She crossed her arms and stared at him.

David's glare held no warmth. "Madge is a survivor. Like you need to be."

Eliza's hands clenched into tight fists. "So we leave her to rot like spoiled offal while we play 'ouse in the woods?"

"We plan. We prepare. We wait." He rose from his chair in one fluid motion. "Going back now is a reckless folly. Your power is wild, unpredictable. You'd get us all killed."

The dismissal cut deeper than any blade. After everything—after he'd searched for her, saved her, made love to her—she was just a liability.

"I destroyed that construct, I did."

"You lost control," he snapped. "There's a difference."

Her shadows recoiled from the light flickering around his hands. "I saved Madge from that thing."

"You nearly tore the arena apart. If I hadn't stepped in when I did, she'd be dead. Along with you."

The words hammered against her skull. True. All of it true. But truth felt like acid in her veins.

"Then teach me." She reached toward him, desperate. "You can 'elp me learn control."

"I've told you everything I know." His expression remained carved from stone. "The power comes from lightness, not darkness. Find the balance. Connect to something greater than your rage."

"That ain't enough!"

"It's all I have to say about the matter."

She felt the rage bubble up. She opened her mouth without thinking through the consequences. "It's all you 'ave to say? That ain't good enough. Your Empire killed my family, and now you're killing the only family I have left. The only difference is that at least the Empire is honest about its murdering ways."

He stared at her as though she had struck him. She expected him to give a retort, to argue. But instead, he turned toward the door. "You have everything you need here. Books. Safety. Time to sort it out yourself."

She stared at his retreating form. "Wait! You're *leaving* me?"

"Yes. Apparently, I have more children to kill."

He slammed the door behind him before she could say another word.

Her shadows exploded outward, lashing at everything within reach. They carved gouges in oak wood, shredded pages that held centuries of knowledge. The cottage seemed to flinch from her rage.

When the storm passed, she stood surrounded by destruction. Chairs overturned. Books scattered like broken wings across the floor. Dust rained down from the ceiling.

The front door reopened, and David emerged, taking in the scene with one sweeping glance. He shook his head.

"This is exactly what I mean." His voice carried disappointment that cut deeper than anger. "You can't even control yourself in a safe space. How do you expect to breach a fortress designed to contain magical threats?"

Heat blazed behind her eyes. "You bastard. You caused this! You and your riddles and half-truths and hidden magic..."

He sighed and ran his hand through his hair. "It's obvious I'm doing more harm than good here."

He moved toward the door, grabbing his coat from a peg on the wall. "I think it's best if I go back to the fortress. I'll be back in five days to check on you. I can take personal time on Sunday."

His words struck a chord of terror in her. "David, no. They'll kill you, they will."

"They never saw me leave. My lightbinding kept us invisible, remember?" His smile held no warmth. "I'll make up a story. Claim I was knocked out by your insane power. They'll believe me because they saw it. And looking at this..." He swept a hand around the room. "... that is hardly the truth stretched."

"And Madge?" Her voice was as sharp as a freshly whetted blade. Doors rattled. Furniture shuddered. Her fury seemed to wipe away whatever love remained in David's eyes.

"I'll get her out when the ward rotation happens. When I can do it without getting us all killed."

The promise should have eased the agony clawing at her ribs. Instead, it felt like another dismissal. Another reminder that she was useless.

"Take me with you."

"No!"

"I can help—"

"You will get *detected*." His hand found the door handle. "The second you step outside, they'll know where you are. Your power signature is too strong, too chaotic. You might as well send up signal flares."

"But you were invisible when we escaped. Why can't you just do it again?"

"The wards learn, Eliza. They've already adapted to my lightbinding signature. They might not know who it came from, but they know it's there. Thus the wards will prevent its use, so I can't use that trick again." His voice turned grim. "But what you unleashed in the arena wasn't shadow magic. That was true Shadowbinding. The power your ancestors designed to be invisible to magical detection."

She stared at him. "You mean they can't detect it?"

"They can't adapt to what they can't see. But you can't access that power at will—not without your third eye fully developed. Which means when you do go back, you'll have the element of surprise. If you can control it."

"More riddles!" she screamed. "One minute you tell me that I can't step outside because of ward detection. The next you tell me they can't detect me!"

"And that is exactly why you cannot come with me. You do not understand the simple difference between shadow-working and Shadowbinding. One can be detected, the other cannot, and..."

He held his hands up in front of him, palms out. "I simply cannot keep on trying to explain this to you, Eliza. Until you understand the difference, you must stay here. *Must.* To do otherwise is to walk yourself to the gallows, and I simply will not allow that."

The cottage walls pressed closer around her. Prison walls

disguised as a sanctuary. "So I just wait 'ere? Doing nothing?" Her voice shattered on the last word.

"You learn control. You study. You sort out how to be something other than a walking magical disaster." His gray eyes found hers. "And you stay alive. Because if you die, this was all for nothing."

He opened the door. Afternoon light streamed in, painting him in bright light as he left her behind.

"Wait," she said.

He paused but didn't turn around.

"Can I do that? Make myself invisible like you?"

"No." The answer fell like a guillotine blade. "I manipulate light. You cannot."

The simple statement carved another piece from her heart. Even their powers weren't equal.

"Then what can I do?" Desperation leaked into her voice. "What use is this shadow magic if I can't even help the people I love?"

He looked over his shoulder, and for one moment she glimpsed what she thought was pity.

"According to the ancient texts, when you've developed your third eye, you'll be able to do anything you want. Aside from invisibility, that is. But you'll be so powerful you'll make invisibility look like a quaint parlor trick." His voice softened just enough to remind her of the man who'd held her in his arms just hours ago. "Until then? You stay here."

The door slammed shut behind him, as if a ghostly wind had followed him out.

Eliza stood frozen in the ruined room, listening to his footsteps fade down the forest path. The cottage settled around her, timbers creaking with age.

Third eye. What in heavens did that mean, exactly? And how was she supposed to develop it without guidance? From dusty texts?

She sank to her knees among the destruction, shadows pooling around her like spilled ink. She caught her reflection in the cracked hallway mirror—wild hair, tear-streaked cheeks, eyes that held too much power and too little understanding.

A memory stirred at the edges of consciousness.

The woman from her dreams. Her real mother from India—at least, the woman whom she believed must surely be her mother. The face that haunted her visions, always just out of reach. Beautiful and yet dreadful at the same time, shimmering with an aura of pure power.

A blue circle.

Small and perfect, hidden beneath carefully arranged hair. But sometimes, when her mother thought no one was watching, she would touch the mark and whisper words in a language that made shadows dance.

Understanding crashed over Eliza like a North Sea wave. The mark hadn't been a tattoo or a chalk mark. It had been power. A focus. The focus she'd somehow invoked in the arena. Although, then, she hadn't really understood what it was. She still didn't— not in the sense that she could awaken it at will and ask it to do her bidding.

Perhaps her third eye was simply waiting for *her* to guide it.

The possibility sent tingles of excitement racing through her. Power beyond what she'd already accessed. Abilities that might let her save Madge, fight back against the Empire, become something more than David's broken liability.

But the hope lasted only moments before reality crushed it flat.

She had no idea how to develop a third eye. No teacher. No guide. Only fragments from a woman who'd died with all her secrets intact.

She was alone.

David had left. Madge was trapped.

The tears came without warning. Her hot, desperate sobs shook her entire frame. She pressed her face against her knees and let the grief pour out. For Madge. For her family. For herself: the last Shadowbinder.

Outside, winter wind whistled through towering trees. Inside, the cottage waited with patient silence, holding her broken pieces together while she learned what it meant to be truly alone.

But in the depths of her despair, something stirred. Not comfort—she was beyond that now. Something harder. Angrier.

If David thought she was too emotional, too weak, too wild to matter—she'd prove him wrong.

She'd sort out this third-eye business. Master her power. Save Madge herself.

And when she was done, when she was everything they'd never believed she could be, she'd make them all pay for underestimating her.

The shadows around her purred with anticipation, as if they too were tired of being dismissed.

24 SHADOWS AND SOLITUDE

Mastering her shadow power was not as easy as lighting a lamp. As much as Eliza tried to control it, her magic had other ideas.

At first, she thought: *I'll show him.* She made a plan to simply focus on her shadows, make them stay put, stretch from the window light in the proper direction. She would take a few minutes to control herself, find her center, then she would follow him, run after him, show him that she was his partner, his equal, a woman worthy of being at his side in battle.

But her shadows had other ideas. When she tried to coax them into perfect shadows, they wobbled and strained at her feet as though she were looking through warped glass.

You're too emotional.

David's words circled around her mind. She pressed her fists against her eyes, trying to block out the memory of his face—controlled, distant—every trace of the man who'd made love to her scrubbed away.

"Madge," she whispered to the empty room.

The name cracked something open inside her chest. Madge, still trapped in that hellish place. Still suffering while Eliza sat safe in a warm cottage, wrapped in protection she didn't deserve.

Her power stirred in response to the anguish, darkness seeping from her skin like blood from a wound. She should call it back. Should demonstrate the control David claimed she lacked.

Instead, she reached for the memory of her mother: a

controlled, patient woman whose every move had purpose. *If you're there, Mama, please help me.*

Shadows flowed from Eliza's fingertips, not wild this time but purposeful. She shaped them into the jasmine flowers from her childhood garden, the delicate petals her mother had tended with such care. But the darkness wouldn't hold the form—it twisted and writhed, becoming thorns instead of blossoms.

Frustrated, she pushed harder. The shadows lashed out, carving deep grooves into the cottage walls in spiraling patterns that looked nothing like flowers. They shattered the remaining intact teacups on the mantel, sending porcelain fragments scattering across the floor.

When the power finally exhausted itself, she knelt among the debris, breathing hard.

She'd tried to create beauty, but made only destruction.

The realization struck without warning, bringing with it a memory so vivid it stole her breath. The blue mark on her mother's forehead.

"Mama, why do you have that mark?"

Her mother's hand had stilled on the jasmine petals. "It's my third eye. It helps me see, little one. See things others cannot."

"Can I have one too?"

"Yes, little one. When you're older. When you understand what it means to carry such responsibility."

The memory faded, leaving Eliza kneeling among the ruins of her tantrum. The third eye. That's what David had mentioned— cryptically, like everything else he'd told her. *When you've developed your third eye, you'll be able to do anything you want.*

She pressed her fingers to her forehead, feeling nothing but smooth skin and bone. No mark. No power. No answers.

Exhaustion crashed over her. The emotional explosion had drained her reserves, leaving her hollow and shaking. She needed to clean this mess, needed to think clearly about what came next.

* * *

Over the next three days, Eliza threw herself into methodical exploration of the cottage and its secrets. She swept up glass and debris, stacked torn books, and pieced together the damaged volumes.

Most of the books dealt with magical theory or Imperial history, dry academic texts that offered little practical guidance. But buried among them, in the Shadowbinder history texts, she found fragments that quickened her pulse. A torn page from *Principles of Shadow Manipulation* that described how shadows, if guided right, could topple St. Paul's Cathedral. Half a chapter on "Bloodline Abilities and Their Manifestation." A single paragraph about "Focusing Techniques for Untrained Practitioners."

She read everything at least three times, piecing together fragments. The information was frustratingly incomplete—some passages had been obscured with black ink—but patterns began to emerge.

Shadowbinding wasn't just one ability. It was a collection of related skills that all stemmed from a practitioner's relationship with darkness: Basic shadow manipulation, which she'd already mastered to some degree; enhanced perception, which explained her growing ability to sense emotions and magical signatures; something called "shadow integration"—the ability to become one with darkness.

But all of these required what the texts referred to as "focal concentration"—a technique for gathering diffuse magical energy into a single point of control. She grasped the idea—she'd practiced it in the fortress—but if she was honest with herself, she didn't realize that what she was doing was drawing in power to one point for the purpose of compressing it. Compressing shadows, according to the text, was "akin to compacting gunpowder in the breech of a gun." She didn't know exactly what a breech was, but she remembered seeing a soldier jamming a rod down inside the barrel of his long gun. Had that memory been from India? The memory was hazy, almost cartoonish, so it was possible she'd simply seen it in a storybook. Either way, the message was clear: compact the shadows in preparation for an explosion.

"The untrained practitioner," read another passage, "often finds their abilities scattered and reactive. Power flows outward in response to emotion, creating discord rather than purpose. The development of the focal point—commonly referred to as the third eye—allows for intentional direction of energy and significantly enhanced capabilities."

The third eye wasn't a physical mark at all, then. It was a technique.

But if it was a technique, then why did she remember seeing the mark on her mother's forehead?

Another memory surfaced then, her tiny hand holding her mother's in a bazaar. She'd begged for a pomegranate, her favorite fruit and a special treat in the autumn. The sign on the seller's stall stated they cost one anna apiece, and as her mother counted out the change, she sighed and dug in her purse.

"What's wrong, Mama?"

"Oh, I forgot my money," she said. "Silly me. I don't have enough change for the—"

Eliza tried to hold back the tears, but she felt them welling in her eyes and spilling on her cheeks.

Her mother spun up her magic then, a blue blazing circle on her forehead. She grabbed Eliza's hand and walked away from the stall.

Eliza looked over her shoulder and watched her shadows reach behind her and grab one of the deep red fruits. It coiled around it, brought it gently to the ground, and slithered it toward them.

She gasped in amazement, but she was also confused, because the seller was going about his business like he hadn't seen a thing. No one was looking at her mother's bright blue circle. No one was looking at the shadows, skittering over the dirt with a pomegranate carried in the air like a prize cup. No one was looking at them at all.

Eliza snapped the book shut, dissipating the memory. No one had seen the mark except for her. What had David told her about Shadowbinder registries? Something about how they had to use trickery to find the Shadowbinders because their magic was invisible. The mark wasn't chalk or ink. It was a thing that only Shadowbinders could see.

But that wasn't quite true. For some reason, David had seen it. Why that was so eluded her, and there was nothing in the books that suggested third eyes could be seen by Lightbinders. Her shadows stirred at the thought of him, as if suggesting to her the answer: David was connected to her in some inexplicable, magical way that defied rational explanation.

On the second night, Eliza found a journal hidden beneath a loose floorboard in David's bedroom. The handwriting was different from his—older, more formal. Tomas Thorne's personal notes, she realized. His father's private thoughts about the work he'd done.

Most entries dealt with guilt and regret over the massacres he'd participated in. But scattered throughout were observations about the Shadowbinder families he'd encountered. Their abilities. Their methods. Their weaknesses.

"The child shows remarkable instinctive control," read one entry dated sixteen years ago. "When frightened, her shadows move with purpose rather than panic. She seems to gather them behind her eyes before directing them outward—a technique I've only seen in fully trained practitioners. I have not seen the golden eye myself, but David assures me it is there."

The child. Her?

Eliza's hands trembled as she read further. Tomas Thorne had been studying her abilities during their voyage to England, documenting her unconscious techniques for future reference. He'd recognized something in her seven-year-old magic that she was only now beginning to understand.

She'd been using a form of focal concentration instinctively. She'd brought her shadows to a "pinprick" before, reining in her shadows and hiding them. Now she understood she'd actually been gathering *power*, not shadows, concentrating it for more effective use.

She just hadn't realized what she was doing.

The revelation sent her back to the damaged texts with renewed purpose. If she'd been unconsciously using the technique since childhood, then she already possessed the foundation. She just needed to understand how to build on it.

By the third day, frustration had carved hollows under her eyes and left her hands shaking with exhaustion. She'd attempted the focusing exercise dozens of times, trying to consciously recreate what she'd done as a child. Each attempt brought splitting headaches that left her nauseated and dizzy. Her shadows resisted deliberate concentration, preferring to flow wild and free rather than bend to her conscious will.

She sat before the cottage's fireplace that evening, glaring at the flames as if they held answers they refused to share. The rebuilt fire crackled cheerfully, mocking her struggles with its steady, controlled burning.

"Why won't you obey?" she asked her power.

The darkness writhed in response, offering no answers.

She thought of David's casual mastery over light, the way radiance bent to his will as naturally as breathing. How had he learned such control? The journal entries suggested Tomas had trained him from childhood, patient instruction building on natural talent. The diary spoke of pride, of growth. She wondered what she could have become if she'd had that opportunity to grow up with loving parents and the right tutelage. Could she become that thing now, or was it too late?

Thinking about Tomas's descriptions of David's innate power stung worse than physical pain. What if Shadowbinders were simply inferior to Lightbinders, destined to be the weaker half of some cosmic balance?

No. The thought blazed through her mind with fierce certainty. Her mother had been powerful—she remembered that much clearly. Her mother's shadows had moved with purpose, never chaotic or wild. She'd possessed knowledge and control that could steal a pomegranate right in front of a fruit seller's eyes.

If her mother could master these abilities, so could her daughter.

Eliza closed her eyes and reached for her power again, but this time she approached it differently. One passage in the methods book talked about working *with* the shadows instead of trying to manipulate them. So, instead of forcing her shadows to obey through sheer will, she attempted to understand what they wanted. Why they moved the way they did. What purpose their chaotic patterns might serve.

The answer came like dawn after an endless night.

Her shadows weren't chaotic at all—they were protective. Every wild tendril, every seemingly random movement, was an attempt to shield her from threats, real or perceived. They responded to emotions because emotions warned of danger, and danger required defense.

But right now, alone in the cottage's safety, there were no threats to guard against. No enemies to confuse or misdirect. Her shadows were trying to protect her from phantoms, expending energy on unnecessary vigilance.

"I'm safe," she whispered to them. "We're safe 'ere. You can rest."

The response was immediate and profound. Her power settled onto the floor like a tired stray dog settling into its preferred alleyway resting spot. The restless energy that had plagued her for days finally stilled.

And in that stillness, she found the focus she'd been seeking.

Power flowed inward with gentle inevitability, traveling up through her body and concentrating behind her forehead like starlight gathering into a single brilliant point. The pain was like the ache of muscles being strengthened rather than torn.

The cottage around her gained impossible clarity. She saw every detail: the way firelight played across the walls, the exact pattern of wood grain in the floorboards, the dust motes dancing in the warm air. More than that—she could sense the history embedded in the space itself. Not the mystical impressions she'd imagined before, but real traces of human presence. The lingering scent of different soaps on the washstand: rose petal, lavender, coal tar. The slight depression in the chair cushion where David preferred to sit. The way certain floorboards creaked under weight.

But most importantly, she could feel the darkness that filled every corner, every shadow cast by furniture and flame. They called to her now, offered sanctuary, promised concealment if she chose to accept their embrace—if she chose not to hide within shadows, but become one with them.

A delicious warmth coursed through her at the sudden realization. This was it—the third eye David had mentioned. A way of focusing her power that let her perceive and manipulate darkness in ways she'd never imagined possible.

She was no longer just a governess with unpredictable abilities. She was a Shadowbinder, heir to techniques that had made her people dangerous enough to warrant complete extinction.

Eliza smiled.

Soon, she would leave this cottage. Soon, she would put her

newfound abilities to the test in the most dangerous place she could imagine. Blackstone Fortress.

Soon, she would go back for Madge.

25 THE THIRD EYE AWAKENS

The wind sighed through the trees outside the cottage. Eliza had woken early to frost patterns on the glass, eager to begin her practice.

She stood before the largest shadow in the front room—the dark space cast by David's reading chair, where it blocked the morning sun. Yesterday's breakthrough had left her exhausted but exhilarated. Today, she would discover what her newfound understanding could actually accomplish.

Her stomach churned with nervous energy as she approached the shadow. What if yesterday had been a fluke? What if she'd imagined the control she thought she'd gained?

She closed her eyes and drew her power inward to that focused point behind her forehead. The technique came easier now, her shadows responding with eager cooperation rather than the resistance she'd fought for days.

But easier didn't mean effortless. Sweat beaded on her upper lip as she held the concentration. Her forehead ached from scrunching her brow. The power wanted to scatter, to flow wild as it always had, and keeping it focused required constant mental pressure.

When she opened her eyelids, the shadow cast by the chair beckoned.

Eliza's mouth went dry. This was the moment of truth.

She stepped into the shadow.

The sensation was unlike anything she'd ever experienced. Not the simple darkness of closing her eyes, but something deeper.

The cold hit her first—not the chill of winter air, but something that seemed to seep through her skin and settle in her bones. Her breath misted, and goosebumps prickled along her arms. The world felt muffled, sounds reaching her with strange distortion.

Her body remained solid, present, but the shadow embraced her like a sponge accepting water. She could see out from within the darkness, the cottage beyond rendered in perfect clarity, but when she looked down at herself, she saw only shadow.

Panic fluttered in her chest. Where were her hands? Her feet? She flexed her fingers and felt them move, but saw nothing.

She'd become part of the darkness itself.

She shifted her weight within the shadow's embrace. The movement felt natural, as if she'd been born to walk within darkness rather than light. The cottage's morning brightness couldn't touch her here. But was she truly invisible? She couldn't know for sure, unless...

She stepped out of the shadow and moved the hallway mirror into the front room.

When she hopped back into the shadow and looked into the mirror, she gasped. In it, she saw the chair and the chair's shadow. But she did not see herself. She should have been terrified, should have screamed, should have thrown a vase at the mirror and shattered the devilish mirage.

But instead, she felt only peace. She was invisible, protected, hidden from any eyes that might seek her. No, not invisible. At least, not in the same way that David had bent light to conceal them. She was simply a part of the shadows.

The shadow only stretched so far. When she reached its edge, she found herself faced with a barrier of light that her concealment couldn't cross. When she stepped her toes into the light, her stocking became clearly visible. She withdrew her foot, and again it disappeared.

She stepped into the light, her normal form appearing instantly in the mirror. The cottage around her looked ordinary, but the muscle memory of that otherworldly concealment was intoxicating.

This was what the texts had meant by shadow integration, she realized. Not just manipulating darkness, but becoming one with it.

For the next hour, she practiced moving between the cottage's various shadows, moving the mirror as she went from hiding place to hiding place. The space beneath the kitchen table. The dark corner where two bookcases met. The narrow band of shade cast by the window muntin. Each transition grew smoother, more natural, until she could slip from shadow to shadow with the fluid grace of water flowing from an urn.

But the cottage's shadows were limited, predictable. If she was going to infiltrate Blackstone Fortress, she needed to test her abilities against real challenges. Real dangers.

The forest beyond the cottage windows beckoned with infinite shadows.

Eliza donned her cloak and stepped outside into a bright winter day. Her breath immediately formed white puffs in the frigid air.

The snow-veiled woods stretched endlessly in all directions, ancient trees creating a stark canopy of bare branches against the pale sky. Oak and silver birch towered overhead, their limbs heavy with snow that occasionally dropped in soft thuds to the forest floor.

Somewhere in the forest, a woodpecker hammered against bark with rhythmic persistence, the sound sharp and clear in the thin winter air. Her boots crunched through snow that reached mid-ankle, and the bite of winter air made her nose sting. A perfect winter's day to test her new abilities.

She steadied herself against a massive oak whose trunk could have housed a family of four. Moss clung to its northern face, soft and damp even through her mittens. Even in the forest's perpetual twilight, the oak cast a deeper pool of darkness that stretched nearly ten feet across the forest floor.

She found the shadow's edge and stepped into it, feeling that now-familiar sensation of becoming one with darkness. Here, the difference between light and shadow was subtle—a gentle gradient rather than a stark boundary. Her outline blurred, not vanishing entirely, but glinting in the cool gloom—caught between the forest's twilight and the deeper shade beneath the oak.

From within this half-hidden state, she saw the forest with impossible clarity. Every snow-crusted branch, every play of light and shadow revealed itself in perfect detail. But more importantly, she could sense something else threading through the trees like invisible wire.

Magic.

Thin threads of power wove between the trunks—not the wild energy of untrained practitioners, but something controlled and deliberate. The magical lines pulsed with a steady rhythm, like veins carrying blood through a living body. Ward lines. Detection spells. A web of sensors that turned the forest into a monitored zone.

Her pulse quickened as she pressed deeper into the oak's shadow, where her form grew more indistinct. The cottage's protection didn't extend beyond its immediate grounds. Out here, Imperial magic watched for any trace of unauthorized power. It would detect shadow-magic, of that she felt sure.

But from what David had told her, although the Empire could detect shadow-magic, it couldn't detect Shadowbinder magic. She just hoped she knew how to separate the two in her mind so that she only used Shadowbinding.

Eliza studied the nearest ward line, a faint silver thread that ran between two silver birch trees about twenty feet away. It hummed with energy, sweeping back and forth in slow arcs like a lighthouse beam. Every few seconds, it pulsed brighter as it measured the forest's magical baseline.

She would have to cross it to move deeper into the woods.

She chewed her lip as she planned her route. A silver birch about fifteen feet away offered another pool of deeper shadow, but reaching it meant stepping through a patch where the canopy thinned slightly, letting in more light. There, her shimmering form might become visible to careful observers.

Taking a steadying breath, she stepped from oak shadow toward the silver birch.

The transition felt strange—her concealment shifting and flowing as the light changed around her. In the slightly brighter space between trees, she felt exposed, her outline wavering like a heat signature. But as she reached the birch's deeper, snow-mottled shadow, the blurring effect strengthened again.

The ward line swept toward her position, its silver glow intensifying as it crossed the space she occupied. Eliza held her breath, wondering if her half-visible state would register as an anomaly.

It passed right through her without pause.

Relief flooded through her limbs, but she remained cautious. The ward had detected nothing, but a human observer might catch glimpses of movement if they looked carefully enough.

Moving deeper into the forest required navigating between these pools of deeper shadow, timing her movements to avoid the brightest patches where her concealment grew thin. Each transition demanded careful observation of the light patterns, and patience to wait for optimal moments.

Twenty minutes into her reconnaissance, she heard voices approaching.

Eliza pressed herself against the trunk of another silver birch, grateful for the deep shadow it provided. Here, her form was almost completely obscured, just a suggestion of movement in the gloom. Male voices, speaking in the clipped tones of military discipline, grew closer with each passing second.

"—sweep pattern's been irregular since Tuesday," one voice was saying, boots crunching through dead leaves. "Command thinks there might be rebel activity in the area."

"Could be smugglers," another replied.

Through the birch's shadow, Eliza could see them now—two guards in Imperial blue cloaks pulled tight against the cold, their breath visible as they spoke. Weapons hung at their sides, and one carried a device that hummed with detection magic.

"Damn thing's been twitchy all morning," the first guard muttered, tapping the device with obvious frustration.

The detector's humming grew louder as they approached her hiding spot. Eliza pressed herself flatter against the bark, feeling the rough texture bite into her back through her cloak. In the birch's deepest shadow, she was nearly invisible, but if they looked directly at her position...

The device swept past without reaction, but the second guard paused, head tilted as if listening.

"You hear that?" he asked.

Eliza's heart was thumping so hard, she was sure it was about to explode. Had she made some sound? Breathed too loudly?

"Hear what?"

"Nothing. Thought I heard... movement." His gaze swept the area around her tree, passing over her position twice. For one terrifying moment, his eyes seemed to focus on the space she occupied, brow furrowing in confusion.

"Probably a fox," the first guard said, though he unslung his weapon, anyway. "But keep alert. Something's got the detection grid spooked."

They moved on, slowly scanning the forest.

Eliza remained frozen against the birch trunk for long minutes afterward, sweat chilling on her skin in the shadow's cold embrace.

When she finally felt safe to move, her legs trembled as if she were on the edge of a cliff. She had to force herself to breathe deeply. The encounter had taught her a crucial lesson—her concealment worked against magical detection, but human observation remained a threat. In the forest's brighter patches, she'd be a hazy form—like a figure in the mist—easily spotted by trained eyes.

She spent the next hour moving with obsessive caution. The forest revealed its secrets slowly: routes marked by subtle signs, the predictable patterns of detection sweeps that created brief windows of opportunity.

But maintaining her half-hidden state for so long took its toll. Her forehead ached from the constant concentration required to keep her third eye active. The blurring effect responded to her focus—relax too much, and her outline sharpened dangerously. Push too hard, and the magic wavered, leaving her visible in patches.

Over the next hour, she cataloged two more observation posts while fighting the growing fatigue that made her concealment flicker. Three posts formed a loose triangle around the forest edge, connected by patrol routes that swept the area every four hours. Ward lines created overlapping detection nets that would scream an alarm at any significant magical manifestation.

The physical and mental strain of maintaining her half-hidden state was becoming overwhelming. Her muscles cramped from moving carefully through rough terrain made treacherous by hidden roots under the snow, and hunger gnawed at her stomach. Her fingers had gone numb inside her mittens despite the magical warmth of the shadows. Twice, her concentration slipped enough that she had to freeze in deeper shadows until her outline blurred properly again, her breath creating small clouds that she hoped wouldn't give her away.

But she pressed on, driven by the knowledge that every detail might mean the difference between rescuing Madge and disaster.

The patrol schedule revealed the crucial weakness she'd been seeking. Between shifts, there was a twenty-minute window when the observation posts coordinated their changeover. Guards focused inward on their communications rather than outward on surveillance. During that brief gap, someone who could become one with shadows—even imperfectly—could slip through undetected.

Eliza began the careful journey back toward the cottage, her concealment flickering with exhaustion as she fought to maintain even basic concealment. She moved from shadow to shadow like a ghost caught between worlds, never fully visible, never completely hidden.

When she finally emerged from the forest's edge, twilight was painting the canopy in shades of pink. As she approached the cottage, the familiar wards recognized her, and she felt her outline solidify back into normal visibility.

She slipped inside and collapsed into David's chair, her body aching from hours of careful movement and magical strain. But despite the exhaustion, satisfaction burned in her chest. Her abilities had worked—not perfectly, not without risk, but well enough to gather the intelligence she needed.

Eliza rubbed her temples, trying to ease the headache that had been building since her return from the forest. The constant focus required to maintain shadow integration had left her feeling wrung out, like a cloth twisted too tight.

The mark on her forehead pulsed with warmth.

She pressed her fingertips to the spot, feeling the circular impression beneath her skin. It had been growing more noticeable since yesterday's breakthrough, but now it throbbed with urgent energy.

"What you tryin' to tell me?" she whispered.

The pulse strengthened, and suddenly the cottage walls seemed to wobble around her, becoming transparent, as if she was looking through stone and timber to something beyond.

Madge.

The thought struck without warning, accompanied by a flash of gray walls and iron bars. For one disorienting moment, Eliza felt herself pulled forward, her consciousness stretching across impossible distance.

Then it snapped back, leaving her gasping in David's chair. *That wasn't real. Couldn't be real.*

But when she shut her eyes, she could still sense the afterimage. Stone walls. Flickering gaslight. The overwhelming smell of despair.

She thought of Madge again, deliberately this time, focusing on the girl's face while pressing her fingers to the pulsing mark.

The world tilted.

This time, the vision came with devastating clarity. Eliza stood in a cell—not physically, but her awareness filled the space as completely as if she'd walked through the door. Gray stone walls wept moisture in the gaslight. A narrow bed pressed against one wall. And sitting on its edge—

"No." The word tore from Eliza's throat.

Madge sat with perfect military posture, staring at nothing with empty eyes. Gone was the brilliant child who'd challenged Imperial doctrine with clever questions. Gone was the girl who'd giggled over shadow games and worried about nightmares. This hollow-eyed creature wore Madge's face, but everything else had been stripped away.

"Recite your purpose," a voice commanded from beyond the cell door.

"I exist to serve the Empire," Madge replied in a monotone that shattered Eliza's heart. "My power belongs to Her Majesty. My will is subject to Imperial command."

"And your former life?"

"Was weakness to be eliminated. I have no family. No friends. No desires beyond duty."

They'd broken her. Not her body—that remained intact, unmarked. But they'd murdered everything that had made Madge human, replacing it with perfect, empty obedience.

Eliza tried to call out, to somehow reach across the impossible distance, but her voice made no sound in that dank cell. She was a ghost here, witnessing horrors she couldn't prevent.

"Excellent progress," the voice approved. "Rest until the next conditioning session."

Madge lay down on the narrow cot. Her eyes stared at nothing, waiting for the next command to animate her hollow existence.

And then, Madge slowly trained her eyes on Eliza. Her face was blank, but a single tear rolled down her cheek.

The vision shattered, dumping Eliza back into the cottage with brutal force. She doubled over, bile burning her throat as her body rejected what she'd witnessed. Her forehead mark felt like it was on fire, the new ability having torn something open inside her mind.

She retched until nothing came up but acid and horror.

When the heaving stopped, she sat back on her heels, shaking. The vision had been real—she knew it with bone-deep certainty. Somehow, the third eye allowed her to see across vast distances, to witness events as they unfolded.

And what she'd seen was unbearable.

She had to try again. Had to understand the full scope of what she faced.

This time, she focused on David, steeling herself for whatever fresh horror awaited.

His office materialized around her awareness. He sat hunched over his desk, head buried in his hands, surrounded by official documents that told of atrocities in neat bureaucratic language.

He reached for a bottle of whiskey, poured a glass, and downed the drink.

He looked down at the paperwork, and it was as if Eliza was looking through his eyes.

Subject 23-L displays concerning attachment to former attendant. Recommend memory modification.

David's face crumpled. For one moment, the controlled mask slipped, revealing the agony beneath.

"I'm so sorry," he whispered to the empty office. "God help me, I'm so sorry."

The vision flickered, and suddenly his head snapped up as if he'd sensed something. His eyes swept the room, searching.

"Eliza?" he breathed.

The connection severed, throwing her back into her body with enough force to knock her from the chair. She hit the cottage floor hard, her head spinning from the abrupt transition.

The third eye pulsed once more, then went quiet, leaving her alone with the horrifying knowledge of what she'd witnessed.

Madge, broken and hollow, everything beautiful about her murdered by Imperial "conditioning." David, trapped in a nightmare of his own making, forced to participate in atrocities that destroyed him piece by piece.

And herself, the only one who could save them—if she was strong enough. If she was fast enough.

Eliza stared out the window at the darkening woods, shadows lengthening as night approached.

The surrounding shadows seemed to be eagerly awaiting what was to come, though she now understood they would offer subtle protection, requiring patience and understanding—much like a troubled child who had to be coaxed into cooperation. The shadows were not to be beaten into submission. They were to be coaxed and guided with love.

It was time to head to the fortress.

26 MEMORIES OF MOTHER

Sixteen years ago

The blue mark on Mama's forehead glowed like a tiny ring made of blue stars.

Seven-year-old Elizabeth leaned against the doorframe, watching from the shadows as her mother knelt in the center of their sitting room. The shutters were drawn against Delhi's brutal afternoon heat, leaving the space dim and warm, the air heavy and still.

Perfect for what Mama called her "practice."

Darkness flowed around her mother, responding to her slightest gesture. Not wild and unpredictable like Elizabeth's own shadows, but controlled, purposeful, beautiful. The tendrils moved in patterns that reminded her of the dancers who performed at the temple festivals: graceful, precise, telling stories without words.

"You may watch, little one," Mama said without opening her eyes. "But you must be very quiet."

Elizabeth crept closer, bare feet silent on the smooth marble floor. Her mother's shadows noticed her approach, reaching out to brush against her ankles with gentle curiosity. They felt warm, welcoming, like being embraced.

"How do you make them so pretty?" Elizabeth whispered.

Her mother's lips curved in a smile. "The same way you make

them move when you're frightened. Through feeling. But instead of fear, I use love."

"Love?"

"Love for you. Love for our family. Love for the light that makes shadows possible." Her forehead mark pulsed brighter. "Shadows exist because of light, beta. They are not opposites— they are partners."

Elizabeth watched the darkness dance, trying to understand. When her own shadows moved, it was because she was scared or angry. But Mama's shadows moved like they were happy, like they were celebrating something wonderful.

"Can you teach me?"

"Someday." Her mother opened her eyes, and Elizabeth gasped. They weren't brown anymore, but deep violet shot through with silver threads. "When you're older. When your third eye opens."

"Will I have a mark like yours?"

Her mother's hand moved to touch the blue circle on her forehead. "Yes. When you find it. Each Shadowbinder finds their own path to the darkness."

Elizabeth bristled at the unfamiliar word. "Shadowbinder?"

"What we are, beta. What you will become." The shadows around her mother began to fade as the violet left her eyes. "We are the guardians of balance. Where there is too much light, we bring shadow. Where there is too much darkness, we guide it toward the light."

Elizabeth frowned. "But Papa says the Empire doesn't like our magic."

Something sad flickered across her mother's face. "Papa is right. They fear what they don't understand. There are men who think our magic makes us dangerous."

"Are we dangerous?"

Her mother was quiet for a long moment, stroking Elizabeth's hair. "We can be, if we choose to be. That's why the training is so important. Why we learn control."

Elizabeth nestled against her mother's chest, feeling the steady rise and fall of her breathing, the soft cotton of her sari warm against her cheek, listening to the steady pulse of her heartbeat.

The house around them felt safe, protected by shadows that loved them.

* * *

Three days later

Elizabeth bounced on her toes as she walked through the academy gates, her shadows wiggling around her feet like excited puppies. She tried to make them stay still like Mama taught her, but they never listened.

"Elizabeth!" David ran across the courtyard, light sparkling around his fingers. "Look!"

He made a tiny elephant that danced on his palm. Elizabeth clapped her hands together, forgetting to keep her shadows quiet. They reached toward the light elephant like they wanted to pet it.

"Can I try?" she asked.

"Light magic is different," David said seriously, like he was a grown-up instead of eight years old. "But we can practice together! Father gave me this book about magic friends."

He showed her a book with pretty pictures of ships and golden skies. "It's about people who work together to fight sea monsters. It's for you. My father said you can borrow it. But you must promise to keep it on you."

"Really?" No light-worker had ever let her borrow their books before. The other children said her shadows made books dirty.

"Of course! We're best friends."

Best friends. The words made her tummy feel warm and sparkly.

As she walked to the school door, David turned in the other direction.

"You're not coming in?"

"No," he said, waving. "Papa says I have to stay home this morning for something important. But he said I should bring you the book first. See you later!"

In class, she hid the book under her desk and looked at the pictures while Mrs. Pemberton talked about boring Empire stuff. The pictures showed people making magic together—light and shadow swirling in pretty patterns, just like when she and David played in the garden.

Then the bells started ringing wrong. Too fast, too loud, like when there were fires.

Soldiers came in with big scary guns that hummed like angry bees. Elizabeth hugged David's book tighter as a mean man with slits for eyes yelled at the children to move to different sides of the room.

Light children here. Shadow children there.

Elizabeth didn't understand why they had to separate. She looked at her friend Raj. His face went white, like when he was scared of thunderstorms. He was shaking his head at her, mouthing words she couldn't understand.

"The shadow children need special lessons," the mean man said with a smile that made Elizabeth's tummy flip a somersault.

Priya, the girl who sat next to her in class, grabbed Elizabeth's hand. "I don't want special lessons," she whispered, tears already rolling down her cheeks. "I want to go home."

But the soldiers were pushing them toward the door with rough hands. Elizabeth stumbled, still clutching David's book, as they herded all the shadow children like they were goats being taken to market.

In the courtyard, the bright sun hurt her eyes after the dim classroom. She blinked, confused, as more soldiers formed a line in front of them. Their guns weren't like the ones she'd seen guards carry—these glowed with scary light and made sounds like growling animals.

Raj backed away. "No. Please, no..."

"Ready for elimination, men," the mean man bellowed, causing the men's guns to power up like magic.

Elizabeth didn't know what those big words meant, but Raj's terror was spreading through the group like fire through dry grass. Meera started sobbing. Priya's fingernails dug into Elizabeth's hand so hard they drew blood.

"I want my mama," someone cried.

The soldiers raised their weapons.

That's when Elizabeth understood. Not with her head, but with her body, with the sick feeling in her stomach and the way her shadows were screaming, *danger danger danger.*

They were going to hurt them. They were going to—

The first shot hit Raj in the chest. Not a normal bullet, but something made of angry red light that punched through him like he was made of parchment. He didn't even scream. Just looked surprised as his knees folded and he fell down wrong, too limp, too still.

Elizabeth's bladder let go.

Hot wetness ran down her legs as the other children scattered, screaming and crying and calling for their parents who couldn't hear them. The soldiers followed with their horrid weapons, hunting children through the garden like it was a game.

Meera made it three steps into the garden before lightning-magic caught her between the shoulder blades. She pitched forward into the roses, and the pink flowers splattered red.

"Mama!" Kumar screamed as he ran past Elizabeth. "Mama! Help! Ma—"

The sound cut off mid-word. When Elizabeth turned to look, Kumar was gone. Just a scorch mark on the grass where he'd been standing.

Priya was still holding her hand, both of them frozen in terror as turmoil exploded around them. Then a soldier turned toward them, his weapon humming as it charged up, and Priya tugged Elizabeth's hand.

"Run!" she yelled, just before the red light swallowed her whole. Her hand went limp, then slipped from Elizabeth's grip.

Elizabeth ran.

Her shadows went crazy with fear, reaching everywhere at once, creating patches of darkness. She stumbled through the garden where she and David played hide-and-seek, where the flowers usually smelled like Mama's hair, where she'd felt safe just yesterday.

Behind her, children screamed. Weapons hummed and crackled. Voices called out for parents, for teachers, for anyone to help them. But the screaming kept stopping. One voice, then another, then another, cutting out like records grinding to a halt.

She tripped over something soft and looked down to see Arjun, who used to share his sweets with her during lunch. His eyes stared at nothing, and there was blood on his school uniform.

Elizabeth threw up all over her shoes.

She was crying so hard she could barely see, snot running down her face as she crawled into the jasmine bushes like a hurt animal. The thorns poked her arms and legs, adding new pain to the wetness in her pants and the awful, sick feeling in her tummy.

The garden grew quieter. No more screaming. No more running footsteps. Just the crackling of fires that had started somewhere and the heavy boots of soldiers.

"Sweep the grounds," a voice called. "Lord Morrison wants confirmation. No survivors."

Elizabeth held her breath until her lungs burned, pressed so deep into the bushes that thorns cut her face. She could hear them getting closer, calling to each other as they found bodies.

"This one's finished."

"Got another here."

"Check behind those trees."

She was shaking so hard the whole bush trembled with her. Maybe they would think it was just the wind. Maybe they wouldn't look here. Maybe—

A pair of shiny black boots stopped right in front of her hiding place.

"Here you are."

She was too scared to move, too scared to breathe, too scared to do anything but clutch David's book and stare up at the soldier who was going to kill her.

He pointed his weapon at her face. The end glowed like a tiny red sun.

"Don't," she whispered, the word barely making a sound. "Please don't. I'll be good. I'll be really, really good."

But the soldier wasn't listening. He fixed his eye on the sight, and Elizabeth closed her eyes tight, waiting for everything to stop hurting.

"Stand down."

The voice was different. Older. When Elizabeth opened her eyes, she saw a new man—an officer with white threading his dark hair and gray eyes with silver threads: David's eyes.

"Sir, orders are—"

"I'll handle this one personally." The officer's voice was sharp like Papa's when he was angry. "Report back to Lord Morrison. Tell him the academy has been cleared."

After the soldier left, the man with David's eyes knelt down beside her in the ruined garden and ran his hands over her head, her arms. "Oh, thank God, you're not hurt—I should have been here earlier—thought I was too late—"

Elizabeth was still shaking, still crying, still smelling like pee and vomit and fear. She held out the Lightbinder book as if it was magic that could protect her. "Please don't hurt me."

The man reached out with hands that glowed with the same pretty light David made.

"Come here, little one."

He picked her up, even though she was dirty and smelly and probably getting his uniform messy. As they walked away from the burning school where all her friends were dead, she felt warm light surrounding her. It came from the man, and though she didn't understand what it was, she knew it felt like safety.

As they walked by an armed guard, he snapped a salute. It was as if he didn't see her at all, like she was the littlest of fairies at the bottom of the garden.

Once they were out of the school gates, the stranger pointed to a carriage at the end of the street where a small figure waited at the carriage door. David.

The man shoved her forward. "Run!"

27 THE JOURNEY

Present Day

Eliza stood at the cottage threshold, her cloak wrapped tight around her shoulders. Dawn crept through the frost-laden forest canopy, casting long fingers of pale light between towering pines heavy with snow and gnarled oaks whose bare branches glittered with ice. Behind her lay warmth, safety, the promise of a life free from Imperial pursuit. Ahead stretched miles of hostile territory blanketed in snow, magical surveillance, and what was perhaps the most fortified prison in the Empire.

Somewhere in that fortress, Madge was suffering.

Eliza stepped outside and pulled the door shut behind her. The cottage's protective wards pressed against her skin like invisible webs, testing her resolve. She had spent the previous evening testing her third eye, taking peeks at the surrounding forest, at the fortress gates, at the traffic trundling under the portcullis. She had learned that as long as she kept to brief "visits," the emotional and physical load was manageable.

The forest welcomed her with familiar shadows. After yesterday's reconnaissance, she knew every patrol route, every observation post, every weakness in the Imperial surveillance network. Her abilities responded to her confidence, darkness flowing around her as she moved between patches of concealment.

As the cottage disappeared behind dense foliage, Eliza shut her eyes and concentrated on her third eye. She needed to see what she was walking into. But before she could fully visualize her path, a branch snapped somewhere in the forest, jerking her back to awareness. A deer emerged from the shadows. It stopped, stared at her, then bowed its head to nose through the snow for something to eat.

Eliza stilled, darkness coiling around her like protective serpents. The forest stretched ahead, innocent and empty.

She pressed forward.

The journey to Blackstone took an entire day of careful movement through hostile territory made treacherous by winter conditions. She followed deer paths that wound between towering elms and sprawling chestnuts, snow crunching softly underfoot despite her attempts at silence. Twisted hawthorns created natural barriers, their thorny branches heavy with snow, providing cover from observation while leaving telltale traces of her passage. She stayed within shadow wherever possible, pausing frequently to let Imperial patrols pass, always mindful that her footprints in the snow could betray her route.

Her newfound abilities made the travel easier than it should have been—she could sense magical signatures from great distances, slip between detection wards that would have caught her days ago, move through darkness like it was her natural element.

As her confidence grew, she found herself using her third eye more and more to check on David and Madge. David reviewing more reports, his hands shaking as he read about "successful conditioning protocols." Madge staring at her cell wall with dead eyes, no longer even moving unless commanded. Each new image revealed fresh horrors, driving Eliza forward with renewed urgency until she was practically running through the shadows despite the need for caution.

By late afternoon, the forest began to thin, snow-covered ground giving way to the cleared approaches around Blackstone's massive walls. Through gaps in the canopy, she caught glimpses of the fortress rising against the gray winter sky, its black stone stark against the white landscape. Guard towers rose at regular intervals, their peaks bristling with detection arrays that swept methodically across the snow-covered fields below.

But it was the main road that caught her attention.

A well-maintained thoroughfare led directly to the fortress gates, wide enough for multiple wagons to travel side by side. Unlike the narrow forest paths, this road bore clear Imperial authority—carved markers every hundred yards, ward stones that monitored all traffic, magical barriers that could be activated to trap anyone attempting unauthorized passage.

A steady stream of wagons rolled toward the fortress gates along the snow-packed road, their wheels cutting deep ruts in the slush. The horses' breath steamed in the cold air as they pulled loads of food, medical supplies, and mysterious crates marked with Imperial seals. Drivers huddled in their cloaks against the bitter wind, no doubt eager to complete their deliveries and return to warm hearths.

Eliza settled into concealment beneath a spreading maple, studying the timing and patterns of the supply convoys. Wagons arrived every few minutes, most carrying mundane goods that barely warranted inspection. It was the food carts that offered the best opportunity—driven by local farmers whose nervous deference to Imperial authority made them unlikely to notice aberrant shadows.

As the sun began its descent toward the western horizon, she spotted her chance. A vegetable cart driven by a man with a hunched back whose hands shook as he held the reins. His horses were clearly terrified of the fortress—ears pinned back, eyes rolling white, dancing sideways with every step, whinnying in distress. Their nervous movements created shifting, writhing shadows that would perfectly camouflage any additional darkness.

Eliza shut her eyes and sought her strength, pulling it inward to that concentrated spot behind her forehead. When she opened them again, the world had gained that sharp clarity that marked her third eye's activation. Every shadow offered protection for those who knew how to accept its embrace.

The vegetable cart rumbled past her hiding spot, and she slipped from tree shadow to wheel shadow to the nervous, shifting darkness cast by the terrified horses. The animals stamped and whinnied, their fear creating perfect concealment—shadows that moved unpredictably, writhing and dancing in ways that would mask any unnatural movement from magical detection.

The transition felt natural now, like stepping from one room to another rather than crossing the hard boundary between light and shadow.

Hidden within the horses' dancing shadows, surrounded by the smell of manure, she began the final approach to the fortress. Somewhere beyond those black walls, Madge sat in her cell, her spirit broken. And David endured his own torment, forced to witness horrors that violated everything he'd once believed about honor and duty.

But they weren't lost yet. The visions had shown her the truth, but they'd also revealed hope. David's reaction to sensing her presence suggested their connection ran deeper than either had realized. And Madge's conditioning, while horrific, still showed cracks—responses that seemed learned rather than natural, suggesting the real child might still exist beneath the Imperial programming. She had no solid evidence for this thought, and she might have dismissed it as fanciful but for the feeling in her gut that she was right: Madge could be saved. She knew it as surely as she knew the setting sun would rise the following morning.

As the fortress gates loomed ahead, bristling with ward stones and defensive magic, Eliza felt her resolve crystallize into something unbreakable.

The vegetable cart lurched forward, wheels grinding through the slush as Eliza pressed herself into the horses' writhing shadows. Her heart slammed against her ribs with each jolt, but she forced her breathing to stay silent, controlled. The terrified animals provided perfect cover—their fear-scent thick in the air, their shadows dancing wildly as they shied away from the fortress walls.

"Papers," a guard commanded at the first checkpoint.

The driver's hands shook as he fumbled for his documents. "Just vegetables, sir. Turnips and potatoes for the kitchens."

Eliza felt the guard's magical probe sweep over the cart like warm honey washing over her skin. The detection spell passed through her hiding place, but her shadow integration held. To the guard's enhanced senses, she was just another piece of darkness cast by nervous livestock.

"These animals are spooked," the guard said, suspicion

threading his voice. "What's wrong with them?"

"The fortress scares them, sir. Always has. They can sense the magic, I think."

A long pause. Eliza held her breath.

"Move along. But keep those beasts under control."

The cart rolled forward, but Eliza's relief lasted only moments. Through the shadows, she glimpsed more checkpoints ahead— three additional barriers between her and the fortress proper, each one bristling with more sophisticated detection magic.

At the second checkpoint, a different guard circled the cart. He stopped inches from where Eliza hid, magical energy crackling around his probe as he examined every shadow.

Fear clawed up Eliza's throat. The guard was so close she could smell the stale sweat on his uniform, see every hair of his wiry ginger beard, feel the heat radiating from his magical probe. Her heart pounded so hard she was certain he'd hear it.

The guard furrowed his brow and stepped closer, inspecting the space where she stood. The probe crackled louder, and she saw recognition in the guard's eyes.

"Got something here," he yelled, studying his probe.

Her shadows responded to her terror, writhing beyond her control, reaching toward the guard with hungry tendrils. This was exactly what David had warned her of. The guards could not detect calm Shadowbinders.

But they could detect emotional Shadow-workers.

28 INFILTRATION

No. Eliza sucked the wayward darkness back into herself, willing her pulse to slow, her breathing to steady. *Calm. Like coaxing a frightened child.*

The shadows reluctantly obeyed, settling back into the chaotic patterns cast by the terrified animals.

The probe crackled down to its baseline level. The guard tapped it, confusion furrowing his brow. He stepped closer to the cart.

Eliza slinked to the right.

The guard extended the probe to the cart's surface but stepped back when one of the horses reared and whinnied.

"Something's off about this cart," he said to his comrade.

"It's the horses. They're always nervous here. Country animals can't handle fortress magic."

"No, this is different. They're not just scared—they're panicked. And the probe, it..." He tapped the probe again. "It went off."

The second guard, a tiny man with a mustache that dangled past his shirt collar, stepped forward. "Gash, mine went off yesterday on a barrel of turnips."

He waved his probe over the cart, stepping so close that Eliza had to shift carefully around him. She might be invisible, but her body was still there—waiting to be brushed against. Waiting to be discovered.

Her pulse thundered as the guard's probe intensified. She forced herself to become smaller, denser, pressing her consciousness into the deepest part of the horses' shifting darkness. The animals whinnied and stamped, their terror creating chaotic patterns that masked her presence.

"There's a bit of a spike, but I don't see anything unusual," the mustached guard said impatiently. "Probably residual magic. Let's move them along. We've got twenty more wagons to process."

"Fine. But I'm noting the irregularity in my report."

The cart lurched forward again, but Eliza could feel sweat beading on her forehead despite the shadows' coolness. It took all her strength to keep her shadows contained in the pinprick behind her eyes.

The portcullis groaned upward, and the cart rolled through into Blackstone's heart, Eliza slinking along beside it.

Eliza had infiltrated the most secure fortress in the Empire.

But celebration felt premature as she glimpsed the scope of what surrounded her. Covered walkways connected sprawling courtyards, dozens of doors led into dozens of buildings of unknown purpose, swarms of civilian workers scurried from place to place like ants following trails. And everywhere, guards. Patrolling in precise patterns, stationed at every corner, their magical awareness creating a web of surveillance that would challenge even her enhanced abilities.

The cart rumbled through the east courtyard toward a loading dock where kitchen workers waited with empty baskets. Eliza closed her eyes, reaching for her third eye, drawing power inward until the world sharpened behind her lids. The fortress revealed itself in layers—stone and steel overlaid with magical energy that flowed like luminous rivers through the structure.

The kitchens blazed with heat and activity. Beyond them lay the dining halls. Training yards occupied the fortress's center, their familiar grounds scarred by magical combat and stained with old blood.

But it was the administrative wing that drew her focus. A separate building connected to the main fortress by covered walkways, its upper floors housing offices where the Empire's darkest work was planned and documented. David's office was there, and the building bustled with constant activity—clerks processing reports, officers conducting meetings, officials moving between departments. More people meant more eyes that might notice shadows behaving strangely.

She scanned desperately for her next hiding place, but the courtyard was too well-lit, too exposed. She needed to move before the driver brought his horses to a complete stop.

A narrow alley lay between the kitchen building and what looked like servants' quarters. Deep shadows pooled there, untouched by the courtyard's magical lighting.

She slipped from horse shadow to wheel shadow to the darkness cast by a water barrel, moving in quick transitions that strained her concentration. Each jump required perfect timing, absolute focus. One mistake would expose her to dozens of hostile eyes.

The alley welcomed her with blessed darkness. She pressed against the wall, gasping silently as the cart continued toward the loading dock. Behind her, kitchen workers began unloading vegetables with the casual efficiency of routine. None had noticed shadows moving wrong.

But she couldn't rest yet. The alley was a temporary shelter at best—too exposed, too close to areas of high activity. She needed to reach David's office, which meant navigating the administrative sections without triggering alarms. There, she hoped to meet him and make a plan for Madge's rescue.

Through her third eye, she traced potential routes. Getting there would require crossing a second courtyard and navigating corridors thick with Imperial personnel. The pathway looked manageable, but the timing would be crucial.

Movement in the first courtyard caught her attention. Kitchen workers were dispersing, their tasks complete. Soon, this area would be less crowded, offering better opportunities for movement.

She settled deeper into the alley's shadows and observed the fortress's rhythms. Guards changed shifts every two hours on the dot. Servants moved in predictable patterns—kitchen staff to dining halls, maintenance workers to areas requiring repair, administrative personnel flowing between the main fortress and the office building.

She identified the gaps. Brief windows where corridors emptied, when guard attention focused elsewhere, when the fortress's defensive web showed weaknesses.

Her confidence grew as she noted each opportunity. This wasn't impossible—it was just incredibly dangerous.

A commotion near the kitchen entrance drew her attention. Two guards were arguing with a cook about missing inventory, their voices carrying across the courtyard.

"Three bags of flour, unaccounted for," one guard said.

"I counted everything twice," the cook protested. "Your numbers are wrong."

"Imperial supplies don't go missing without explanation."

While they argued, other guards drifted closer to observe the dispute. For precious seconds, attention focused away from the shadows where Eliza hid.

She moved.

Shadow to shadow across the first courtyard, using buildings and equipment to mask her transitions. Her abilities responded with growing fluency—each jump smoother than the last, each concealment more natural.

A servant emerged from a side door just as she slipped past, forcing her to freeze in the darkness cast by a stone buttress. The woman passed within arm's reach, humming softly as she carried linens toward the laundry. If she turned her head, if she noticed shadows that moved wrong...

But the servant continued past, oblivious to the strange shadow lurking mere inches away.

Eliza reached the first covered walkway. The passage connected the main fortress to the administrative building. It was brightly lit with magical illumination, but the stone pillars and archways created irregular patches of shadow between them. She would have to wait for the right moment, when foot traffic thinned enough to risk a crossing.

Reaching through her third eye, she peered through the walkway's windows and into the administrative building's interior. Corridors lined with office doors, their brass nameplates gleaming in magical light. Clerks and officials moved with bureaucratic purpose, carrying armfuls of paperwork. She was headed to the right place.

She couldn't see him, but she was sure that somewhere in that building, David sat at his desk. How surprised he would be to see her. Shocked even—at her transformation from emotional mess to powerful magician. The thought of the amazed look on his face sent fresh determination racing through her mind.

The walkway's foot traffic began to thin as night set in. Guards maintained their positions, but civilians moved less frequently between buildings. Kitchen duties were complete, administrative work was winding down for the day.

Her window of opportunity was coming.

But as she prepared to move, exhaustion threatened to cripple her. Hours of maintaining shadow integration had drained reserves she didn't know she possessed. Her consciousness felt stretched thin, her connection to darkness growing unstable.

She needed rest, needed time to recover her strength. But time was a luxury she couldn't afford. Any delay meant more conditioning for Madge, more torment for David, more risk of losing control of her shadows and risking exposure.

Fear and determination warred inside her as she gathered herself for the next phase of her infiltration. The walkway stretched ahead, bright with magical light but empty of observers. Beyond it lay a second courtyard—smaller than the first but buzzing with activity. That space served as a buffer zone before the administrative building, its stone expanse constantly crossed by officials and clerks going about their daily business.

She'd made it this far against impossible odds. Now she had to navigate through the heart of Imperial bureaucracy without being spotted by people who might casually notice shadows behaving strangely.

Eliza stepped from shadow into light, crossing the threshold that would take her deeper into the fortress.

The walkway felt endless under the harsh magical illumination. Each step echoed. But she reached the far end without being seen, slipping quickly from pillar shadow to pillar shadow. At the end of the walkway, she stepped into the shadows cast by the second courtyard's ornamental pillars.

Here, the challenge multiplied. Unlike the utilitarian first courtyard, this space hummed with constant activity. Officials in fine uniforms crossed between buildings, their conversations echoing off stone walls. Clerks hurried past with armloads of documents. Guards maintained watchful positions at every entrance.

Too many eyes. Too many chances for discovery.

But David's office waited somewhere above, and with it, a plan for Madge's rescue. Eliza pressed herself deeper into the pillar's shadow and began planning her approach to the administrative building's entrance.

The most dangerous part of her infiltration was just beginning. The administrative building's entrance loomed ahead, guarded by two sentries whose attention drifted between the courtyard and their quiet conversation about weekend leave. Eliza waited in the pillar's shadow, muscles tensed for the sprint across open ground.

But something was wrong.

A third figure emerged from the building—a man in deep purple robes whose fingers traced whirlwind patterns in the air that left sparkling traces of light. His movements held the distracted focus of someone maintaining multiple spells simultaneously, and when his gaze swept the courtyard, it lingered too long on shadowed spaces.

Eliza shrank as deep as possible into the darkness, but the magician's head tilted like a hound catching scent. His fingers stilled mid-gesture, pointing directly at her hiding place.

"Guards! In the shadows, right there!"

29 THE HUNT

"Sir?" One guard straightened to attention.

"Something's disturbing the ambient magical field," the magician in purple robes said. "Small fluctuations. Probably nothing, but..." The magician's hands moved again, weaving detection spells that made the air shimmer like heat waves. "There. And there. Shadow magic signatures."

Eliza's blood curdled. Her integration with darkness had hidden her from simple detection spells, but this man was methodically mapping every magical disturbance in the area. She needed to move before he traced the anomalies back to their source.

The courtyard's far side offered another pillar, closer to a service entrance. If she could reach it while the magician focused on other areas...

As she slipped from shadow to shadow, the magician traced her path with his outstretched finger. He couldn't detect her Shadowbinder magic; she was sure of that. But a cold sweat of fear settled in as she realized her path left traces, perhaps magical ripples that a skilled practitioner could follow like footprints in snow.

"There!" The magician's voice cut through the air. "Guard! Something just moved between the pillars!"

Shouts erupted across the courtyard. Guards poured from doorways, their weapons blazing with intense light that bleached the darkness. Eliza dove for the nearest alcove as detection spells swept the area. In her panic, shadows erupted from her feet. She recalled the shadows into her third eye in an instant, but it was too late.

"Shadowbinder!" The magician's voice carried triumph and terror in equal measure. "The Shadowbinder is here!"

The word resounded around the courtyard. Guards who'd been moving through dull routines suddenly radiated deadly focus. Weapons designed to kill rather than capture appeared in their hands, barrels humming with energy. She recognized them as the same weapons from her dreams—the ones that had evaporated her classmates. She was seconds from joining them—if she didn't think fast.

But thinking fast while her heart was thundering proved almost impossible. Out here, she couldn't reach the main building without exposure, and if she exposed herself, that would be the end.

More alarms joined the first—not the simple bells used to mark time, but a deep, resonant tolling of an alarm. Throughout Blackstone, footsteps thundered on stone as the entire fortress, it seemed, mobilized for the hunt.

Eliza leaned against the alcove's back wall, the cold sweat feeling feverish now. She closed her eyes, forced her pulse to slow, and reeled her shadows into the pinprick behind her forehead.

Be still, my friends.

That's when she realized the guards knew *what* she was, but not *where* she was. That advantage wouldn't last long with detection spells flooding the area—and her less than perfect shadow containment—but it might be enough to reach the administrative building if she moved fast while the chaos was still erupting. Once the guards slowed into formation, once they held their ground and pointed their weapons in silent focus, once the magician had perfect stillness with which to detect her—it would all be over.

A service door stood twenty yards away, unguarded. She gathered herself to sprint across the open ground.

"Search pattern seven!" the magician commanded. "Standard containment protocols!"

Whatever that meant, it couldn't be good.

No choice. She had to move.

Eliza burst from the alcove, shadows streaming behind her like dark wings. The distance to the service door stretched endlessly as shouts erupted behind her. A fiery blast lashed out, missing by inches as she dove through the doorway.

But she had no time to fall apart. No time to be emotional. She had to move with purpose and not fear.

But the building's interior offered new challenges. Servants scattered from her path, screaming about intruders and monsters. The hubbub drew more guards, more weapons, more magic designed to incinerate her from existence.

She sprinted down a corridor lined with supply rooms, but it ended in a stone wall with no way forward. A dead end. Behind her, boots thundered closer with each heartbeat.

Think. The building had to have service passages, maintenance shafts, something that connected different levels. She shut her eyes and invoked her third eye, scanning through the walls for pathways invisible to normal sight.

There—a narrow stairwell hidden behind a false panel, used by servants to move between floors without disturbing important meetings. She pressed against the wall until the mechanism clicked, revealing steep steps that climbed into darkness.

"Check every room!" voices shouted behind her. "She's on this level!"

Eliza climbed as quietly as possible, but the wooden steps creaked under her weight. Each sound felt loud enough to wake the dead, and if they heard her moving upward...

Light blazed below as guards entered the stairwell. Their weapons cast harsh illumination that chased shadows from every corner, making concealment impossible.

"She's on the stairs!" someone yelled. "She's going up!"

Fire magic roared up the narrow shaft, scalding the air. Eliza threw herself against the second-floor door, bursting through into another corridor just as flames licked the space where she'd been standing. Pain exploded through her foot—not just heat, but something *wrong*. The fire carried corruption, a foulness that sank beneath skin and bone. Her shoe had melted into her flesh, leather and skin fused into a blackened mass that sent white-hot agony up her leg with each step.

This level buzzed with a different energy. Administrative personnel in fine clothes hurried between offices, their arms full of documents that probably detailed the Empire's darkest work. They seemed not to hear the alarms, likely thinking whatever the threat was, it couldn't possibly be on *their* level. Their presence meant witnesses, complications, people who would remember seeing her fleeing through their workplace.

She needed concealment, but the corridor's magical lighting left few shadows deep enough to hide in. Only the alcoves between office doors offered any darkness, and those would be searched within minutes.

She spun up her golden circle.

A main staircase spiraled upward toward the building's upper floors, where senior officials worked behind reinforced doors. More security, but also more architectural complexity—rooms within rooms, private passages, spaces where she might find brief sanctuary.

She sprinted up the stairs three at a time, her burned foot sending spikes of agony through her leg with each impact. Behind her, the hunt spread through the lower floors as fast as a warehouse fire. Guards shouted orders, administrators screamed about security breaches, and underneath it all, the steady pulse of detection magic that grew stronger with each passing moment.

The third floor offered a maze of interconnected offices, but it also held something that made her heart race with hope—shadows cast by heavy furniture, thick carpets that muffled footsteps, and most importantly, a brass nameplate that read "Major David Thorne."

David's office. Close enough to touch, but separated from her by guards who would kill her on sight.

"She's on the third floor!" The magician's voice echoed up the stairwell. "Seal all exits!"

More boots on stairs. More weapons charging with deadly energy. And now they knew where she was, which meant they'd concentrate their search on this exact area.

Eliza limped toward David's office, but movement in the corridor ahead made her freeze. Two guards emerged from a side passage, their weapons sweeping the hallway.

"Empty," one reported into a communication device on his shoulder. "Moving to the next section."

They passed within arm's reach of where she pressed herself against an office door, hidden in the narrow band of shadow cast by its frame. Her burned foot throbbed with each breath, and she could smell her own singed flesh beneath the acrid scent of magical fire.

"What's that smell?" one of the guards asked.

"They just fired the stairwell. Probably roasted a rat," the other said.

The guards moved on, but their voices carried back from the next corridor. "Check every office. If she's up here, she's running out of places to hide."

A new sound joined the noise below—children crying. Through the building's walls, she could hear young voices raised in fear and confusion as alarms disrupted their controlled routines. Guards were probably herding them into secure areas, treating them like zoo animals rather than terrified children.

The rage boiled up inside her, so blistering it was an effort to contain her shadows. These monsters had stolen hundreds of children from their families, broken their spirits through systematic torture, and now they were terrifying them further just to catch one desperate woman trying to save a child. No, that was a lie. They were trying to catch a *Shadowbinder*, something so feared that they had tried to purge them all from the earth. But why? She was just a woman who wanted answers, who wanted nothing more than to rescue Madge and live a peaceful life, perhaps in David's cottage surrounded by nature. What was so fearsome about the likes of her that it drove the British Empire to genocide?

Her shadows reached toward the guards with hungry tendrils that wanted to wrap around their throats. She forced the darkness back, but the effort left her shaking. Loss of control now meant death for everyone—herself, Madge, David. They would surely torture her until she spilled their secrets.

"Third floor clear!" voices reported from different sections.

But that couldn't be right. She was on the third floor, hidden mere yards from where they searched. Unless...

Understanding washed over her. They weren't just looking for her physical form. They were scanning for magical signatures, and her shadow integration was now sophisticated enough to fool their detection spells. As long as she remained motionless, became truly one with the darkness she hid within, they might pass her by entirely. The magician was a different matter. But although he'd detected her moving in the open courtyard, would he be able to detect her trail in the nooks and crannies of this third-floor corridor? She prayed he could not.

The guards returned, scanning the corridor more slowly this time. Their weapons swept every shadow, every alcove, every space where a human might hide. But their spells found nothing unusual—just ordinary darkness cast by ordinary furniture.

"Moving to the fourth floor," they reported.

Eliza waited until their footsteps faded before allowing herself to breathe again. The corridor stretched empty before her, David's office door tantalizingly close. But the scent of burned flesh from her foot would draw any guard with enhanced senses once they realized that what they were smelling was human flesh and not rat.

She had perhaps seconds before they realized their mistake and returned to search more thoroughly. Seconds before the magician came to the third floor and looked for minute disturbances: a breath, a slight wobble of the walls, a shadow out of place.

The distance to David's office felt infinite, but she limped forward anyway, stepping from alcove to alcove. Each step sent fresh agony through her damaged foot, but the pain was nothing compared to the hope that blazed in her chest.

Sanctuary waited just ahead—if she could reach it before the hunters realized their prey had slipped through their fingers.

David's door stood slightly ajar, golden light spilling from the gap. Eliza reached for the handle with shaking fingers, exhaustion and pain making her movements clumsy.

Behind her, new voices echoed up the stairwell.

"Search the third floor again. Something's not right about those scans."

She pushed through the door and collapsed against its far side, gasping as safety embraced her. But even as relief flooded her veins, she knew this respite was temporary.

The hunt was far from over.

30 FALSE SANCTUARY

David's office embraced her with golden lamplight and the lingering warmth of banked coals. Eliza collapsed against the door, her body shaking as remnants of fear crashed through her. The wood desk sat exactly where she remembered, papers scattered across its surface.

But it was her foot that demanded immediate attention.

The fire magic had melted her shoe into her flesh, creating a twisted mass of leather, fabric, and charred skin. Each heartbeat sent fresh agony racing up her leg, and the smell of her own burned meat made bile rise in her throat.

She bit down hard on her lip to keep from screaming.

Think. She needed to hide before someone followed the smell of charred flesh.

When Eliza closed her eyes, she saw her power more clearly. Pain shattered her concentration repeatedly, waves of fire radiating from her ruined foot. Her shadows resisted the pull, wanting to spread out and search for threats, but she wrestled them into submission.

Behind her forehead, power condensed into a tight spiral of controlled energy. But maintaining the focus required absolute stillness, complete mental discipline.

And she couldn't stop herself from whimpering.

The sound escaped, a soft keen of agony that would carry to anyone on the other side of the door. She grabbed a sheet of parchment from David's desk and stuffed it between her teeth, biting down until the parchment crackled.

The taste of ink mixed with blood as she bit through her lip, but the parchment muffled the worst of her sounds. Each breath came as a thin hiss through her nose, each shift of position a careful calculation of how much pain she could endure without losing control.

Outside, mages roared past in the corridor. Garbled voices shouted orders. But none stopped at David's door, none tried the handle that would reveal her hiding in plain sight.

Where was David?

She'd hoped he would be here, planning an escape, planning her return, planning *something*. Instead, she found only an empty chair. Had the alarms driven him to some emergency meeting? Was he helping with the search that hunted her through these very corridors?

Minutes crawled past with agonizing slowness. Her foot throbbed, each pulse a reminder of how close she'd come to being burned alive. The parchment in her mouth had turned to soggy pulp, but she didn't dare remove it for fear of crying out.

She needed to see where David was. Needed to understand why his office sat empty when she'd risked everything to get to him.

She reached for her third eye. The focus sent spikes of pain through her skull, but she pushed through it.

The vision formed slowly, fighting through layers of agony and exhaustion.

Stone walls. Harsh magical lighting. The familiar scent of fear and disinfectant that marked Blackstone's detention levels.

As she traveled through the fortress in her mind, she left the agony of her foot behind.

David stood in a cell, in full Battle Mage uniform.

Beside him, Madge faced a wall covered in Imperial propaganda—portraits of Queen Victoria, maps of the Empire's territories, slogans about duty and service. Her posture was perfect, her hands clasped behind her back.

"Sir, the alarm—" a voice said.

"For the fiftieth time, private, she must finish the oath. Unless you want to explain to the Queen why one of her most prized subjects has gone soft in the head!.'"

"Yes, sir. As you wish, Sir."

"Recite the oath," David commanded, his voice carrying authority she'd never heard before.

"I exist to serve the Empire," Madge replied in that same hollow monotone from Eliza's earlier visions. "My power belongs to Her Majesty. My will is subject to Imperial command."

"And what happens to those who refuse to serve?"

"They are eliminated as threats to stability."

"Good." David circled behind her. "Your conditioning is progressing well. You may rest."

Eliza's gasp of horror shattered both the vision and her concentration. The golden circle collapsed as shock drove every other thought from her mind.

The truth washed over her, destroying every assumption she'd built about David's character.

He wasn't a reluctant participant in the Empire's crimes. He was orchestrating them.

She crumpled a new parchment sheet into a ball and shoved it into her mouth, biting down to gag the renewed pain from her foot. But as much as her foot burned, her anger was far more furious.

The rescue from Blackstone hadn't been mercy; it had been calculation. He'd known she would return for Madge, had counted on her desperation to drive her back into his hands. While she'd struggled to master her abilities in the cottage, believing he was maintaining his cover, he'd been conditioning the girl they'd both sworn to protect. But why? Why save her at all if his intent was to destroy her upon her return?

The answer was obvious. He'd needed Eliza to develop her Shadowbinder abilities. For some nefarious purpose here in the fortress.

She could use her third eye to find out, perhaps. But something inside her knew that if she attempted to reach out again, he would know she was there. No, it didn't matter why he did what he did. All that mattered was rescuing Madge. And she would have to do it without David Thorne.

She chastised herself for her stupidity. Twenty-four hours

missing from the fortress. She didn't need to wonder how he'd explained that absence to his superiors. He hadn't needed to explain anything because his superiors had orchestrated her escape. To follow her back to any rebel networks she might contact, perhaps. To use her love for Madge as bait in a trap. None of it made any sense. How could they have known that she would use her magic in the arena? The only answer was that the Magisterium must have precognition magic, which was, of course, the stuff of storybooks. The lack of a clear explanation, her inability to sort it all out—even with her third-eye ability—was enough to make her want to scream.

Her foot blazed as she shifted position, but physical pain felt distant compared to the agony tearing through her chest. David— the boy who'd shared his light with her shadows, the man who'd kissed her intimately—was her enemy.

Had always been her enemy.

Every gentle word, every moment of connection, every promise of escape had been lies designed to manipulate her into exactly this position. Alone, injured, trapped in the heart of Imperial power with nowhere to run. It didn't make any sense; she knew it didn't. But nothing about the British Empire made sense. Their purges, their destruction, their decimation of magical children.

Footsteps approached in the corridor outside. Measured, familiar, carrying the confident stride of someone who owned every inch of this place.

David was coming.

Eliza struggled to reactivate the golden circle, but pain and betrayal shattered her focus. Her shadows writhed chaotically around the office, responding to emotions too powerful to contain. Instead of hiding her, they announced her presence like rooks congregating around an animal carcass.

31 REUNION AND FURY

The footsteps stopped outside the door.

Eliza braced herself against the wall, shadows boiling around her like black fire. Her foot screamed agony with each heartbeat, but rage burned hotter than pain. The betrayal sat in her chest like swallowed glass, cutting deeper with every breath.

She'd trusted him. Loved him. Let him touch her body and soul while he played the Empire's game.

The door opened.

Eliza spat out the parchment and struck without warning.

Shadows wrapped around his throat like hungry pythons, squeezing until his face flushed red.

"I saw you." Venom dripped from every syllable. "Standing over 'er like she were livestock. Making her recite that filth."

He didn't fight back. Didn't even raise his hands to defend himself. It only fueled her fury.

"Fight me, damn you!"

"No." His voice came out strangled. "If this is what you need."

"What I need?" The shadows tightened until tiny blood vessels began to burst in his eyes. "What I need is you never to 'ave walked into me life!"

"Then kill me and be done with it." He met her gaze without flinching. "If that's what you think I deserve."

His calm acceptance made her want to scream. She released him suddenly; he staggered, gasping for air.

"Those words you made 'er say..." Her voice trembled. "I watched you destroy everything good left in that child."

"I watched it too." He leaned against the desk and rubbed the angry red marks on his throat. He raised his hand and cast a spell in the air. His magic flowed weakly, but soon formed a barrier between them and the corridor.

"We'll have to hide here until the hubbub dies down," he rasped. "An hour, perhaps, until we can move."

"Move? What makes you think I want to go anywhere with you after what I seen?"

He inhaled and blew out a deep breath. "I've seen horrors too, Eliza. I was with Madge for every session. Every broken response. Every piece of her spirit they tried to steal."

"You joined in!"

"I *survived*." Steel entered his voice. "They never saw me leave the arena during your escape. Never knew I helped you flee."

"Impossible."

"Lightbending. Complete invisibility. You saw it! You were there! How could you have forgotten so quickly?"

His excuses did nothing to cool her rage. "You could have warned me. Could have—"

"Could have *what*? Sent a message to the cottage and risked exposure? Got us all killed for sentiment?"

"Then explain yourself!"

"I did! Are you not listening?" His gray eyes blazed with silver. "We had a whole conversation in the cottage, Eliza! I feigned unconsciousness when your power exploded. Said when I woke up, I was deep in the forest with no memory of how I got there, that your power had flung me far from Blackstone. I hobbled back and played the wounded warrior."

"You left me in that cottage alone, then you came 'ere to continue with your games..."

He slammed his fist on the desk. "I wasn't playing *their* games, Eliza. I was playing *ours*."

"You could have got 'er out three days ago when you arrived. Used your invisibility magic to rescue 'er."

"What is wrong with you? Why do you insist on me having to repeat everything we discussed? The wards *learn*, Eliza. I told you that I cannot use that trick again."

"Fine! But that still don't explain why you left me there alone!"

"I had to. So you could concentrate on yourself instead of me. I made you focus on your power." No apology in his voice, just brutal honesty. "Caring would have got you killed."

"But Madge's conditioning sessions—when did you—"

"They assigned me to her case that same day. I had to do it, Eliza. Had to. Would you prefer someone else take charge of her conditioning? For God's sake, stop this..."

As his voice trailed off, he caught sight of her foot. "You're injured."

She ignored his attempt to distract from the conversation. "You tortured 'er, you did."

"I *conditioned* her, mildly. It is not too late to reverse it." He stared at her foot. "But first, let me take a look at your foot. It looks like it's been inflicted with corruption—"

"Forget me bloody foot! Tell me why you did nothing to stop it!"

"I did everything I could without exposing us all." He met her eyes. Pain carved his features raw. "I falsified reports. Recommended lighter conditioning protocols. Argued for more time between sessions."

"That ain't enough!"

"It's all I could do!" The words exploded from him. "One wrong move, one hint of sympathy, and they would have replaced me with someone who would have enjoyed breaking her completely. Who would have recommended solitary confinement, silence rules, mental deprivation, flogging. Would you have preferred that for her?"

The air crackled with residual magic, shadows and light still reaching for each other.

"Of course not. Why didn't you tell me then?"

"Have you not been listening? You were at the cottage! You were supposed to stay there and learn!"

"I did!"

"I see that," he said, rubbing his neck again where her shadows had left bruises blooming purple against his skin.

The sight of those marks sent something twisting through her chest. Satisfaction and regret tangled together, leaving her breathless.

David stepped closer and kneeled at her feet. "You think I wanted to leave you there?" he whispered, placing a gentle hand on her knee. "You think it was easy to walk away when every instinct screamed to stay?"

"You acted like it were easy."

"I acted like I had to act. Cold. Calculating. Everything they expect from a loyal Imperial officer." His gaze returned to her foot, and he let out a long sigh.

As much as she tried to feel the anger, force it to stay, it began to dissipate at the sight of his slumped shoulders and worried look. "It felt real."

"It had to feel real." He lifted his hand to touch her cheek. "But watching you break when I said those things—that was the hardest thing I've ever done."

Anger returned, flowing back at gale force. "You made me think you didn't care!"

"Eliza, caring about you is the only thing that's kept me sane in this place."

She held a hand up, palm out. She closed her eyes, not to summon magic, but just to take a breath. When she opened her eyes, she said, "I thought you'd chosen that lot over us."

"Never." The word came out fierce, absolute. "I chose survival. I chose to keep us all alive long enough to actually escape instead of dying in a blaze of righteous fury."

Her throat tightened. "I wanted to burn this place down."

"I know." His thumb brushed across her cheekbone, his touch feather-light. "I could feel your rage from miles away. It called to me."

"Then why—"

"Because rage without strategy is suicide." His forehead touched hers, breath mingling in the space between them. "And I need you alive more than I need you righteous."

The raw honesty in his voice undid something in her chest. All the fury, all the hurt, all the desperate fear—it cracked open like an egg, spilling truth she hadn't wanted to face.

She'd been terrified. Not just angry—terrified that she'd lost him forever.

"I thought you was gone," she whispered.

"I'm here." His hands framed her face, fingers tracing the tear tracks she hadn't realized were there. "I'm here and I'm not going anywhere."

When his lips found hers, it wasn't gentle. It was desperate, hungry, alive with days of separation. Her shadows wrapped around his shoulders while his light caressed her skin, magic dancing between them in ways that made her bones sing.

She kissed him back with everything—all her rage and relief and stubborn, stupid hope pouring into the connection. He tasted like home and danger and promises that might actually be kept this time.

"I was really angry," she gasped against his mouth.

"Good." His teeth caught her bottom lip. "Angry keeps you fighting. Angry keeps you alive."

"I wanted to 'ate you."

"I wanted you to." His embrace grew tighter, as if he were afraid she might slip away. "Hate would have been safer."

"But I couldn't."

"I know." He kissed her temple, her cheek, the pulse point at her throat. "I felt it every time our magic touched. You couldn't hate me any more than I could stop loving you."

The word love hung between them, weighted with everything they'd risked and lost and found again.

"David." His name escaped as half plea, half surrender.

"Tell me." His voice turned rough, demanding. "Tell me what you need."

"You." The admission came out broken. "I need you to be real. To be mine. To stop playing games that could get us all killed."

"No more games." His mouth moved against her throat, teeth scraping sensitive skin. "No more lies. No more choosing strategy over what matters."

"Promise me."

"I promise." The vow vibrated against her pulse. "After tonight, we disappear. All three of us."

Her foot throbbed, dragging her back to immediate concerns. "How long does she 'ave?"

His face went pale. "Days. Maybe less. Before the real conditioning starts."

"Real conditioning? What's that look like then?"

"Memory modification. Personality reconstruction. They'll strip away everything that makes her who she is." Terror flickered in his eyes. "Which is why we have to get her out tonight."

"Tonight?" Pain shot up her leg. "That ain't happening. I can barely walk."

"I can help with that. But we must move fast. They'll notice I'm missing soon. And they know you're here, so by the morning half the empire's forces will have surrounded Blackstone."

She stared at him, trying to reconcile the man who'd kissed her breathless with the stranger who'd played Imperial games while a child suffered. Both were real. Both were necessary.

Both were hers.

"Touch me," she said suddenly.

"What?"

"Your light. Touch my shadows. Let me feel if you're telling me the truth about everything."

He hesitated, then reached out with power that pulsed like a heartbeat. The moment his radiance met her darkness, truth blazed between them.

His terror during their arena escape. His agony during Madge's sessions. His desperate calculations to minimize harm while maintaining cover. His bone-deep love that had driven every impossible choice.

And underneath it all, blazing like a star, was something she hadn't expected. Relief so profound it staggered her. Relief that she'd found him. That she was safe. That he could finally stop pretending and just be the man who loved her more than his own life.

"David." His name came out as absolution.

"Now do you believe me?"

"I believe you." She reached for him with shaking hands, fingers tracing the bruises her shadows had left on his throat. "I believe all of it."

His hands glowed with concentrated light. When his power touched her burned flesh, the screaming agony dulled to a manageable throb. His light found every shadow in her soul, not banishing them but embracing them. Showing her that darkness and radiance could coexist, could strengthen each other instead of warring for dominance. But the healing wasn't complete; he couldn't fully repair the damage, only numb the worst of it.

"Better?" he asked, voice rough with emotion.

She tested her weight gingerly. Pain still shot through her ankle, but she could walk. "It'll 'ave to do. How long will it last?"

"An hour, maybe two. Then you'll need real medical attention."

She pulled him up to face her, hands framing his face the way he'd done to hers. But as soon as she stood, the pain stabbed like a hot poker through her ankle.

An hour later, the worst of the pain had subsided. The sounds outside in the hall had diminished to the occasional set of footsteps, the odd bellow from far away.

"Let's go save our girl," Eliza said.

"Our girl?"

"Madge. She's our family now, ain't she?" Fierce protectiveness blazed through her. "What's your escape plan then?"

"There are service tunnels beneath the fortress. They'll take us directly to the detention levels." He stood, offering his hand. "Your shadows to hide us, my light to guide us through the dark."

She took his hand, feeling electricity dance between their fingers. The connection was still there, scarred but unbroken. Stronger for having survived doubt and fear and the sort of love that chose trust over safety.

"When do we leave?"

"Now. Before someone realizes the search is missing its most dedicated participant."

Together, they moved toward the door and the most dangerous gamble of their lives.

But as they stepped into the corridor, Eliza felt certainty settle in her bones. Whatever happened next, they would face it as partners. As lovers who'd chosen each other despite every force arrayed against them.

Light and shadow, united against the darkness trying to destroy them all.

32 THE ALLY

The service tunnels reeked of old magic and older secrets.

David's light blazed ahead, illuminating stone walls that wept moisture. Eliza's foot screamed with every impact against rough stone. Still, David's healing magic dulled the worst of the pain— enough to keep her moving through this labyrinth beneath Blackstone's foundation.

"Almost there." His voice carried strain from maintaining both the light and her pain relief. Sweat beaded his forehead despite the tunnel's chill. "Stay close."

She pressed her shoulder against him, drawing comfort from his warmth.

The tunnels branched endlessly, disappearing into darkness that seemed to swallow sound.

Her foot caught on uneven stone. Pain blazed up her leg, and she stumbled against David's side. His arm circled her waist immediately, steadying her.

"I've got you." His breath warmed her ear. "Lean on me."

The simple words sent heat through her chest. Even here, in the bowels of the fortress, he made her feel safe. Protected. It made her want to turn into him and kiss him breathless.

"Focus," she whispered to herself as much as him.

"Always." His fingers pressed against her waist. "We get Madge. We get out. We go home to the cottage."

Home. The cottage felt like a dream now, all golden firelight and soft shadows. Would they ever see it again?

The tunnel opened into a circular chamber carved from rock. Ancient symbols covered the walls, their meanings indecipherable, but their power vibrant. Gas lamps flickered in iron sconces, casting dancing shadows that made the space feel alive.

A figure stepped from the darkness.

Eliza's breath caught. The man was built like a siege engine—broad shoulders straining a threadbare uniform. Scars carved through thinning red hair, stocky as a barrel, boots caked with mud.

"Thorne." His voice was gravelly, weathered by age.

"Haggard." David stepped forward, keeping Eliza slightly behind him. "This is—"

"The Shadowbinder."

Not a question. A statement that made her shadows stir restlessly around her feet.

Haggard smiled, showing a set of mangled and yellowed teeth. "I 'eard about yer arena performance. Rattled the ole fortress."

She blushed from her neck to the top of her head. "It weren't on purpose."

"Don't matter. You shook 'em. That's what counts."

David moved closer to the grizzled man. "We need your help. The girl—Madge Windermere. We have to get her out."

"The light-worker, eh?" Haggard nodded grimly. "She won't last but 'nother week."

"You'll 'elp us then?" Eliza asked.

"Will I 'elp you?" Haggard chuckled, moving to an iron chest against the chamber wall. "I've been plannin' this rescue since David told me of yer arrival. Question is whether yer strong enough to pull it off."

His fingers traced symbols on the chest's surface. Locks clicked open. From within, he withdrew a vial filled with amber liquid that seemed to pulse with its own light. Beneath the glass lay a scorched strip of linen with a small brass token pinned through it. Haggard's thumb brushed the token once, tracing the crookedly punched letters of SINDY, before he offered the vial.

"Compliance draught." He held it up to the gaslight. "Six hours of soft mind. Three drops under the tongue and it binds to the first voice heard within three breaths of dosing. If a guard speaks first, she's theirs for the duration. If it's your voice, she's yours."

Eliza's stomach twisted. "You want us to drug her?"

"I want you to get 'er out alive." Haggard's voice turned fierce. "After the conditioning, she won't trust on sight. The draught forces an anchor. Make sure the first voice is the right one."

Memories of her hazy youth flooded back. The laudanum drops. The shakes and sweats when she'd weaned herself off the drug. "We can't do this. Not without her knowing. To give a drug to a young un, it ain't right, it ain't right at all..."

Her voice trailed off. She was afraid that if she spoke more words, it would unleash the shadows threatening to spill from her soul.

David placed a hand on her arm. "It's okay, Eliza. I trust Haggard. He knows what he's doing. And we don't have any other choice."

He was right, of course. They had no other option. Was that the sort of thing William Clarke had wrestled with before administering the laudanum? Was he worried about her safety? Had he sat up all night, watching Eliza's shadows, knowing that he had to drug her, drumming up the courage to do what was wrong for the sake of her life?

But was that really their only option? "She knows you," Eliza said. "You 'elped to condition her. You can just tell her to follow us, right?"

David shook his head. "Not safely. She's not fully conditioned yet, Eliza, which is a good thing. If she were, it would be easy for me to command her to follow me. But you wouldn't want that... once a child is fully conditioned, there's no returning from it. But right now, she's still Madge. She's still a twelve-year-old with a strong will and opinions. Without the draught, she could balk or bolt. With it, we have a chance."

"What's the price then?" Eliza asked, staring at the bottle.

Haggard shrugged. "She might feel a bit faint, maybe a bit shaky. Not often, and it don't usually bother folks much. I took it myself once or twice."

"That ain't very reassuring," Eliza said. "You're ten times her size."

"True enuff," Haggard said. "But it won't kill 'er. And there's an antidote to break the tether once yer clear."

David's gaze cut to Eliza. "The plan, then, is that we walk in silence once we're near her. No one speaks but me until she's bound."

Eliza nodded. Her stomach curdled at the thought of drugging Madge, but she realized David was right. Getting out of the fortress was a risk to their lives. They couldn't take the chance that Madge would dig her heels in and resist before they even got beyond the walls. "Alright," she said. "Are you sure it's the only way?"

David nodded. She thought she saw fear in his eyes, but tried to ignore it. They had few options. Leave Madge here, and she'd face a grim future—possibly one where her soul was no longer hers. Leave without the potion, and all their lives would be at risk.

"Why you in the resistance, Haggard?" she asked, needing a reason to trust him.

Haggard straightened, and something vulnerable flickered across his scarred features. "Me wife were an attendant. Nineteen when they took 'er for the Tournament trials." His voice cracked slightly. "Sindy 'ad healing magic. Thought she could protect the children."

David's hand found Eliza's, squeezing gently.

"She got fed to the construct in the first round." Haggard's hands clenched into fists. "Twenty years I been planning what comes next."

"And now?" Eliza asked.

"Now we burn it all down. And David 'ere tells me you and Miss Madge might be the light that destroys the darkness."

He moved to a map spread across a stone table, red ink veining a warren of tunnels. "The girl's in maximum security—deepest level. Three barriers between you and 'er." He drew a knife from his belt and tapped the map with the tip. "First, Avern Gate—a black ward banded across the catacomb mouth. It sleeps between bells; cross only on the lull. Second, the Silver Spiral along the sluice. It drinks light and sings to the watch. Bank yer glow to a candle, or it will wake the tower. Third, the Iron Choir grate—rattle it an' every guard in the sump comes running."

Eliza repeated the wards in her mind: Avern Gate, catacomb. Silver Spiral, sluice. Iron Choir grate, somewhere past the others. Before she had a chance to ask him exactly where it was, he traced a narrow run with the blade.

"Patrol sweeps the sluice every seven minutes. We move in their wake."

His knife stopped at a hatch mark. "If the exit's blocked, take the ash chute—three ladders, forty rungs apiece. Don't look down. Cover yer mouths; the soot's caustic."

"This is a lot to remember," Eliza said. "You'll guide us?"

"As much as I can," Haggard said. "I'll take you to as far as I can."

David studied the layout. "How long do we have?"

"Thirty minutes before the guard rotations and headcount," Haggard said. "After that, they'll know we're missing and every Battle Mage in the fortress hunts you. Keep yer feet, and it's a straight run. Lose time at a barrier and yer dead on the stairs."

He pulled a second vial from the chest—clear liquid that caught the light. "Antidote. Give it to 'er once you're clear. Should bring her back to 'erself within the hour."

"Should?" David raised an eyebrow.

"Nuffin's guaranteed in war." Haggard began rolling up the map. "But it's worked before. Yer girl should be fine."

He fixed them with his weathered stare. "Once we move, there's no going back. They'll know someone inside 'elped you. This place will tear itself apart lookin' for traitors."

Eliza touched the pouch containing the compliance draught. The leather felt warm and heavy. "When do we go?"

"Now." Haggard extinguished the gas lamps with a gesture, leaving only David's golden light.

He moved toward a passage leading deeper into the fortress. "Follow me."

As they plunged into Blackstone's depths, Eliza felt her shadows pulse with anticipation. David's light wrapped around them both, warm and protective. Whatever waited in the darkness below, they'd face it together.

33 INTO THE DEPTHS

The air grew cooler and mustier with each descending step. David's light carved a bubble of gold around them, but the darkness beyond pressed close, hungry.

"Sixty steps to Avern Gate," Haggard said, his voice barely above a whisper. "After that, we're in the belly of the beast."

Eliza's foot screamed against the uneven stone, each impact sending fresh fire up her leg. David's magic wrapped around the injury like a warm bandage, but it wasn't enough.

"How much deeper?" she gasped.

"Three levels." Haggard checked a brass timepiece that gleamed in David's light. "Seventeen minutes before the guard change. We must move faster."

The tunnel opened into another circular chamber where five passages branched like the fingers of a skeletal hand. At the center stood the Avern Gate—a threshold of black iron inscribed with runes that seemed to crawl on its surface. Ward-light pulsed along its surface in slow, hypnotic patterns.

"Signature scanner," Haggard explained, approaching a panel beside the gate. "Tastes every drop of magic that tries to pass. One whiff of unregistered power and it screams loud enough ter wake the whole of bloomin' Essex."

David's light dimmed to a weak glow. "What do we do?"

"This." Haggard withdrew the brass token from his pocket, pressing it against the panel. Mechanisms clicked and whirred behind the stone. "Me auf'rization code. But you need to throttle yer abilities to nuffin while we pass."

Eliza felt her shadows writhe in protest as she pulled them tight against her consciousness. The effort brought her intense pain, but the darkness obeyed, coiling behind her eyes like sleeping serpents.

David guttered his light until only the faintest golden thread remained, barely enough to see by.

The gate recognized Haggard's token. Iron bars slid aside, revealing the passage beyond.

"Come on then, 'urry up," Haggard snapped. "Thirty-second window before it resets."

They hurried through the threshold. The moment Eliza's feet touched the far side, the gate's scanning magic brushed against her consciousness—gentle at first, then probing deeper. She held her breath, shadows clenched tight, as the ward tasted her magical signature and, finding no purchase, let them pass.

The bars slid shut behind them with a sound like closing coffins.

"One down," Haggard said, relief evident in his voice. "Now comes the interesting bit."

They descended through tunnels that grew narrower with each level, stone walls pressing close enough to brush their shoulders. The air turned stale, thick with the smell of old magic and despair. Somewhere distant, water dripped with metronomic persistence.

"Patrol comin'," Haggard warned, holding up his hand.

Footsteps echoed ahead—measured, mechanical, the sound of guards who'd walked these routes a thousand times. David's light died completely, plunging them into absolute darkness.

Eliza let her shadows flow outward, creating a bubble of concealment around them. The darkness embraced them, wrapped them in protective obscurity. When David's hand found hers in the blackness, she squeezed his fingers.

Two guards passed within arm's reach, their conversation carrying in the stale air.

"—temperature's rising in the deep cells. Conditioning's ramping up."

"Good. Sooner they break the new ones, sooner we can get out of this dungeon."

Their voices faded as they continued their patrol. When the last echo died, Eliza drew her shadows back and David rekindled his light.

"That were incredible," Haggard said, staring at Eliza's hands. "Ain't seen nuffin' like that before."

They pressed deeper, following passages that seemed to curve back on themselves in defiance of geometry. The Silver Spiral stretched ahead—a corridor lined with gleaming metal that caught and twisted David's light into impossible patterns.

"Don't look direct at the walls," Haggard warned. "The silver plays tricks with yer perception. Follow the floor seams and you keep on movin'."

The moment they entered the spiral, Eliza's sense of direction shattered. The passage seemed to loop endlessly, turning left when logic insisted they should be turning right. Her foot wobbled on a deep crack in the stone, and pain blazed through her foot.

She stumbled, gasping, and David caught her as she fell. But the spiral's disorienting magic made the pain worse, amplifying every nerve signal until she had to bite her lip to keep from crying out. Heat was building inside the boot; a light-headed sway kept brushing at her balance.

"The walls," she whispered, watching silver patterns writhe in her peripheral vision. "They're tryin' to trap us."

"Stay focused on my voice," David said, his light pulsing in a steady rhythm like a heartbeat. "Ignore everything else. Just stay with me."

They pressed forward, the barely-there floor seam their only anchor in the spiral's confusion. When they finally emerged into a normal stone corridor, Eliza's legs nearly gave out with relief.

"How much farther?" she asked, leaning heavily against David's side.

"Almost there." Sweat beaded Haggard's forehead despite the tunnel's chill. "One more thing to pass."

The Iron Choir stretched before them—a latticed gate of black metal that hummed with contained energy. Beyond it lay the final corridor, where shadows pooled thick around cell doors that had swallowed countless hopes.

"It sings when magic passes," Haggard explained. "The

'armonic resonance is tuned in ter guard frequencies. They'll 'ear it three levels up."

Eliza stared at the gate, dread settling in her stomach. She'd never seen a gate so complex, so ominous, so *alive*. "How do we get past it, then? D'you 'ave another token?"

"We can't." Haggard checked his timepiece again. "It's gonna make noise. No gettin' around it."

David moved closer to the gate, studying its construction. "Can we disable the alarm?"

"No." Haggard shook his head. "When it blasts, I'll head back to the Spiral and tell the patrol that there's some kids runnin' to Avern Gate. That'll give you some time." He glanced at his timepiece. "She's in cell forty-three. By my count, you got nine minutes to get out of 'ere before the whole place is on alert and lookin' for yer."

Haggard unlatched the gate's central lock. He looked into Eliza's eyes. "You make 'em pay, you 'ear me? For Sindy, or 'em all."

Eliza drew in a deep breath, realizing this was goodbye. No, not just a goodbye, but the point of no return. "Twenty years you waited. We won't waste it."

He nodded once before slipping away.

When David and Eliza passed between the iron bars, pain exploded through her burned foot as some sort of suppression field interacted with her magic.

She bit down on her sleeve to muffle her scream, but the gate registered her passage anyway—a low, musical note that rang through the stone corridors.

They froze, waiting for alarms, for running feet, for the end of everything.

Then, behind them, Haggard's voice echoing down the hall. "Avern Gate! They were 'eaded to Avern Gate!"

David broke into an almost jog, dragging Eliza alongside him as they reached the cell block.

Cell doors lined both walls, each one secured with locks that gleamed with suppression magic. Numbers were carved into the stone above each threshold—humans reduced to digits.

They moved past cells whose occupants stirred restlessly in

drugged sleep. Past doors that stood empty, their former prisoners graduated to fates Eliza didn't want to contemplate. Past spaces where darkness held secrets too shocking for light.

At the corridor's end, they stopped before cell number forty-three.

A faint glow breathed beneath the door—irregular, fitful, like candlelight struggling against wind. Through the observation slot, shadows shifted in patterns that spoke of restless sleep and dreams that brought no peace.

"She's here," David whispered.

Eliza pressed her face to the slot, peering into the darkness beyond. Her heart hammered against her ribs as she glimpsed a small figure curled on the narrow cot, light flickering weakly around her fingers even in sleep.

Madge. Alive. Waiting to be saved.

Or betrayed.

34 THE RETRIEVAL

David's fingers trembled as he withdrew the brass key Haggard had pressed into his palm. The lock turned with a whisper, and the cell door swung inward on silent hinges.

Madge sat on the narrow cot, spine straight as a ruler, hands folded in her lap. Her eyes stared at nothing, reflecting the golden threads of light emitting from David's hands. Everything about her posture screamed compliance—perfect, hollow, inhuman.

But a single dried tear tracked down her cheek, silver in the darkness.

Eliza's heart shattered at the sight. This wasn't the brilliant, defiant girl who'd questioned the Imperial doctrine with smart questions. This was what remained after weeks of systematic breaking—a child-shaped shell, programmed to obey.

David stepped into the cell. "Subject 23-L. Stand," he said, with the crisp authority of Imperial conditioning.

Madge rose immediately, movements fluid but empty. Her light flickered weakly around her fingers—a ghost of the blazing power that had once shattered windows across Mayfair.

"Come."

She moved toward him without question, feet silent on stone.

"Madge," Eliza whispered, holding an arm out.

When Madge passed, her head tilted slightly at the familiar voice whispering her name. For one heartbeat, recognition flickered in those vacant eyes, and Eliza imagined she would collapse into her arms, sobbing, *Miss Clarke, you came!*

But then, she looked through Eliza as if she were nothing but air. A moment later, she stood in front of David, eyes focused on nothing.

David held up the compliance draught. "This will help," he said, though whether to Madge or himself, Eliza couldn't tell. His hands shook as he uncapped the vial.

"Three drops under the tongue," he whispered. "Stay silent until—"

"Yeah, I know," Eliza snapped, a little more harshly than she'd intended. It wasn't that she was angry with David—it wasn't that at all. She was just resisting the urge to forget the draught, forget their plan, scoop Madge up in her arms, and run for the gate.

David tilted Madge's chin up. The amber liquid caught what little light there was, seeming to pulse with its own malevolent energy. Three drops fell onto her tongue like liquid fire.

One breath. Two. Three.

"Madge." David's voice turned gentle, stripped of Imperial steel. "You're safe now. We're taking you home."

The change was immediate. She nodded once, the movement more human than anything she'd done since they'd entered. "Okay."

"I want you to walk softly and quietly, okay?" he asked.

"Yes."

"Stay close to me. Follow where I lead."

They moved toward the door, Eliza's shadows flowing around them all in protective concealment. For twenty precious seconds, the rescue unfolded exactly as planned.

It started small—a soft wheeze as she swallowed, as if the air had turned to grit. Then Madge stumbled.

"David," Eliza whispered.

He turned just as Madge's knees buckled. The sound in her throat had changed from a wheeze to something wetter, more desperate. Her skin mottled pale and gray in the wan light.

"Something's wrong." David caught her before she could fall, his magic flowing immediately into her body. But his light offered no relief—her breathing turned ragged, labored.

Madge's eyes found his, wide with confusion and growing

terror. She tried to speak, to follow his last command, but only managed a gasping whistle.

"She's 'aving some sort of fit," Eliza said, medical knowledge from tending injured children flooding back. "Because of the draught. It's poisoning her!"

Guilt carved lines across David's face—the look of a man who should have known, should have asked, should have found another way.

A full-body convulsion seized Madge, her back arching as she struggled for air. The light around her fingers blazed wild and chaotic, responding to her panic.

"The antidote," David said, reaching for the second vial.

"No." Eliza caught his hand. "That breaks the binding, not the poisoning, right? We 'ave to keep 'er breathing!"

Several years ago, she'd heard whispers in the governesses' network of a young charge who'd died from convulsions after ingesting peanuts. Eliza had never forgotten the grisly retelling. The doctor in attendance had said that tilting a head back could prevent such deaths.

She knelt beside Madge and David, tilting Madge's head back to open her airway as much as possible. The girl's lips were turning blue, her struggles growing weaker as her body fought a battle it was losing.

David threaded his light into her chest, trying to ease the constriction in her lungs. "Come on, Madge," he whispered. "Breathe! You must breathe!"

She seemed to hear him, her wide eyes fixed on him as she heaved in dry, whistling breaths.

In the distance, chimes began to ring—not the measured tolling of shift change, but something sharper. Higher pitched. The alarm Haggard had warned them about.

"We 'ave to go," Eliza said. "Now."

David lifted Madge upright and scooped her into his arms. Her head lolled against his shoulder.

"Can you carry 'er the whole way while runnin' your magic on her breathing?" Eliza asked.

Sweat beaded his forehead from the effort of healing and lifting simultaneously. "I have to."

They slipped from the cell into corridors that had grown more dangerous in the moments they'd spent getting Madge to breathe. Guards' voices echoed closer than before, accompanied by heavy boots pounding stone. The patrols moved with different energy now—searching rather than patrolling.

Eliza's shadows wrapped around the three of them, but without David's magic to dull the pain in her foot, the effort pushed her abilities to their limit.

"How much farther to the tunnels?" she gasped.

"Two levels." David's voice was tight with strain.

In his arms, Madge's breathing grew shallower. Her skin had taken on a waxy pallor that spoke of her body failing, of a child's body losing its fight against the toxin in her blood.

"Breathe," David repeated, the word both command and desperate prayer.

But Madge's eyes had rolled back, showing only white. Her chest barely moved.

Around them, the fortress was on the hunt. Soon, the monsters would be upon them.

35 FLIGHT

The service tunnels shuddered as alarms reverberated through Blackstone's bowels.

David stumbled through passages that had grown treacherous in minutes, his light guttering. Madge hung limp in his arms, her breathing so shallow it barely fogged the freezing air.

"This way 'ere." Eliza's shadows flowed ahead, scouting for patrols that moved with new urgency. Her burned foot screamed against rough stone, but fear kept her walking.

Above them, the fortress had awakened fully. Boot-falls thundered through corridors. Officers barked orders that echoed down stone shafts. The measured cadences of routine had become an active hunt.

A figure emerged from an alcove—Haggard, his scarred face grim with understanding. He fixed his gaze on Madge's blue lips and dying breaths.

"Nervous shock," he said.

"The draught," David gasped. "Something went wrong."

"Damn." Haggard worried his jaw. "Change of plans. The exit I 'ad in mind's no option coz they're sealing the primary shafts. We take the ash chute."

The tunnels branched ahead, narrowing into passages carved from rougher stone. Ancient soot streaked the walls, residue from decades of forge-smoke. The air grew thick, caustic, burning Eliza's throat with each breath.

"Cover yer mouths," Haggard warned, pulling his scarf across his nose.

They pressed deeper into Blackstone's industrial depths, past furnaces that glowed with hellish light, past chambers that stunk of toilet waste. Above a pile of ashes, the chute stretched above them—a vertical shaft lined with iron rungs, disappearing into smoky darkness.

Then the bombardment began.

Magic struck the tunnels like artillery fire—controlled demolition spells that brought ceiling stones crashing down in calculated patterns.

"They're collapsing the exits," Haggard said, understanding blazing in his eyes. "Tryin' to trap us down 'ere."

"But how do they know where we are?" Eliza asked, forgetting for a moment that the walls in Blackstone fortress listened. She waved a hand in front of her. "Stupid question. Sorry."

A quake shook the ash chute, sending ancient mortar raining down. One of the iron rungs tore loose, clanging against stone as it fell.

David stared up the shaft, leaning forward and grimacing, obviously struggling with Madge's weight. His light had all but disappeared now. "I can't carry her and climb. I'm losing strength by the second."

Eliza hoped he had enough magic left to keep Madge breathing. She was afraid to check. What use would it be? She could do nothing for Madge in this hellish place.

Haggard stepped forward. "I'll take 'er. You lot go first."

Another bombardment struck, closer this time. The tunnel mouth behind them collapsed in a roar of falling stone, sealing their retreat. Through the dust and debris, voices shouted— Imperial forces moving to secure the remaining exits.

"No time," Haggard said. "Move!"

Eliza climbed first, using her shadows to test each rung before she put her weight on corroded iron. David followed, his light barely strong enough to see by, exhaustion making his hands shake on the ladder.

Below them, Haggard carried Madge with ease. But even his strength had limits—sweat streaked his face, and his breathing grew labored in the choking air.

What felt like a hundred rungs later, the shaft opened into a chamber where multiple passages converged—a hub in the fortress's underground network. As they emerged, ward-light blazed along the walls. The chamber exit—their route to freedom—was sealing itself, stone blocks sliding together.

"The warded arch," Haggard said, staring at the sliding stones. "It's closin'."

The passage beyond led to the surface, to freedom. But the archway was contracting with each bombardment strike, its keystone blocks grinding toward each other like closing jaws.

"Can we make it?" David asked.

Haggard studied the arch's rate of closure, the distance they'd need to cover. In his arms, Madge stirred briefly—a reflexive swallow, a flutter of eyelids—then went still again.

"Not all of us," he said quietly, passing Madge carefully to David. "You take 'er from 'ere."

Understanding passed between them without words. The arch would close before they could all escape. Someone had to hold it open.

Someone had to stay behind.

"A brick!" Eliza said. "Use one of the fallen bricks to keep it open!"

Haggard shook his head. "It ain't strong enough to keep it open. And when that door seals, it starts a chain reaction all the way to the surface. If I go through with you, we'll all be trapped. Nah. I'll stay put. I won't be able to keep it open fer long, so you scurry on out like you got fire behind yer."

Eliza opened her mouth to protest but Haggard gave her and David a gentle shove forward. He moved toward the arch, magic already flowing from his hands. "Go. Take 'er an' run."

"Haggard, no—" Eliza protested.

"This is what I been planning fer twenty years." Power blazed around his palms as he pressed them against the arch's keystone. "Twenty years since they fed my Sindy to their monsters."

His magic flowed into the stone, binding his life force to the ancient ward-work. The arch stopped closing, held by will and sacrifice.

"You're the one, eh?" Haggard's voice carried strange peace. "The one who'll free us from this nightmare."

Eliza stared at him, not understanding.

"The Shadowbinder." Haggard smiled, even as his strength flowed into the stone. "I can see it in ya. The power to end this."

Eliza's gut told her the words were true, but her head swam with uncertainty. "I don't know how—"

"You'll learn." The arch groaned, pressing against Haggard's magic. "You best get goin' now."

Another bombardment struck. The chamber shook, dust cascading from cracks that spider-webbed across the ceiling.

"Now!" Haggard's voice strained as the arch fought his hold. "Before I can't 'old it anymore!"

"Thank you, Haggard," David said, shifting Madge in his arms.

"Thank you," Eliza said, though she knew this would be the last time they would see him.

Her shadows flowed around David and Madge, offering what concealment they could. Together, they ran for the arch.

The passage beyond stretched toward blessed darkness—a natural cave rather than carved stone, leading up toward the surface world.

Before they rounded a bend, Eliza took one last look behind her. Haggard's magic blazed brighter as the keystone pressed down. His face was serene despite the agony, no doubt convinced that his sacrifice served a greater purpose.

"You get 'em," he yelled. "For what they did to my Sindy."

The arch collapsed.

Stone crashed down in a thunderous roar that shook the earth above. Dust billowed through the passage, choking off the last light from the chamber behind.

When the echoes faded, only silence remained.

David stumbled through darkness, his light reduced to barely a thread. In his arms, Madge's breathing rattled, her body fighting a losing battle. Eliza pressed close beside them, her own strength failing.

They'd escaped. But at what cost?

36 CONVERGENCE

Eight hours later

Light stuttered at the edge of Eliza's vision as David knelt beside her. Madge lay on the sofa, her breathing a desperate whistle that filled the silence between heartbeats. Eliza sprawled on blankets before the fireplace, her burned foot swollen beyond recognition, red blotched covering her leg like a giant hogweed rash. Eliza's fever spiked high, burning hot; it was the sort of heat that cooks the mind.

"Come on," David whispered, gathering light in his hands and laying it over Madge's throat and chest. Her lips were blue-gray, her breaths no longer perceptible.

His hands hovered, as if he was unsure where to place them; each time he turned, the light thinned. Blood beaded at his nostril and tracked to his lip. "Breathe, I command you to breathe," he muttered, shifting to Madge's mouth and throat.

"No," Eliza gasped, voice slurred with delirium. "Don't take me there. I won't go."

She wasn't talking to him. Her gaze fixed on empty air, her vision hazy with fever and something else. Something that made shadows writhe around the cottage walls.

Whispers drifted from the corners—voices speaking in languages that predated English, calling her name with ancient authority.

Elizabeth. Come, child. Come home.

David's light guttered; his shoulders sagged. Madge's breathing stopped entirely while Eliza's fever roared unchecked.

Light surged through his hands into Madge; her ribs lifted, then lifted again.

The effort rocked him; his light spasmed, and he tore his hands away.

"I can see 'em," Eliza whispered. Her fever-bright eyes tracked movement. "Standing in the doorway. Waiting."

The shadows deepened, reaching toward her with tender hunger. Not threatening—welcoming. Like arms opening to embrace a long-lost child.

"Madge! Madge" David yelled. Pleaded?

Madge stirred, her hand twitching at the sound of his voice. A rasped word escaped her throat—not quite his name, but close. Her eyelids fluttered, consciousness surfacing briefly before sinking again. Was Eliza imagining this? Was the fever taking her again, or was Madge recovering? Please, please, let it be true, she thought, talking to no one and everyone at once.

"Stay with me," David said, although Eliza did not know who he was talking to.

Her back arched, not with pain but with recognition. The whispers grew clearer, forming words that resonated in frequencies below hearing.

Choose quickly, daughter.

Somewhere behind the voices, Madge rasped, and the room tipped like a deck in heavy seas. Then the walls widened impossibly, billowing out like sails. The dark filled with faces, a procession moving through the cottage shadows—figures in robes that shifted like living darkness, their faces bearing the same sharp bones as Eliza's, the same defiant glare in their eyes. Generations of Shadowbinders walking in a death parade.

Welcoming her home.

At their head came two figures more solid than the rest. A man with kind eyes and scarred hands. A woman whose beauty carried power like perfume, a blue circle pulsing faintly between her brows.

Her parents, Leo and Kamala. *Come home, daughter*, they said without words.

Eliza's breathing slowed, her pulse thinned—no longer fever's disarray but a calm tilt toward a threshold.

"No." David's light pressed into her chest, shattering the Shadowbinder vision. "You don't get to leave. Not like this."

Light surged wild and desperate from his hands to Eliza's chest and then over to Madge. He swayed, eyes unfocused. But perhaps it was her swaying, not him, swaying, quivering, rocking in a cradle. So much love in this place, so much comfort in the shadows.

In the fever-space between worlds, Eliza leaned into the shadowed place that held no geography—just her parents' faces and the choice they offered with infinite patience.

"Come with us, beta," her mother said, voice carrying all the love that had been stolen sixteen years ago. "No more pain. No more struggle. Just peace."

Her father's scarred hands reached toward her, the same hands that had lifted her in his arms a hundred times. "You've suffered enough, Elizabeth. Let us carry you now."

Behind them, the ancestral parade waited—centuries of Shadowbinders who'd fought the Empire's hunger and lost, who'd been broken and buried and forgotten. Their eyes held no accusation, only understanding.

Death would be so easy. So gentle. After years of searching for a hint of belonging, she could rest in the arms of those who knew her. Loved her as no one else could.

But as she reached toward her parents' embrace, another image blazed through her consciousness. David, shaking with exhaustion as he fought to keep both her and Madge alive. The man who'd searched for her across years, who'd risked everything to save a Shadowbinder child.

And Madge—brilliant, defiant Madge, who needed someone to fight for her future instead of mourning the past.

"I can't," Eliza whispered. "Not yet."

Her mother's expression didn't change, but pride blazed in those ancient eyes. Golden threads wove through her blue circle. "Then claim what is yours, daughter."

The choice crystallized before her—a door of absolute night that promised rest, and a thread of golden-blue light that pulsed with her heartbeat, connecting her to the living world.

She grasped the thread.

Power blazed through her, not chaotic shadows, but something deeper. Older. The accumulated strength of every Shadowbinder who'd ever lived, flowing into her body like molten starlight.

The golden circle beneath her skin pulsed. A pressure built behind her eyes, knowledge pressing at the edges of consciousness.

Not yet complete. But no longer dying.

Her parents smiled as they faded, the ancestral parade dissolving into ordinary cottage shadows.

"Live, little queen," her mother whispered. "Live and remember us."

David slumped beside the makeshift beds; the light was absent from his hands.

With trembling fingers, he shaped a brief flare; it stitched itself into the window—short, long, short, then a doubled burst. Even through fever haze, Eliza inexplicably knew the sign: an urgent summons for help, two lives in peril.

The message slipped into the dark, racing toward whoever, or whatever, might answer.

37 THE HEALER

A woman's voice drifted through Eliza's fever haze. "Tell me who is worse and why in one sentence."

David's voice, strained and desperate: "Madge is worse, because of nervous shock from a compliance draught, and Eliza has wound fever from a foot burned with corrupted fire."

The fever pulled Eliza under again, but she fought to surface.

"How long since onset?" the woman asked.

"Six hours. Maybe seven."

Footsteps moved around the cottage—brisk, purposeful. Not David's exhausted stumbling, but the measured pace of someone who was all efficiency.

"The corrupted fire has hastened the onset of fever." The footsteps neared Eliza's side. "And this one, you may have left it too late to send a message. I will do what I can."

Glass clinked against glass. Eliza forced her eyes open enough to see a woman, her fair hair decorated with a corded black snood over her bun, kneeling beside Madge's makeshift bed, a worn leather bag open at her feet. She drew liquid into a brass syringe.

"Hold her arm steady. Do not let her thrash. She needs calming potion."

"Calming potion?" David asked. "But she is calm, Dr. Coulty, she's—"

"Not calming of the mind, David. Calming of the body."

The doctor slid the needle into Madge's arm. Within moments, the death rattle that had filled the cottage began to ease, replaced by something closer to normal breathing.

"Nettle extract with valerian root, bird's-foot trefoil, and healing magic," the woman said. "It should buy us time, but the condition could return within twelve hours."

The fever dragged Eliza down again, but she could hear the doctor working—the scratch of a match, the hiss of a spirit stove being lit, the gentle bubble of water beginning to boil.

"Warmed mist for the airways. Keep a light cone over her, David. Threads, not flares."

David's voice was barely a whisper: "I don't have much left."

"Then save what you do have for when she needs it most."

Cool hands touched Eliza's forehead, then moved to her wrist. Fingers found her pulse, as a wispy voice counted the beats.

"Good Lord," the doctor muttered. "One hundred and thirty. How long has she been this hot?"

"Since we got back. The fever—"

"It's an infection." Hands moved to Eliza's foot, probing gently around the tender flesh. "Red streaking past the ankle. We could lose her to septicemia."

The next minutes blurred together in a haze of pain and fevered awareness. The doctor's voice giving crisp orders. David moving to obey, his responses getting slower as he sighed heavily. The sound of water boiling, the sting of something sharp and clean being poured on her wounded foot.

"Silver wash. Should help with the surface contamination." The doctor's hands worked with gentle efficiency, cleaning the worst of the burned tissue. "I am going to try something experimental. Mold broth. I have seen it work on similar infections."

Eliza felt the poultice slide over her wound, cool and soothing against the angry heat. Then, bandages were wrapped a dozen or more times around her foot.

"Now fluids. Loss of humors on top of everything else."

Something warm and slightly sweet touched Eliza's lips. Salt and honey dissolved on her tongue, followed by the bitter edge of medicine.

"Drink," the doctor commanded, and somehow Eliza found the strength to obey.

The fever began to ease, just slightly. Enough for her to open her eyes and focus on the woman kneeling beside her. The doctor's face was lined with age and experience, but her eyes glimmered with magic.

"I know what you are," the doctor said quietly. "The Shadowbinder."

Eliza tried to speak, but only managed a whisper: "How d'ya know?"

"Because I've been treating magical children for thirty years. I know extraordinary power when I see it, even when it's burning up with fever." The doctor's expression softened slightly. "I also know what the Empire does to people like you. And I had words to say about it. That is why they struck me off the rolls. You're a lucky young lady that I ended up in this Godforsaken part of Essex."

She moved back to Madge, checking her breathing, adjusting the position of the mist apparatus.

"Your friend here is stable, but she is not safe. Nervous shock can return without warning. You will need to watch her through the night."

David slumped in a chair, his face pale with exhaustion. Blood had dried beneath his nose, and his hands shook when he tried to summon even the faintest light.

"You're spent," Dr. Coulty told him, not unkindly. "Drink this." She pressed a cup into his hands. "Salt water and sugar. It will help with the magical depletion."

"How long?" David whispered. "How long do I stay awake and watch?"

"Until morning tells you which way the night decided." The doctor packed her instruments back into the leather bag with efficient movements. "They are stable. Not safe. Keep counting breaths, check temperatures every quarter hour. Send for me if either is harder to rouse or their breathing turns shallow. For you—no magic bigger than a candle flame, or you will collapse and be no use to anyone."

She paused at the door. "I will be back at first light."

"Thank you," Eliza whispered.

Dr. Coulty twisted her mouth into a grimace. "You get some

rest. You'll be fine, young lady."

Eliza knew this was a lie. She wasn't fine, and neither was Madge. Did all doctors lie to patients close to death? Did patients who struggled to avoid death somehow bring the reaper closer if they feared him? She didn't know, but she did know this: she wasn't afraid of death. Death would be a homecoming.

38 AWAKENING

Eliza heard David's faint voice minutes, hours, days later—she had no idea.

"One hundred and two. That's getting better," he whispered.

Eliza's eyes cracked open. David sat hunched over charts, his beard grown scraggly—days of growth, maybe a week. When had she last seen him clean-shaven?

She drifted toward consciousness, hearing the scratch of pencil on paper. Through fever-heavy lids, she glimpsed him hunched over a parchment chart, scribbling notes by candlelight. His face was drawn, shadows pooling beneath his eyes.

"Count it with me," he said to Madge's sleeping form. "In for four, out for six."

Madge's breathing followed his rhythm, steadier than hours before but still shallow. Her light flickered weakly around slack fingers.

Eliza let her eyes close again, floating in the space between sleep and waking. But something had changed. The pressure behind her forehead—constant since her confrontation with her parents' spirits—built to a sharp point.

Then released.

Her vision snapped clear. Not the hazy awareness of fever, but something diamond-sharp that sliced through darkness. Every shadow in the cottage revealed itself in perfect detail, from the gentle pools cast by furniture to the dense blackness beneath

David's chair.

They aligned themselves without effort. Obeyed without struggle.

Instinct moved her shadows before conscious thought could interfere. Darkness cupped around David's weak light, not smothering but focusing, creating a lens that gathered the scattered radiance into something concentrated and gentle.

The effect was immediate. His light steadied, no longer wild with exhaustion but channeled through shadow into precise streams that penetrated Madge's chest without burning.

"Hold it there," David breathed, wonder threading his voice. "Perfect."

Understanding blazed through her. The shadows weren't separate from his light; they were its partner. Where she shaped darkness, his radiance could flow in harmony instead of desperate flaring.

"I can hold the shape," she rasped, testing the connection between their powers. "Give me your light and keep it thin."

David let his magic flow through her shadow lens, and together they wove a shield around Madge. Not just a protective shield, but one filled with love and strength and hope. *Wake up*, the shield said, *you're safe now.*

But something else flowed through their connection— fragments of memory that belonged to neither of them. *I can't control the light, Mama,* whispered through the golden thread. *Mama, why don't the governesses like me?*

Madge's lips moved in sleep, forming words that carried the echo of a life before conditioning: *When will Miss Clarke be here?*

These were not Eliza's memories, but Madge's, bleeding through their magical connection. A flash of morning light on Madge's bed, the mansion door slamming shut, the thundering of small footsteps down the stairs.

More fragments followed as the connection flowed. The smell of Lady Windermere's lavender water. The weight of Lord Windermere's hand on her shoulder during a church service. The sound of her own voice repeating *I exist to serve the Empire.*

Each recovered piece brought disorientation—Madge's body twitching as contradictory memories warred in her sleeping mind.

The conditioning scripts that demanded compliance battled against returning fragments of who she'd been.

"Easy," David whispered to Eliza, adjusting his light to something gentler. "Don't push. Let her mind sort itself."

Eliza felt the urge to pry deeper, to use their connection to tear away every trace of Imperial programming. But she sensed the damage that would cause—memories forced to surface too quickly could shatter what remained of Madge's sanity.

"Slow and steady," she murmured, drawing her shadows back to a whisper. "The antidote..."

"I gave it to her an hour ago," David said. "She'll be fine."

Dawn crept through the cottage windows, pale yellow light mixing with the gold of their combined magic. Birds began their morning chorus in the forest.

Madge stirred, her eyes opening with gradual awareness instead of the snapping attention conditioning had demanded. When she saw David, confusion flickered across her features.

"I know you," she said, voice small and uncertain. "But I don't understand why I should be afraid."

"You don't have to be afraid anymore," David said gently, his words carrying safety instead of control.

"Where am I?"

"Home," David said. "We're at my cottage, a long way from the fortress."

Madge turned toward Eliza. "Miss Clarke. You came back for me."

"I promised, right?"

"But him," Madge said, pointing a shaky finger at David. "I don't... I don't understand. I feel his warmth, but he looks like... looks like the man in the fortress..."

"Shhh," Eliza said, placing a hand on Madge's arm. "He's a friend. And you're safe with us."

"But..."

"All in good time, Miss Madge. But you rest, you 'ear me?"

Madge nodded and closed her eyes.

They both rested in the growing light, arena survivors bound by magic and choice. David's exhaustion had eased with Eliza's help, his power no longer stretched to breaking. Madge breathed without the desperate wheeze that had marked her poisoning.

But it was the quiet that struck Eliza most deeply. The stillness inside her own mind, where shadows had once writhed with chaotic energy. Her third eye opened and closed at will, revealing layers of perception she'd never imagined possible.

The darkness answered without resistance. Obeyed without rebellion.

It was quiet inside. At last.

She met David's tired smile with her own, their powers still entwined in gentle harmony. Outside, the forest stirred with morning sounds. Inside, they'd found something worth more than vengeance or answers.

But the artificial comfort of the cottage could not last forever. She would allow herself a little time to recover.

And then, she would plan.

39 HEALING LIGHT

Three days after her fever broke, morning care had become a ritual.

Steam rose from the basin as Eliza changed her foot dressings, the clean linen warm against her fingers. The honey and mold broth had worked—red streaks faded to pink lines, angry swelling reduced to manageable soreness. She tested her weight gingerly, pain shooting up her leg, but it was bearable now.

David pressed the brass thermometer beneath Eliza's tongue, watching the mercury rise. "Ninety-eight and six," he announced, clearly relieved. Normal temperature for the third day running.

Madge sat propped against pillows on the sofa, breathing easily but exhausted by the simple act of staying upright.

David leaned over her, patting her arm. She smiled at his presence, though she did not open her eyes. Light flickered weakly around her slack fingers, responding to his touch with trust instead of programmed compliance.

"Ward strength," David muttered, moving to the cottage's threshold. He pressed his palm against the doorframe, testing the magical barriers.

"It's weakening," he said, sweat beading his forehead despite the morning chill. "Needs recalibration, but I don't have the strength for it right now." He slumped against the doorframe. "When the Empire search parties come this way, we're not ready for them."

Eliza shifted on her bed by the fireplace.

"How long before you're battle-ready?" Eliza asked.

"A week. Maybe two." David settled into the chair between them, dark circles shadowing his eyes. "Magic takes time to recover from depletion."

The vulnerability in his admission sent unease through her chest. They'd escaped the fortress, but they weren't safe. Not yet.

David pulled a scrap of paper from his pocket, paper yellowed with age. The royal seal was crimson wax, embossed with Victoria's crown, and the parchment carried the stale smell of dust and bureaucratic decay. "I forgot to show this to you before. What with looking after you and Madge. I found it in the fortress archives."

"What is it?"

"A ledger entry from the pre-purge registration. It has your birth name and a few details of your parents."

Eliza stared at the letter, her skin crawling at the sight of the official seal. The same cold efficiency that had cataloged her people for extermination reduced human lives to neat columns of data. The thought of her name buried somewhere else in those records made her stomach turn.

"How do I know this is accurate? I mean, the scribe could've made a mistake, right?"

"Because the details match what I remember from when we were children. Your father's occupation—Leonard was an artist who painted landscapes for merchants. And your mother, Kamala, had your green eyes, Eliza. Green as thyme."

So, her father's name wasn't Leo, but Leonard. She remembered him then, standing on their porch in the bright sun, painting a green landscape in oils. She'd asked him why he was painting hills that looked so unnaturally green and a lake that looked so whitish-blue it could have been a melted glacier. He laughed then and told her he wasn't painting India, but England. "You'll see it one day, little one. This is Lake Windermere, in the Lake District of England, where your ancestors came from."

The memory fizzled as fast as it came, leaving a gnawing emptiness. What had truly happened to her parents? Would she ever find out?

"Eliza, this is proof you are Elizabeth Windermere. Do you

know what that means?"

In truth, she wasn't sure she was ready to hear it. If Leonard Windermere was her father, then that meant she was probably Madge's cousin, unless an incredible coincidence was afoot. Either way, she had chosen Madge as kin not through an official document or bloodline, but through choice.

"It means Madge and I are related."

"It could mean more than that. You might have a stake in the Windermere fortune."

Eliza coughed out a laugh. "And do what with it? Buy me a new petticoat and a set of lace doilies? I got no use for an 'ouse that'll take a month to dust. I got everything I need right 'ere."

David smiled, folding the letter and returning it to his pocket without argument. The gesture felt like acceptance, like choosing her present over her past.

The words surprised her with their certainty. For years, she'd believed the answer to her identity lay in records and registries, in documents that might illuminate the hidden memories of her past. But sitting here, surrounded by the people she'd chosen, she understood something different.

Names weren't carved in stone. Family wasn't determined by blood alone.

* * *

Later that day, Eliza discovered an old account book hiding in the recesses of the bookshelves. Marbled green boards with leather corners were rubbed thin by handling. Faint mildew stained the spine. Inside the front cover, a fern had been flattened between the boards, its delicate fronds preserved in amber.

Faded entries filled the first few pages in handwriting that wasn't David's: *Lamp oil, one quart. Eggs, 16. Salt pork, two pounds.* Simple domestic accounts from someone who'd lived here long before rebellion had claimed the cottage.

Then blank pages, waiting to be filled.

The ink thickened as she worked, her pen nib catching on paper grain. She ruled columns with a careful hand. Left pages for vitals and practical matters—the medical log their survival depended on. Right pages for something more deliberate. Names. Lives that mattered.

1 November, noon: Madge, 98 degrees. Breathing well. Cottage Ward strength, low.

2 November, evening: Dressings changed. Honey and mold broth. Food stores, two loaves, carrots.

On the right-hand page, she wrote three names:

Madge Windermere. David Thorne. Eliza Clarke.

"What are you doing?" David asked, watching her work.

"Keeping track of who matters." She drew a thin line beneath the names, then added another entry in smaller script: *Leonard and Kamala Windermere, died in the Purges. Sindy. Haggard's wife, died in the arena.* Below that: *Haggard—died protecting us.*

Not just medical records, then. Something more important. A ledger of souls she was responsible for, both living and dead.

She was in half a mind to scratch out the word *us* and replace it with *me*. He'd said she was the prophesied Shadowbinder. Somehow, scratching out the word and replacing it would cement that idea, but she wasn't sure she was ready for what that meant.

The steam kettle whistled on the hob, and Madge flinched. Her eyes went wide, fingers clenching until light sparked between them.

"I'm sorry," she said immediately, the words tumbling out. "I didn't mean to react. I'll control myself better."

The automatic apology cut through Eliza's chest. Even here, surrounded by safety, Madge's body held the memory of punishment for any unguarded response.

"Breathe with me," David said quietly, settling beside her. "In for four counts, out for six."

He demonstrated, his chest rising and falling in a steady rhythm. Madge followed, her breathing gradually slowing from panic to something approaching calm.

Watching him tend to Madge, Eliza felt a warmth bloom through her chest. This man, whom she once thought a demon, was now their savior. She reached for a wool blanket, wrapping its soft edge around Madge's clenched fists. "Feel this. Tell me what you notice."

"It's... warm," Madge whispered, fingers relaxing slightly. "Soft. It smells like lavender."

"Name three things you can see in this room," Eliza prompted.

"The fireplace. Your notebook. David's tea cup." Each item

seemed to anchor her further in the present moment.

"You can do that whenever you feel startled," Eliza said. "Look around you for things you can see, feel, and touch."

"I feel better already. It's like magic," Madge said. "Is it your magic doing that, Miss Clarke?"

"No, that's all yours, Miss Madge."

Her face crumpled. "I don't feel very magical. I'm sorry I—"

"Hush now. You don't need to say sorry for being startled," Eliza said gently.

Confusion flickered across Madge's features. "But I showed weakness. Lost control of my power."

"There's no such thing as weakness here." David rose to remove the kettle from the fire. "Only healing."

But the whistle had triggered something deeper. Madge's breathing quickened, her gaze fixed on nothing as memory surfaced.

"The arena," she whispered. "There was steam. From the boy who—" Her voice broke. Tears streamed down her cheeks, but she didn't move to wipe them away. As if crying required permission she'd never been given.

"That weren't your choice to make," Eliza said.

"But I chose it then. I chose to live while he died."

"You chose to *survive*." David's voice carried gentle firmness. "That's what any reasonable person would choose."

"Is it?" Madge's light flared wildly around her hands. "What if surviving makes me a monster?"

The word felt like a stab to Eliza's heart. Would Madge ever heal? It was like she'd latched onto the thought of being a monster, and she couldn't let it go. Her earlier reassurances of Madge not being a monster hadn't worked. So what *would* work? She didn't know. But then again...

"Let me ask you a question, Miss Madge. You reckon I'm a monster?"

Madge's eyes widened, and her face went slack with shock. "Of course not!"

"But I've killed many more than you. In the arena, I killed a bunch of mages by squeezing 'em with me shadows. And when me shadows poured up the arena walls, I killed many observers without thought of who they were or what their purpose might be for being there."

Madge stared at her. "But..."

"No buts, Miss Madge. The fact is, you're no more a monster than I."

Madge tilted her head, as if contemplating the suggestion. She shrugged her shoulders. "I suppose."

"You suppose right," Eliza said, vowing to repeat the mantra as many times as necessary.

David knelt beside the sofa, offering her a slice of bread spread thick with butter. "What you choose today, Miss Madge, is to eat, rest, and breathe. That's enough."

The simple act—holding food, accepting nourishment—seemed to anchor her. She took a small bite, then another, her light settling to a gentle glow.

* * *

Ledger entry: 3 November, afternoon: Madge, normal temperature. Appetite returning. David, managing five-minute ward sessions.

Eliza's hand moved across the page, recording progress in careful script. Each entry was a small victory against the forces that had tried to destroy them.

* * *

6 November, morning: Foot dressings dry. Walking short distances. Ward strength improving.

As evening shadows lengthened across the cottage floor, David dozed in his chair. The strain of maintaining even basic chores had finally claimed him, his breathing deep and exhausted.

The cottage ward flickered.

Eliza felt it through her newly awakened senses—the protective barrier wavering like candleflame in wind. David's attempts at resetting the ward system had failed, leaving them all exposed.

She concentrated her energy to the focal point on her forehead, shadows responding with eager cooperation. But instead of creating her own barrier, she shaped darkness around David's failing light, cupping it like hands around a flame.

David stirred, blinking slowly. "What—"

"Just 'elping," Eliza said. "Play with your light. I'll hold the shape."

He sat forward, gathering threadbare light around his hands. She curved her shadows into a lens, focusing his radiance into a concentrated beam that required less power to maintain.

Not her magic replacing his, but her shadows supporting his light, creating harmony where exhaustion had brought chaos. The effort required no strain, felt as natural as breathing.

The ward flickered, buzzed, and strengthened to full capacity.

And it had felt as simple as ABC.

Her control had truly changed. The wild, emotional magic that had once betrayed her at every turn now obeyed instantly with gentle precision.

* * *

17 November, evening: Madge walked to the garden gate. No fever episodes.

The garden gate stood twenty paces from the cottage door, wrought iron painted green that had weathered to sage. Madge's fingers wrapped around the cold rail, and she breathed deeply of air that carried no stone dust, no institutional disinfectant. Just earth and sun and a crisp breeze.

"I can stand," she said with quiet wonder, as if the simple act of supporting her own weight was miraculous. "Without help. Without permission."

Madge's hand drifted to her pocket, fingers touching something hidden there. "Miss Clarke?" Gratitude threaded her voice. "The stone you gave me, it helped. When they tried to break my mind, I'd hold it and tell myself you were coming back."

She withdrew the protection stone, its surface glowing faintly in the garden light. "You should have it back now. I'm safe."

Eliza's throat tightened. This child wanted to return the one thing that had anchored her through hell. She glanced at David, catching his slight nod. It was his stone, but her choice to make.

"Keep it," she said firmly. "It's yours now."

"Are you sure? It must be valuable..."

"Some gifts ain't meant to be returned, Miss Madge. They're meant to be kept by the people who need 'em most."

Madge closed her fingers around the stone, tears brightening her eyes. "Thank you."

* * *

19 November, morning: Madge remembered a hymn from home. Asked if she's allowed to sing it. Food stores replenished by a messenger sent by Dr. Coulty.

The entries marked their slow climb back toward something resembling normal life. But it was the question that appeared one morning that caught Eliza off guard.

"Miss Clarke?" Madge stood by the window, watching sparrows flit between the trees. "Might I ask about my parents? Do you think—" Her voice faltered. "Do you think they're worried?"

The innocent question pierced Eliza's chest. Of course they were worried. They'd lost their daughter to Imperial machinery, and probably spent every waking moment wondering if she was alive.

"They love you," Eliza said. "They're probably really sick with worry."

"Could we—" Madge's light flared slightly with hope. "Could we send them a message? Let them know I'm safe?"

David looked up from his breakfast, considering. "I could send a pigeon."

The cottage's small aviary occupied a lean-to structure behind the kitchen, cedar wood weathered silver by seasons. Inside, three birds perched on roosts David had carved himself. The space smelled of grain and straw, clean but wild.

David selected a bird, its feathers gleaming black-blue in the morning light. "This one knows the London route," he said, stroking its neck until it cooed softly. "Fast, reliable, trained to avoid Imperial interceptors. It will fly to the London loft. One of the couriers will deliver your message."

"But what if the Magisterium gets hold of it?" Eliza asked.

"The pigeon's home is London. Once I release it, it simply flies home. It will never be able to find its way back here."

Madge dictated her message while Eliza wrote: *Mama and Papa—I am safe and well. Cannot come home yet but am protected by good people. I think of you every day. Your loving daughter.*

Minutes later, the pigeon launched from David's palm, disappearing into the afternoon sky with the precious cargo. They watched until it vanished beyond the treeline, three figures united in hope and anxiety.

"Two hours to London," David said.

"And if they send a reply?" Eliza asked.

"The London loft doesn't have any pigeons that will home back here. It would be too dangerous. But they will have one that will home to Colchester. I will send word in a few days to see if there is a reply. Dr. Coulty can send a messenger there."

* * *

23 November, morning: Madge slept through the night without terrors. Full appetite returned. Foot healed enough for normal walking.

The ledger's pages filled with steady progress, each entry a small triumph. But it was the right-hand page that drew Eliza's attention as evening settled around the cottage.

Three names. Their small family.

Below them, the space reserved for the lost. Haggard's sacrifice earned its own line—a man who chose to die believing in prophecies that might never come true. Underneath, she'd penned in the names of the arena children and attendants that she knew of: Thomas Jones, Marcus, Miss Brooks...

As David slept peacefully in his chair and Madge's breathing held the steady rhythm of natural rest, Eliza took up her pen one final time.

Who we save will tell me who I am.

She closed the book.

Who had she saved? Madge, herself, and possibly David. But was that enough? Supposedly, she was destined to save more lives, become some sort of prophesied Shadowbinder. Should she be thinking of a plan to free the poor souls trapped in the construct? But before she could even consider entertaining that notion, she had to make sure that Madge was safe. Right now, the cottage offered a sanctuary, but for how long?

She brushed the thought away. One day at a time. Today, she had kept Madge safe. Tomorrow would bring new challenges, and she would face them one at a time.

* * *

One week later, David returned from his morning walk to the village with tension carved into every line of his body.

Eliza looked up from where she sat mending Madge's torn

sleeve, needle suspended mid-stitch. "What's goin' on?"

"Message from Dr. Coulty." He pulled a folded paper from his coat, the edges damp with morning mist. "The Windermeres sent a reply."

Madge's head snapped up from the book she'd been reading, her light flaring bright enough to illuminate the whole cottage. "What did they say?"

David hesitated, his gaze moving between them. The pause stretched too long, weighted with whatever news he carried.

"Out with it, then," Eliza said, setting down her sewing.

"They're being watched. Constant Imperial surveillance since Madge disappeared. They can't travel, can't send more messages, can't do anything that might suggest they're in contact with fugitives."

Madge's face crumpled. "I can't visit them?"

"No. And they can't visit you either." David moved to the sofa, settling beside her. "I'm very sorry. They're prisoners in their own home."

He unfolded the paper, revealing Lady Windermere's careful script. "They say they love you. That they're proud of your courage and happy that you're safe. And that they understand why you can't come home yet."

Madge took the note and read it, tears slipping down Madge's cheeks. She smiled. "They understand."

"Your mother thinks that keeping you safe matters more than seeing you again." David's voice grew thick. "They'd rather know you're alive and free than have you home and imprisoned."

Eliza's throat tightened. Lady Windermere's sacrifice—accepting separation from her daughter to protect her—cut deeper than any blade.

"There's more," David said quietly. "They've been threatened with treason charges if they're found to be concealing information."

"And are they?" Eliza asked.

David shook his head. "They genuinely don't know where we are. Which is what's keeping them alive."

Madge clutched the letter to her chest. "May I keep this?"

"Of course." David squeezed her shoulder. "But we can't risk sending another message. Not until the surveillance lessens."

"How long will that be?"

"Months. Maybe longer." The admission hung heavy in the air. "The Empire doesn't forget easily."

Eliza watched Madge's face as understanding settled. No more messages. No reunion on the horizon. Just the endless ache of separation from everyone she'd known before.

But instead of breaking down, Madge straightened her shoulders. "Then we make the best of what we have."

She looked at David and Eliza. "We're family now, aren't we? The three of us?"

"Yeah," Eliza said, warmth kindling in her chest. There would be a time to tell Madge about their connection, once she was stronger. Once Eliza had sorted out in her own head what it actually meant. "We are."

David guided Eliza to the kitchen on the pretense of making tea. "We must talk," he whispered. "It's time."

"Time to talk about what?" she whispered back.

"Time to talk about our future. And our passage to America."

40 TETHERED HEARTS

Morning frost glazed the cottage windows as Eliza bent over her ledger, recording the previous night's ward strength: *Full power maintained.* Her foot held steady as she shifted her weight, the angry red infection now just a thin pink line across her ankle.

David emerged from the woodshed with an armload of split logs. He'd spent the morning chopping fuel against November's bite—work that required no magic, just steady effort and time.

"Breakfast?" he asked, brushing sawdust from his sleeves.

They gathered around the scrubbed pine table as they had every morning for the past week. Eggs from Dr. Coulty's network of suppliers, bread baked in their own oven, thick jam.

Madge spread butter across her toast. "I dreamed about Mama last night. She was standing in our drawing room, looking out the window. Just waiting."

Eliza felt a pang at Madge's wistful tone. "Sounds like a right peaceful dream."

"It was." Madge's light flickered gently. "But when I tried to go to her, I couldn't cross the threshold. Like something invisible was holding me back."

David set down his fork, concern creasing his brow. "That must have felt awful."

"Yes. I was sad. But also..." Madge searched for words. "Protected? Like the dream was telling me I'm meant to stay here for now."

The silence became too prolonged, too intense. David's gaze met Eliza's across the table, and she caught the question in his eyes. *Now?*

She nodded slightly.

David cleared his throat, choosing words with obvious care. "Madge, there's something we should discuss. Not urgent, just... something to consider for the future."

"What sort of something?"

David's hand found Eliza's under the table. "There are people who help magical refugees start new lives in America. Places where children can learn without fear." His voice stayed neutral, offering rather than pushing. "It's an option. Only if you wanted it."

Madge's fork stilled halfway to her mouth. "Leave England?"

"The Empire's reach ends just off the coast of England. On the other side of the Atlantic, you could be truly free." David leaned back, deliberately casual. "But crossing means risk—public travel, Imperial checkpoints. And it would mean leaving everything familiar behind."

"My parents." The words came out flat, final. "I can't leave them."

"Madge," Eliza said, reaching across the table to hold her hand. "In America, you'll be free. I'm sure that will make 'em 'appy."

Madge looked at her for a long time. When she spoke, tears welled in her eyes. "But at least here I'll have hope to see them. If I'm across the Atlantic, I'll never see them. Never."

"Not true," Eliza said. "It's just eight days' travel. When it's safe, you can return. Or, once the Empire's forgotten about you, your mama and papa should be able to make the trip to see you."

"They could see me here, when the Empire has forgotten about me."

David tapped his fingers on the table. He took a moment to speak, as if choosing his words carefully. "If we stay here, the Empire will not simply forget about you, and they definitely will not forget about Eliza. But if we go, and if we leave just a thread of a trail so that they know we have traveled to America, then their grip will loosen because they know we're out of their reach."

Madge seemed to consider this for a moment. "Okay, I'll think about it. But I'm not going to abandon my parents."

"Of course not." David's response was immediate. "I wouldn't ask you to do that."

"They're prisoners because of me. Watched every day, questioned about my whereabouts. How can I sail to freedom while they suffer surveillance in their own home?"

Eliza squeezed Madge's hand. "Your survival ain't betraying them. It's honoring their sacrifice."

"Is it?" Madge's voice cracked. "Or is it just selfishness disguised as nobility?"

"It's staying alive long enough to choose your own future," David said gently. "When you're old enough, strong enough, wise enough to make real decisions instead of desperate ones."

Madge shook her head, tears spilling. "And what about the other children? The ones still trapped in Blackstone? How many more will die in tournaments while I'm safe across an ocean?"

The question pierced Eliza's chest. This child, barely recovered from systematic torture, still carried others' suffering on her shoulders. "You can't fight for 'em right now," she said quietly.

"Can't I?" Fire blazed in Madge's eyes. "If I have power they fear, if I could somehow—"

"You're twelve years old." Eliza's voice turned firm. "Your responsibility is to heal, not to carry the Empire's sins."

"But they're my friends' sins too. Thomas Jones died because I fed Miss Brooks' fire. Because I chose my life over his." Madge's hands clenched into fists. "How do I live with that if I don't try to prevent it from happening to others?"

"We can plan in America," Eliza said. "I promise you that, Miss Madge. We ain't abandoning no one."

Silence settled over the kitchen. Wind howled outside, November asserting its grip with icy fingers. The fire crackled against the cold while they grappled with impossible choices.

"Tell me about the crossing," Madge said finally. "Not to decide—just to understand."

David considered the request. "Ship to Boston. Eight days at sea, maybe ten. From there, contact other magical families."

"And the risks?"

"Passenger manifests. Port authorities. Imperial agents who watch for unusual bookings." His honesty was brutal but necessary. "It's not a guarantee of safety, just a chance at it."

Madge absorbed this information, her expression thoughtful rather than frightened. "And once we're there? What sort of life would we have?"

"Different. Harder in some ways—starting over with nothing, learning new customs. But freer. Children attend schools where magic is celebrated, not weaponized."

"Children like me?"

"And others. Fire-workers, earth-shapers, shadow-workers. You wouldn't be alone in your abilities."

Hope flickered in Madge's eyes, quickly suppressed. "It sounds wonderful. Too wonderful, perhaps."

"Dreams often do sound like that," Eliza said. "That don't make them impossible."

Madge picked at her toast, her appetite apparently fading as the pressure of decision pressed down. "I can't choose now. Not while my mind still holds their conditioning, their words. What if I'm choosing based on programming rather than my own will?"

"Then we wait," David said simply. "As long as you need."

"Months?"

"If necessary."

"Years?"

"If that's what healing requires." David's smile was gentle but absolute. "We have time, Madge. Time to understand what you truly want."

Relief flooded Madge's features. "You won't pressure me? Won't nag me if I'm taking too long?"

"Never," David said firmly. "Your choice, your timeline."

Madge reached for both their hands, her light pulsing with something approaching joy. "Then yes. Let's wait."

"Agreed," David said.

"Until then," Eliza added, "we focus on today, right? On breakfast and books and all the ordinary things that make life worth living."

Madge's laughter was the first genuinely carefree sound she'd made since their rescue. "I'd forgotten about ordinary things. About choosing what to do with whole hours."

"We'll help you remember," David promised.

They finished breakfast in comfortable silence, each lost in their own thoughts but connected by the simple pleasure of shared domesticity. When Madge returned to her book by the fire and David went to repair a loose shutter, Eliza opened her ledger once more.

30 November: Discussed America. Madge chooses to wait and heal first. No pressure. Decision delayed until she's truly ready.

Eliza thought of America, of freedom, of living beyond the Empire's grip. But she wasn't thinking of setting up a cozy cottage somewhere in New England and forgetting about the Empire. She was thinking of revenge.

In America, they would have the freedom to plan a revolution.

41 NEW BEGINNINGS

Spring light streamed through the forest, chasing away winter's lingering shadows.

Eliza knelt in the garden bed behind the kitchen, her fingers dark with soil as she transplanted seedlings David had started on the windowsill. Tomatoes, onions, herbs that would flavor their meals through summer. The earth smelled alive—rich and loamy after months of frost.

Her foot pressed firmly into the ground without pain. The angry red infection had faded to nothing more than a pink smear across her ankle, barely visible unless she looked for it.

"Miss Clarke." Madge's voice carried from the cottage doorway. "The bread's ready."

Eliza brushed dirt from her hands, noting how steady Madge's tone had grown.

Inside, the cottage hummed with domestic rhythm. David pulled golden loaves from the oven, flour dusting his forearms. The sight sent warmth spiraling through Eliza's chest—this man who commanded battle magic reduced to wrestling with stubborn dough and temperamental yeast.

"Smells really nice," she said, sitting down at the kitchen table.

"Only took three attempts to get the timing right." His smile carried satisfaction earned through small failures.

Madge sat and poured tea. "I've been thinking," she said, pausing mid-bite. "About our conversation before Christmas."

Eliza's hands stilled on the bread knife. "Which part?"

"America." The word carried weight—not fear, but careful consideration. "I think I'm ready to discuss it properly now."

Eliza's pulse quickened, but she kept her voice level. "What's changed your mind then?"

"I've been watching you both." Madge's light flickered gently around her fingers as she poured milk into her cup. "The way you move through the cottage, tend the garden, plan for seasons. You're building a home. But I know it's not what's meant for us. It feels... temporary."

"We're building whatever you need," David said.

"But it's not enough, is it?" Madge met his gaze directly. "For any of us. I'm twelve years old, and I should be learning things beyond hiding and healing. You should be able to walk through villages without a disguise. Miss Clarke should—" She paused, looking at Eliza now. "You should have a life that's yours, not one chosen for you by circumstance. And all of us should be planning to join the rebellion. We can't do that here."

The observation cut deeper than accusation. Madge was thinking beyond her own comfort, her own survival.

"The cottage is home enough for now," Eliza said gently. "And me entire life has been led by me circumstances. That ain't your burden to bear."

Madge stirred sugar into her tea, the spoon making tinkling sounds as she spoke. "That's maybe true. But your future is based on what I decide. That doesn't seem fair to either of you. Sometimes I dream about attending a real school. And I know I can't do that here."

Outside, nightingales called to each other in a forest awakening from winter sleep.

"There would be others like you there." Eliza said. "Other magical children."

"Others who survived tournaments?" Pain flickered across Madge's features. It wasn't the raw agony of early recovery, but a deeper sadness that had learned to coexist with hope. "Or others who were luckier?"

"Not tournaments. They don't 'ave those in America."

Madge absorbed this, her expression thoughtful rather than

overwhelmed. But Eliza saw the way her lips scrunched, the way her eyes crinkled—as if she was having trouble imagining a place where freedom was a given and The Empire was a far away threat.

"I've been having dreams of long granite steps that slip off into a misty harbor full of sails. I think it's America, and my dream is telling me I could be happier there. Here, I'm just reminded every day of what I've lost. What we've all lost."

"I ain't lost nothing of value since we met," Eliza said. "If anything, I feel like I gained family." She bristled at her thoughtlessness. Madge might never see her family again, and it wasn't fair to suggest her "new" family could replace the one that was lost. "Sorry, Miss Madge. I didn't mean to suggest that..."

Madge cupped her hand over Eliza's. "No, don't apologize. You *are* family. We're all family now. I like the idea of a big family, anyway. There's always room for more. But as much as I love it here, with you both, here isn't real life, is it?" Madge's gaze moved between them. "I want real life. I want friends, hobbies, choices that matter beyond what flavor jam to put on my toast."

The truth in her words resonated through the cottage kitchen. They had built something precious in these last few months— safety, family, the luxury of time without urgency. But sanctuary was meant to heal, not to hold forever.

"What about your parents?" David asked. "You do realize what we're asking of you? To leave them here in England?"

Madge's light pulsed brighter, but her voice stayed steady. "They want me safe above all else." Tears gathered in her eyes, but didn't fall. "I think they'd understand if safety meant crossing an ocean."

"We could ask 'em," Eliza suggested. "Send another message."

"Could we?" Hope blazed in Madge's expression. "I thought you said it was too dangerous."

David considered, fingers drumming against the table. "We could code the message. Make it look like mundane correspondence." His expression grew thoughtful. "Nothing that suggests fugitives or flight plans."

Madge leaned forward, energy crackling around her in excitement rather than fear. "What would we say?"

"Do you have any cousins?" David asked.

"No," Madge said. "Why?"

"We could send a note saying that their beloved niece Margaret is traveling to America this summer to seek a better climate for consumption. Say that she's seeking their blessing, and she hopes they will consider visiting."

"Ooh, a code!" Madge's face lit up. "That's exciting! Like the Caesar Cipher. Did you know he used to shift letters by a certain number in correspondence? We could do that!"

David shook his head. "Great idea, but your parents might think they received poppycock and throw it away."

"Okay, then we'll use my non-existent cousin. But how would we know it's a positive response?"

David drummed his fingers on the table. "Well, we can't ask for a return reply, because your parents are still being monitored. It's too dangerous for them to send anything."

The three of them sat there, deep in thought for minutes. David slurped his tea, Eliza chewed on a delicious buttered nobby, and Madge stirred eggs around her plate.

Madge put down her fork. "I've got an idea! The tip!"

"Explain," David said.

"In the note from my dear cousin Margaret, ask for my parents to tip generously, perhaps five shillings. Then, put a P.S., saying, *Of course, if you hate the idea, dock the messenger a shilling for delivering bad news!*"

David leaned back in his chair and smiled. "Madge, that's genius."

"How long will that take?" Eliza asked.

"If I send a pigeon today, they'll get the message tomorrow, maybe sooner. As far as the tip, we'll have to glean that information via word of mouth. It could take days, perhaps weeks. I'll talk with Dr. Coulty and see how it can be arranged."

David rose from the table, already moving toward his writing desk. "I'll prepare the message now, if you're certain."

"I'm certain." The words carried weight beyond their simplicity—not just agreement to send a letter, but acceptance of everything that might follow.

They spent the next hour crafting careful sentences that would pass Imperial scrutiny while conveying their true meaning. Madge dictated while Eliza wrote, David offering suggestions for phrasing that sounded properly innocent.

Dearest Aunt and Uncle Windy. I continue to recover well in the countryside air. My companions believe a journey to visit our American cousins might benefit my health further. The voyage would be long, but the climate there is said to be excellent for young people with delicate constitutions. Would you think such travel wise? Your loving niece, Margaret.

P.S. Do tip the courier five shillings.

P.P.S. Of course, if you think this is a silly idea, then dock the messenger a shilling for delivering bad news.

P.P.P.S. I hope you will visit. I will forward my address when I am able!

"Windy?" Eliza asked.

Madge chuckled. "They'll not know straight away it's from me. I used to call us 'The Windy's' and they hated it."

Eliza smiled—not because of the childish name but because of Madge's glee and enthusiasm for the plan. "You sure about this? That's a lot of postscripts, and your parents might balk at the lack of formality."

"That's the point," Madge said. "That, and the reference to the Windy's, they'll realize that it isn't any ordinary note."

David glanced at the final draft. "If the Magisterium intercepts this, they will assume it has come from distant family."

"What about the 'delicate constitution,'" Eliza asked.

"It explains why a healthy child might need to travel to a different climate." He folded the message, sealing it with plain wax.

Minutes later, the pigeon launched from David's hands, disappearing into the forest canopy.

"Now we wait," David said.

"And plan," Eliza added. "If the answer's yes, we'll need to move quick."

They spent the evening discussing logistics with careful optimism. Routes to Liverpool that avoided Imperial checkpoints. Documentation that would pass casual inspection. The delicate balance between preparation and premature commitment to a future that might never arrive.

But beneath the practical considerations, something deeper had shifted. They were planning beyond survival. Imagining lives that extended past hiding and healing into something resembling normalcy.

As April melted into May, they fell into new routines shaped by possibility. Madge practiced her light magic with increasing confidence, no longer afraid her power would betray them. David made new shutters and stocked up on travel supplies, preparing for a departure he hoped would come. Eliza tended her garden with extra care, not knowing if these seedlings might have to sustain them through another winter if their plan failed to come to fruition.

When Dr. Coulty arrived one morning with the supply delivery and news from her courier network, they gathered around the kitchen table.

Eliza's heart hammered in anticipation. Dr. Coulty hadn't visited all winter, so she had to be carrying important news.

"Your reply came through Colchester yesterday," Dr. Coulty said, withdrawing an envelope from her worn leather bag. "Clean passage, no Imperial interference."

David opened the message with steady hands, though Eliza caught the slight tremor in his fingers. He read silently first, his expression neutral.

"Well?" Madge asked, barely breathing.

David read the letter aloud. "Dear Dr. Coulty, Thank you for your inquiry. Our records show that the messenger received a five-shilling tip for the correspondence placed to the Windermere residence on March 31st."

Five shillings. The generous tip that meant approval, understanding, blessing.

Madge's light blazed bright, her joy unleashed after months of careful control. "They said yes. Mama and Papa said yes!"

Dr. Coulty smiled at their celebration, but her expression carried additional weight. "There's more news. I made inquiries about the nature of magic in Boston, as you asked, David."

This was the first Eliza had heard of such an inquiry.

David caught her questioning glance and placed a hand upon hers. "And what did you hear?"

"Your instinct was correct. There are at least two

Shadowbinder families in Boston."

Eliza gasped. Surely she hadn't heard that correctly. "Two Shadowbinder *families*?"

"Yes," Dr. Coulty said. "And that's just in Boston. There are more Purge survivors in America than you might imagine."

The words settled into the cottage kitchen like a benediction. Not just escape, but community. Not just survival, but the possibility of belonging somewhere designed for people like her, of the possibility of discovering new friends and perhaps distant relatives.

As afternoon light slanted through windows, casting golden patterns across the table where they'd planned their future, Eliza felt certainty crystallize.

They were going to America. Going to build lives that belonged to them instead of hiding from lives the Empire had tried to steal.

Spring had brought more than warming weather to their cottage sanctuary. It had brought hope, and plans, and the promise that healing could grow into something larger than itself.

42 THE PROMISE

Eliza knelt between the vegetable rows, her fingers working soil that had become familiar over weeks of tending. The earth smelled of growth and possibility—like promises about to bloom.

"Sit still test today," she called to Madge, who was weeding between the herbs. "Ten hours without emotional magic. Can you manage it?"

Madge's light flickered once—a brief pulse of excitement—then steadied to nothing. "I've been practicing. Watch." She settled cross-legged on the grass, hands folded in her lap. Light died completely around her fingers.

For the first hour, Eliza watched from her weeding, placing the occasional ripe strawberry into a punnet for the journey.

"Tell me about Boston again," Madge said. No emotional spikes. No magical leakage.

"Don't know much about it." Eliza moved to the beans bed, picking bugs from the leaves. "But Dr. Coulty says cobbled streets, trading ships, and harbor-side shops that sell everything from whale oil lamps and beaver hats to ice-cream."

"Real ice-cream?"

"Real everything. Markets where folk sell maple sugar and plain old magical wares instead of Magisterium-approved gadgets. Places where being different ain't dangerous."

Madge absorbed this, her breathing steady. Light remained contained, though Eliza caught the slight smile that curved her lips.

Progress beyond anything they'd dared hope for all those months ago when they'd arrived at the cottage.

By evening, Madge had passed her test. Ten hours of sitting, reading, eating, stretching—all without a single pulse of uncontrolled power. She kept the composure of someone who finally trusted her own abilities.

"Well done," David said, genuine pride threading his voice. "You're ready for the trip."

The words settled around them with the weight of inevitability. Tomorrow, they'd leave this sanctuary that had become home. Leave safety for the unknown promise of freedom.

That evening, David found Eliza in the garden. She was deadheading roses—a futile gesture since she wouldn't see the next bloom cycle, but her hands needed occupation while her mind processed the magnitude of departure.

"Walk with me?" he asked.

They strolled the cottage perimeter, checking ward stones that pulsed with steady light. The magical barriers that had protected them would fade within days of their leaving, returning the space to ordinary forest. Someone else would find this clearing eventually, create their own sanctuary, plant their own dreams in soil that had sheltered theirs.

"Nervous about tomorrow?" David asked.

"Excited." The admission surprised her with its honesty. "Feels like I been waiting me whole life for this. Like everything that came before was just preparation."

They paused beside a patch of daisies that starred the grass like a fallen constellation. David knelt, his fingers working among the stems with careful precision. "Since we'll be traveling together as a family, we should probably make it official."

Eliza raised a brow. "Make what official?"

His nails pierced the stems as he threaded the daisies into delicate loops. "Well, we can't have people questioning why an unmarried couple is traveling with a child. It might raise suspicions."

Warmth crawled up her neck as understanding dawned. "David Thorne, you proposin' marriage for the sake of avoiding Imperial scrutiny?"

"Among other reasons." The daisy chain grew in his hands—white petals bright against green stems. "I'm proposing because I love you. Because I want to build whatever comes next together. Because when I imagine growing old, it's with you."

He held up the finished ring, a delicate and perfect fairy ring brought to life. "Eliza, will you marry me?"

The question lingered between them like a held breath. Behind them, the cottage glowed with lamplight and the promise of one final night in their sanctuary. Ahead stretched an ocean and the possibility of lives that belonged entirely to them.

She thought of the ledger entries she'd written over months of healing. *Who we save will tell me who I am.* But kneeling here with David's love shining in his eyes, she understood something deeper.

Who she chose to love would define her future.

"Yeah, I'll marry you." Her words came out strong, certain. "But not because of disguises or Imperial papers."

"Then why?"

"Because I choose you. Choose us. Whether or not we ever find any of me family, whether or not the Empire thinks we belong together." She held out her hand, watching him slide the daisy ring onto her finger. "I choose you."

The petals were soft as silk against her skin, the stems cool and slightly damp from evening dew. It wouldn't last—by tomorrow, the flowers would begin to wilt. But that felt right somehow. Their love wasn't built on permanence but on the daily choice to keep building it, no matter what appearances dictated.

His thumb brushed across her knuckles where the ring rested. "We should tell Madge."

They found her by the kitchen window, packing her few possessions into a cloth bag. She looked up at their joined hands, her gaze fixing on the daisy ring. Her grin spread from ear to ear. "You're engaged?"

Eliza held up her hand, displaying the ring as if it were a real ruby. "We're going to pretend we're married for the trip."

"I suppose this means I need to call you Mum now?" she asked, with a cheeky tone to her voice.

"I suppose you might 'ave to, if we're to keep up appearances."

Madge rushed over and threw her arms around David and

Eliza. "That makes us real family then!"

Eliza still hadn't told Madge about their common ancestors. She would, when the time was right. When they were safe in America. Perhaps, on an evening when Madge missed her parents the most, Eliza would tell her a story of Shadowbinders and Lightbinders and how their joint heritage just might save the world.

They spent the rest of the evening in quiet preparation. Clothes packed into worn carpetbags. Food wrapped for the trip. The ledger, with its careful accounting of souls saved and lost, tucked safely between Eliza's spare chemises.

As midnight approached, Eliza made one last entry:

15 June: Departure for Liverpool. All three healthy, hopeful, ready. Beginning new chapter.

In her journal, below David's name, she added a tiny daisy chain. Below her own, a heart. Below Madge's, wings.

Dawn came gray and misty, perfect weather for travelers who preferred to avoid notice. The pig cart arrived as promised—a sturdy wagon filled with squealing livestock, driven by a weathered farmer with protruding eyes as bulbous as a cow's.

Eliza, David, and Madge were dressed in their disguises: patched clothing that marked them as poor but respectable folk seeking work in distant counties. Madge's curls were tucked under a plain bonnet, and she wore an eye patch. Eliza had rubbed blackberry juice over her cheek to give her a diseased appearance—protecting her from strangers' scrutiny. David's papers identified him as a non-magical journeyman carpenter, while Eliza became his non-magical wife. Madge was their niece, slightly touched with light abilities but nothing worth Imperial attention.

"Mind the pigs don't escape," the farmer warned as they climbed into the wagon bed. "And keep yer 'eads down when we pass checkpoints."

Eliza settled between David and Madge, her hand resting in his.

Madge wrinkled her nose at the smell, a potent combination of pig sweat, urine, and feces, lending an ammonia-bite to the air. "How long do we stay in this cart?"

Eliza laughed. "You think this is bad? You should try walking into the shared privies in the East End, Miss Madge. Makes this pig cart smell like roses."

Madge chuckled, covering her nose with her sleeve. "Oh, *do* take me to the East End one day, Miss Clarke," she said with mock excitement.

Eliza narrowed her eyes and pursed her lips as if she was sucking a lemon wedge. "That's only where the bad girls go, right after Father Christmas leaves 'em a lump of coal in their stocking."

Madge burst into laughter, which turned contagious. Even the farmer chuckled as he shouted to the horse, "Walk on!"

The cart lurched into motion, wheels grinding over forest paths that led away from everything they'd known toward everything they'd dreamed of becoming. Behind them, the cottage grew smaller through gaps in the trees until it vanished completely into the morning mist.

Ahead stretched ten days of careful travel, an ocean crossing, and the vast possibility of America. Of communities where magic was celebrated instead of weaponized. Of lives built on choice rather than survival.

"Ready?" David asked as the wagon swayed through morning shadows.

Eliza squeezed his hand, feeling the daisy petals soft against her finger. Around them, pigs grunted and settled into the drive toward market while Madge, still beaming, settled back against the wood side rail.

"Ready," Eliza said, and meant it with every fiber of her being.

43 NEW HORIZONS

Salt spray kissed Eliza's face as she stood at the Britannia's rail, watching the Irish coast shrink to a dark smudge on the horizon. The ship's paddle wheels churned through Atlantic swells, carrying them beyond Imperial reach with each revolution.

Two days out from Liverpool. Far enough that the Magisterium cutters couldn't follow, that ward-sensors couldn't taste their magical signatures across the water. Far enough to breathe.

David's arms circled her waist from behind, his chin resting on her shoulder. "No regrets?"

"None." She leaned into his warmth, feeling the shriveled daisy ring in the pocket. The flowers had died during their ten-day journey, but she'd kept the crumbling remnants. Some promises deserved that sort of faith.

"Good." His breath warmed her ear. "Because I spoke with the ship's chaplain this morning."

Heat bloomed through her chest. "About what?"

"About performing a proper ceremony. Tonight, if you're willing. Just us, Madge, and Captain Morrison as witness."

The offer hung between them, carried on ocean wind and the sound of rigging creaking against the masts. Marriage. Not the desperate practicality of their pig cart disguises, but something chosen. Something real.

"I'm willing," she said.

His arms tightened around her. "I love you, Eliza."

"I love you too." The words felt new on her tongue, untainted by Imperial fear or desperate circumstance. Just truth, spoken freely above waters that belonged to no crown.

Footsteps approached across the deck. Madge appeared at the rail beside them, her traveling dress replaced by a floral-patterned frock one of the passengers had given her. The woman said her daughter had outgrown it, and Madge looked like she could use something cheerful.

The dress was yellow as summer butter, and Madge's light magic danced with happiness. "Look!" Madge pointed toward the western horizon, where sunset painted the sky in shades of rose and gold. "You can see forever out here."

She was right. The Atlantic stretched endlessly ahead, with no Imperial watchtowers breaking its surface. Just water and sky and the promise of land that had never known Victoria's boot on its throat.

"What do you think you'll study first?" David asked Madge. "When we reach Boston?"

"Everything." Madge's smile was as bright as her magic. "Mathematics, natural philosophy, painting."

She spoke without the careful hesitation that had marked her speech for months. No glancing over her shoulder for permission. No flinching at her own enthusiasm. The conditioning had faded to a distant memory, replaced by curiosity that blazed like her light.

"And magic?" Eliza asked.

"That too." Madge held up her hand, letting golden radiance play between her fingers. Not wild with fear or rigid with control, but joyful. Playful. The way a child's power should be. "I want to learn what light can build instead of what it can burn."

Other passengers had gathered at the rails to watch the sunset. Families fleeing poverty, merchants chasing opportunity, young couples seeking fortune in America's promise. None of them Imperial agents. None of them watching three fugitives with recognition or suspicion.

Eliza was just another traveler now. Someone choosing her own horizon.

"Miss Clarke?" Madge turned from the sunset, her expression thoughtful. "When we get to Boston, will you help me write to

Mama and Papa?"

They'd planned this carefully—a letter that would tell the Windermeres their daughter was safe while alerting Imperial watchers that their quarry had fled beyond reach. Once the Empire knew they were in America, surveillance on Madge's parents would ease. Not disappear, but lighten enough that they might walk in their own garden or go for a carriage ride without permission.

"Of course we will," Eliza said.

Wind caught Madge's hair, sending her dark curls streaming like a banner. "Good. I want them to know I chose this. That leaving wasn't abandoning them, but honoring what they taught me about courage."

"They'll understand," David said.

"I know." Madge's light pulsed once, gentle as a heartbeat. "And someday, when it's safe, they'll come see what we've built."

Madge moved to the bow and started chatting to a group of children clustered on the railing.

"She looks so happy," Eliza said.

David tucked a stray strand of hair behind Eliza's ear. "She does. But listen, there's something else we must discuss. About what comes after we're settled."

Eliza felt the familiar warmth behind her eyes where her third eye pulsed with steady power—no longer the flickering glimpse David had caught sight of, but fully formed, blazing with the strength she'd finally learned to control. She understood what he was thinking. "The others."

"The children still trapped in Blackstone. The souls bound in their constructs. We can't leave them there."

"What are you thinking?"

"Alliances. America has magical communities the Empire can't touch. Resources. People who understand what we've escaped from. With your power fully awakened, and networks we can build..."

"We could go back," Eliza finished. "Not as fugitives. As liberators."

The sun skimmed the horizon, painting the water molten gold. In that light, Eliza caught a glimpse of their future—not perfect, but theirs. David working to build alliances. Eliza planning their return, hopefully with other Shadowbinders. Madge in a classroom where questions were welcomed, surrounded by children who understood what it meant to be different.

David checked his watch as stars began to emerge. "Time to go below. The chaplain's waiting."

They made their way to the ship's tiny chapel, footsteps echoing in passages that smelled of brine and possibility. Captain Morrison—a plump man with wire spectacles—waited with his hands clasped behind his back. The chaplain, dressed in a black frock coat with white collar, consulted a prayer book.

Eliza's legs wobbled as they approached the altar. Not from fear, but from the overwhelming magnitude of the moment. How many people got to choose their own beginning? How many were granted the chance to write their story fresh?

"Ready?" David asked, offering his hand.

She took it, feeling their magic pulse in recognition. Light and shadow, meant to dance together.

"Yeah, I am. You 'ave the document with my birth name, right? For the registry?"

He patted his pocket. "I do."

Eliza looked at Madge. "You ready to be me flower girl?"

Madge held up a bag of rose petals, collected from last night's dinnertime floral arrangement. "I am!"

Eliza smiled, drawing Madge into a hug. She slowly withdrew from the embrace, holding Madge at arm's length. Looking Madge in the eyes, she drew in a deep breath, hoping this was the right moment. Her golden third eye pulsed in acknowledgment. *It's time*, it said.

"You're gonna get a bit of a surprise when you 'ear me name at the ceremony. But when we sit down to dinner, I'll explain it all. How does that sound?"

Madge broke into a beaming smile. "It sounds perfect, Miss Clarke! I love surprises!"

Above them, the Britannia's engines drove them toward Boston. Ahead lay eight days of ocean and then America—dangerous, magnificent, free.

But for now, there was this: three souls who'd survived hell and were choosing to write their own ending on waters that promised new beginnings with every wave.

The chaplain opened his book and began to speak words that would bind them not to Empire or duty, but to the simple, radical act of love.

"We are gathered together here in the sight of God, and in the face of this congregation, to join together David Thorne and Elizabeth Windermere in holy matrimony..."

And in the ship's gentle rocking, carried by tides that knew no master but the moon, their story sailed toward tomorrow.

THE END